CHASING
SARAH

BY SUSAN MURRAY - MILLER

Best Wishes

Susan Murray-Miller

All photos are the creation and property of the author.

Cover design by Luna Lake Design

Published by Plaide Palette Publishing

Cherry Valley NY 13320

First Edition Paperback ISBN 978-0-9746558-3-3

First Edition Hardcover ISBN 978-0-9746558-4-0

For my family and friends...
I find inspiration in each and every one of you.

I shall not commit the fashionable stupidity of regarding everything I cannot explain as a fraud.

Dr. Carl Jung

Introduction

The grey dawn light appears as a tiny streak on the horizon. It is a bitter cold March day in a quiet town in upstate New York. Here, in the foothills of the Adirondack Mountain Range, the snow sticks to the tops of the hills. The unkempt grass, clothed in ice crystals, sways stiffly in the gentle, breeze, as the first shafts of light turn the sky a blaze of orange and turquoise blue.

An old pickup truck, swallowed in a tangle of snarled branches and seed pods, a shadow of its former self, rests in a sea of rust, metal, glass and weeds.
A backup beep of a front end loader sounds in the distance, shattering the silence and quieting the moan of the wind. A day's work has started and the peace of this forlorn place is about to be broken.

Headlights appear in the path. A large truck lumbers forward with its cargo of bent and broken hulks. Another truck, empty for the moment, will be loaded with cars headed for the crusher, hundreds of miles away. Lumbering along behind it is a massive front-end loader, which has already picked its victims within the rows of candidates, waiting... silently waiting.

Prologue

It was centuries ago, on this very land that he was banished to this hell, this torment. Good and evil are life's balance, both are within us and sometimes we choose or let others choose that balance for us. He had learned that much in the centuries since that night he was put to death. Now, he lived in waiting as those first stirrings of desire entered him.

The time was coming, he could feel it. His rage and anger were intensifying and with this increased rage came the darkness from deep within, darkness so black, so intense it consumed him.

May

Chapter One

Lydia was an only child and the center of attention in her parents' lives. She was of average height for a twelve-year-old, with piercing green eyes, pudgy cheeks and a turned-up nose. What intrigued people most about Lydia, though, was her unruly red hair and excessive number of freckles that showered her face and arms.

Some of her school mates were not kind to her about this. One day, after an especially trying day at school, her mother sat her down and explained that freckles were kisses from the angels. She should be proud and glad that her red hair was not the result of carrot juice. This helped shore up Lydia's self-confidence to some degree.

Lydia heard the quiet music and smelled the natural aroma oils her mother, Karen, used in her business as a Reiki practitioner, in the room below Lydia's bedroom. Lydia knew something about the practice of Reiki as she had eavesdropped enough times to get the gist of what was going on.
Catching her in the spying act one day, Karen sat her down and explained to her that Reiki was a technique of hands-on-healing for stress reduction and relaxation that also promotes the body to heal by balancing the life force energies. These energies are

present in all living things, and when these energies became misaligned, sickness results. Her mom said that maybe someday Lydia would like to attend the classes to become a master teacher and possibly volunteer her time one day a week at the hospital, just like she did.

Afterward, Lydia would practice on the cat or on whatever friend was visiting at that time. Her friends thought that Lydia was absolutely fabulous when she practiced her healing techniques on them. Karen thought that Lydia was a natural and said so many times, especially to her clients. The only problem was that many of her clients had kids in school and sometimes Lydia would be teased by them. Therefore Lydia, being the tomboy that she was, had refined her self-defense mechanisms to techniques that resulted in black eyes and cuts and bruises instead of healings.

Lydia sat on the side of her bed, swinging one leg idly, as she contemplated her desire to get out of doing the rest of her homework. As the underside of one calf touched the bedspread, its soft tickle reminded her of her cat. Speaking of cat, where was he?

"Spyder, where are you?" she hissed, determined not to disturb her mother or her mother's client in the room downstairs. Lydia inspected the closet, under the bed, in the dresser drawer and behind the door, but no Spyder. Grumbling, she raced out the door, down the narrow hallway and into her parents' bedroom, stopping just inside the door.

Early afternoon sunlight filtered in through the rear window of the bedroom. It had a yellow, almost unearthly light and it filled the entire room. Lydia caught her breath for almost in front of her was the figure of a tall girl with long, dark hair and wearing what looked like a short-sleeved summer dress. It was hard to see clearly as the light was so bright. There was an air of sadness about the girl and Lydia sensed that this girl didn't exist in her time.

Lydia's throat went dry and she started to say something but all that came out was a squeak. The girl looked directly at her and smiled. Lydia's breath came out in short gasps. Then she heard it, that voice that sometimes kept her awake at night. That whisper, faint, alluring and pleading, "*We have work to do, so let's get on it.*"

Lydia was puzzled. "Work, what work?" She blinked several times as the image faded, the light less intense now. She wasn't really scared, she was intrigued. Who was this, a figment of her imagination or just a bunch of dust bunnies congregating into a wispy shape?

Something rubbed against her leg. She quickly came back to reality with a start as she heard the faint meow of her cat. Lydia moved from one room to another in the small Victorian-style house. People in town called it *The Cottage*. She peeked into each of the three bedrooms and the study. Except for the quiet murmurings from her mother's studio and the soft, background music, it was quiet. Her mind returned to the task at hand. What was she looking for, more dust bunnies, more shafts of light? She didn't know, but the encounter made her feel wanting, just like going to a theme park and on the way being so excited you nearly pee your pants and then when you finally arrive find the park closed.

Brought back into the present, she heard the side door on the porch close. Her mother's client had gone. There was no one else in the living room which also acted as a waiting room during business hours, or in the seminar room where her mom gave her monthly Reiki seminars or lectures on topics pertaining to healing.

She heard a scraping noise on the front porch so she bolted down the stairs.

Her father, Matt Bell was lifting the heavy carpet from the front porch. He was still in his police uniform and she marveled at his high polished shoes, heavy and serviceable.

"Lydia," he called, "Lydia."

"Yup," came the rather churlish reply. She stood before him with an apple in one hand and a donut in the other.

"So much for a fully nourishing snack," he mumbled. "Help me with this, will ya. I need to get it off the porch and onto the driveway so I can clean it."

"Let's get on it," she stated, matter of factly.

He laughed at that response. She just looked at him, shifting from one leg to the other.

They finished the rug duty and after it was neatly placed back on the porch, they went in to dinner.

Chapter Two

Olivia Walton's dulcet voice was heard above the commotion in the school hallway on this Friday morning. "Well, where is she then?" She drew her words out in an almost disdainful tone. The words were shrill and loud. This was Olivia, rail thin, long-fingered, tall, steely-eyed Olivia. She was one of Lydia's dearest friends, most of the time. When she went into one of her ghastly moods, it was sometimes hard to take her, but Olivia had a tenacious temperament, one that never let anything or anyone get in her way.

Olivia endured a fair amount of ridicule, but that goes with the territory. Kids teased her for her eccentric behavior and some even called her *Princess Olivia*. Most of the time, Olivia took the teasing and ridicule with a broad back and a deaf ear, but sometimes not. It was during those times that Lydia was made aware of the fondest wishes and dreams of this rather haughty child that lived in the trailer park next to the junk yard. Olivia's father worked for the Town Highway Department and her mother was one of those women who constantly doted on her *can do no wrong* children. She worked at the counter of the local bakery and helped out with baking if needed. She was an amiable and tolerant woman, who seemed to wish upon her daughter the things she had missed out on in life. Olivia's father was a hard-drinking, jovial fellow, with a rather impressive beer belly. Lydia's father and Olivia's father were good friends, frequently seeing each other at volunteer fire department meetings and sometimes having a few drinks together at the local tavern.

Olivia's brother, Josh, was four years older and loved to tease and taunt his sister and her friends. Josh was one of those boys who excelled in sports of all kinds and was well liked by the students of Emeryville's small-town school. Needless to say, Josh's father was quite proud of him and, consequently, any misbehavior on the part of Olivia always ended up with the words, "why can't you be more like your brother?"

Olivia usually threw up her hands, let out one of her raucous bellows, spun around and muttered "oh, for one's lack of a penis!" before storming away.

Chapter Three

Kenny was the anchor in the friendship of Lydia and Olivia, but today Kenny was in a low mood as he walked quickly home from school. His head was lowered, which afforded him the view of the toes of his sneakers at every step. He got along well with most of the kids at school, but the so-called jocks were a different story.

He was a large boy, thirteen years old with an IQ in the stratosphere. He didn't like sports or cars but preferred music, writing, and reading. This made him *bullying fodder* for the likes of Olivia's brother, Josh Walton, and his friends.

Kenny and his sister, Cassie, lived with their aunt and uncle. Their uncle was the head cashier of the bank and their aunt owned a small beauty salon on the property where they lived. The salon was in a converted garage, spacious and friendly, and had those beauty parlor scents of shampoo, ammonia and perfume that go with the territory.

It was funny to see a new salon client squirm if they were not an animal lover, for within its walls was a very small menagerie of assorted pets. This menagerie included a one hundred pound iguana that lived in the customers' bathroom shower, an Egyptian sand tortoise that measured almost two feet across and loved to steal the dog food from Pris, the toy poodle, assorted koi fish in a three hundred gallon tank, several African Grey parrots and a chinchilla named Ralph. Kenny's uncle never allowed any of the animals in the house, although he called the fish *his fish*.

Chapter Four

The day dawned sunny and warm. Karen was in the kitchen fixing her morning cup of tea. Matt had gone to the precinct already. She sighed, glad for this morning respite before attending to her daughter and clients for the day. Birds chirped from the porch and a slight breeze began to blow the curtains outward. She looked at the curtains, now pushed up against the screen, and thought someone had a door open in the other room. "Lydia," she said quietly. *"No Mom, it's just me."* She smiled at the sound of her voice, her lovely Sarah, gone from this life but still very much part of hers. A light filled the room and she found it very peaceful. She remembered the first time her daughter communicated with her from the other side. She was almost expecting it, wishing it. At first it was the shock, but her mother always told her to listen, listen to those inner voices. You can't learn or increase awareness without listening, and today listening seems to be a thing of the past. She smiled to herself and thought of the comfort it brought.

Lydia's voice sounded from the base of the stairs and suddenly the light was gone. "Bye for now my little one," whispered Karen as Lydia burst into the room.

Karen supposed that the two girls might have been vastly different but still pals if Sarah had lived, and this thought comforted her.

"I have a few clients, your father is working and you, my girly girl, what have you in store for today?" she asked her daughter.

"Well, it's Saturday and Olivia and I are going to hang out."

"Ok, carry the cell with you but don't, I repeat, don't use it for anything but emergencies. Understand?" demanded her mother. "I got the bill last month and texting was a major part of it."

As Lydia walked out the door she said, "We might take a walk over to Dottie's or see Mum Mum," referring to her grandmother Eugenia, Karen's mom.

Chapter Five

Dottie woke before dawn on Saturday morning. Her white hair fell past her shoulders, which in the day time she kept braided and wrapped tightly around her head.

She scooted a cat off the bed, removed the light sheet that had become entangled in her feet during the night, and rolled to the side of the bed. She felt pretty good this morning. It wasn't raining and that meant that the ground would be fairly stable for walking in the paddocks. The farrier was coming at 8 a.m. and she had to be prepared. Some boarders were having their horses shod and she had two of her own to do. This morning meant gathering in her subjects for their hoof trims and re-shoeing, if necessary, plus the usual morning routine of feeding, grooming and checking all her *kids*-- as she called them-- for any health or mental problems. "Just like a big bunch of three-year-olds," she would proclaim loudly. "I should have been a teacher, then I'd only have them for six hours a day instead of twenty-four."

Her little house bordered the junk yard, and one part of its fence formed a side of her training paddock. She always thanked Tom the owner, "that beastly old drunk," by baking for him at Christmas time. How many times had she offered to take that boy of his in, but his remark to that idea was always the same: "mind your own damned business, woman."

On summer evenings she took walks or rode her horse to the back fields just before the woods that bordered the junk yard. It was quiet and sometimes depressing among the old cars. She wondered what their stories were and imagined that if they could talk, enough would have tales to tell to probably fill a library.

Dottie was happy where she was, she had made peace with herself many years ago. Her husband, David L. Bowmaker Esq., had disappeared years ago, or so she told everyone. He was an attorney and he worked for all the *low-life* in Alabama. After she married him, it became apparent that life with David was not going to be easy.

After their twin daughters were born, his abuse started in earnest. Violent and unpredictable was his *modus operandi,* and she had the scars to prove it. After returning home from work one evening, she had to face the fact that both her little girls were gone. Informed that she was next, she snapped, and when her rage subsided she changed her identity and fled in the middle of the night to Emeryville.

She was always small but on the chunky side. Now, at the age of sixty-nine, she looked much older but she had lost the weight, thanks to chores and horses. Her wrinkled, sun-browned face, lean, almost gaunt figure and snow white hair spoke of a grandmotherly image. She had piercing grey eyes and always wore flannel shirts, blue jeans and cowboy boots. She was good with horses, and people came from distances to seek out her advice.

Matt, Lydia's father and a local policeman, was especially fond of her and often referred to Dottie as the mother he never had.

Chapter Six

He seemed hesitant as he sat down in the chair at the side of Matt's desk in the police station. A wizened old man of seventy-five, with deep brown eyes and a head of very unruly white hair, Ben was small in stature with a slight stoop. He always wore the clothing of academia; suit jackets of tweed, old and faded now, with a buttoned polo shirt and faded dress pants. He had a limited wardrobe, but he always wore something different from the day before. It was always clean and neat.

His hesitant mannerisms translated to nervousness, and this intrigued Matt.

Matt relaxed and hoped that he could put him at ease. He really didn't want to listen, but something deep within told him to. "Hi Ben, what's up?" he said quietly.

"Well, it's just not something you talk about all the time, ya know, legends and such, but this is real bad, real bad. You see, I've been doing a lot of research on this topic myself. State library, county archives, locals," hesitating, he took a deep breath. "Something bad will happen here real soon," he blurted out, "something real bad."

"Okayyyy" countered Matt, with a lot of hesitancy in his voice.

"Please listen," said Ben, "as this is important. You see, I do the weekly history column for the paper and as you know, I married a local girl and settled down here. My family is also from this area. I was born on the Oneida reservation. Now, my wife's family's been here many years and I heard about this thing, only it wasn't mentioned too often. It's kind of a taboo subject, so to speak."

He looked at Matt, his eyes full of anxiety. Matt nodded his head at him, signaling him to continue.

"There's this legend, you see, that every seventy-five years, in this town, horrible things happen because of an incident that happened here many hundreds of years ago. No one remembers what triggered this bloodbath, so to speak, but I do know that horrible things have happened to people here in the past since this has been documented."

Ben bowed his head, shaking it slowly and sadly, then suddenly raising it to look directly into Matt's eyes; he said, "I've been doing a lot of research on this over the last year or so. This is the year and sometime in the middle of August it will happen; August seventeenth to be exact."

Matt opened his mouth, but Ben was already rising from his seat.

"As I said, ask the locals, if you can get them to talk. You'll find things that you won't like and you'll find a pattern," he said. Matt was intrigued, and he didn't know what to think. He wanted to investigate this more. Either way, he couldn't wait to get the morning over with and ask everyone at the cafe about this story.

Chapter Seven

Matt came sauntering into the café and sat down at the counter. He was almost bursting to tell the story of the crazy town historian, at it again. Although Ben was good at his job and had married into a local family whose roots went back into the 1700s, starting an investigation because of a legend was a little too much for him to swallow. He had to think about the reaction of his boss, Chris.

Stools scraped as some of the lunch crowd assembled at the counter while Lucy waited on tables, Suzie, one of the owners, waited on the counter trade. Her husband, Terry, was cooking on the big grill that took up ten feet of one wall. Terry was a tall, medium-built man with an enormous paunch, and Susie was short and very plump. Boisterous, generous to a fault, they were some of the best confidants that a person could have.

As well as a full breakfast menu with lots of hot coffee, the lunch menu consisted of burgers, sandwiches, wraps and salads. The food was over-proportioned, very good and from local sources. They closed promptly at three each day. Suzie's favorite saying to all her customers was "Hell, honey, I can puree a brick and make it taste so good you'll pay to have more."

"Are you kidding me," Suzie retorted, when Matt retold the story that the historian had given him. Terry turned slowly, giving Matt a somber look, like he had something really important to say, but was reluctant to say it. He approached the counter where his wife was standing, the spatula still in his hand, burgers still spattering on the grill.

"This legend or history for that matter involves my family in one of the incidents," Terry said quietly. Suddenly, Terry had everyone's attention. "My grandfather disappeared one night after he had taken the cows to pasture. They searched all that night and into the next morning. The whole town was involved. Then, there was a shout from the lane at the back of the barn. It was just after daybreak. There was my grandfather's body, tacked up on the wall of the barn, just like you would do with a hide after the animal was skinned. Hell, someone even made a comment he reminded him of Jesus crucified. It was awful. The body was taken down and let's see, that was well… it was back in mmmm, let's see, 1938 or so. Oh, by the way, he wasn't the only one who died that day."

"Oh shit," blurted out Matt.

"Now wait," said Terry, "here's the interesting part. When they did remove his body, it was all burned behind it, as if he was burnt from the inside out. When they took him down there was this perfect impression of his body on the barn wall. When you went out the lane to get the cows or were coming in from haying with the horses, there it was, that silhouette and that dark stain that was obviously blood all down the side wall of the barn. The barn is still standing, somewhat. Drove past there the other day but I didn't get out of the truck.

"My grandmother and the family vacated the place as soon as they could. Had to try to sell the place first and they just ended up walking away from it. The bank took it back, God bless 'em. They moved into town and have been here ever since. My father started this place up back in '62. Anyway, that's the legend my grandmother told me many years ago. She stated that she would only tell it to me once, but I had a right to hear it. I never saw them, the burn marks I mean, never had the inclination and personally I don't want to believe it. But there is one other thing that she mentioned." He stopped and took a deep breath. "Every seventy-five years this whole town gets a wake-up call."

Matt was struck dumb. A local legend he knew nothing about? How funny that his mother-in-law, Eugenia, didn't say anything about it. She was a native here, born and raised, but then again natives of a place are always reluctant to say things.

Matt finished eating his customary lunch, one burger, onion rings, a *short* salad and a coffee. As he headed for the door of the café, Suzie waved and shouted above the din, "another crime fighter on the way to destiny."

Matt smiled a wan smile and thought to himself, "Oh, how right you may be."

He had work to do and the least of it was to confront his Chief about this tale. Should he just shake it off, ignore it or plunge head-on into a mess that maybe was just a bunch of fairytales? He could end up being the laughing-stock of the entire town or worse yet, wasting time and money when real crime had to be addressed. He was going to have to think this one out and interview some people who would know the tale. He was starting to get a little irritated about no one telling him of this situation, especially his wife and his mother-in-law. What if something awful did happen? What then?

Chapter Eight

It was slightly overcast as Lydia made her way over to the trailer park on the other side of the school. Olivia's mother would be working at the bakery, but her dad would be home and so would Josh. Her stomach was queasy as she approached the driveway where the light blue double-wide sat. The yard was neat and Mrs. Walton had already planted flowers bordering the driveway and around the cluster of mailboxes near the front of the house.

She did not want to encounter Josh, but there he was. Lydia sighed and watched as Josh bent over the shaft of his motorcycle. He glanced up at her. He smiled, gave a nod and said, "hey twerp."

"I'm not a twerp, and why do you do that to us, call us names?" she said angrily.

"Because I can," he said nonchalantly, as he straightened and stretched his long, lanky figure.

"Don't you get tired of harassing us?"

"Naw, never get tired of doing that, beside what else do I have for entertainment around these parts anyway?"

"Olivia says you might get a job this summer at the junk yard."

"Yeah, I thought that it would be an interesting place to work. All those cars and all those parts," he said dreamily. "I just might be able to fix up my dad's old car."

"I wonder how long you'd last with ol' Tom anyway," she said.

He laughed, "That old drunk SOB? Don't know, but I'm keeping my options open. I suppose you came for the Queen Bee.

She's in the house, bugging dad or something. She's got the diva disease this morning."

"At least we can go to the library or do some exploring," said Lydia.

"Oh, get a job, the both of you," he snarled.

"Who will hire us?" she mimicked back at him.

"Who knows, maybe Tom," he tittered.

She turned and made her way into the small house as Olivia was just pushing the screen door to come out.

"Oh," Olivia said in a high-pitched, sarcastic tone, "there's Joshie Boy" as she wiggled her hip a few times.

"That's me," he said with a laugh, "and some day I am going to give you that spanking you really deserve."

"You lay one hand on me and you'll be sorry," she stated.

He started for her and Lydia, and they ran shrieking down the driveway. He stood there laughing at their retreating backs. Olivia turned around and stuck her tongue out at him which caused him to laugh even harder.

"Whatcha feel like doing?" said Lydia.

"How about exploring, I really would like to go see what's in that junk yard. I mean besides all the old cars." Olivia's voice was serious but expectant.

Lydia said, "Okay, let's go. We can go in through Dottie's, there are more paths there. If we go in on the opposite side we have to go through all those hedges Tom planted, and they have thorns."

"Oh, aren't those thorns ghastly?"

"I also heard from my gram that the college is doing a research project in the back woods," said Lydia.

"Where the swamp is?" said Olivia, incredulously.

"Yes, in the deep part of the woods where the swamp starts. There is a rumor of some sort of vine living there, maybe it's a bush or a tree, anyway, it's hundreds of years old and its arms are miles long."

"Wow," said Olivia, "I'm speechless."

Lydia elbowed her, laughing, and Olivia retorted with a "What?"

When they reached the end of Dottie's road, they cut across in front of the farthest barn and took the well worn path into a tangle of brush that marked the beginning of the Pederson property and the *yard*. A small hill separated the properties, and Lydia scrambled up the slope, sending dirt and rocks flying down toward Olivia, who crouched at the bottom. With feet still planted on the path and looking up at her, Olivia placed her hands on her hips and shrieked, "That was unacceptable."

Lydia glanced back and hissed, "Will you shut up now. We're not supposed to be here."

The old cars loomed before her from her position on top of the small knoll. There was no fence here so they could wander at their leisure on this Saturday morning. Olivia panted to a stop beside Lydia and gazed down at the sight.

"Wow, this is creepy, all those cars," she exclaimed.

In the distance they noticed a small cloud of dust coming toward them. A guy on a four-wheeler turned down a lane of cars and disembarked in front of a small compact car. The flat section on the back of the four-wheeler held a welding torch, and he immediately grabbed a pair of goggles and the torch and went to work cutting off the side of the car. It was a newer car, not like the ones at the very rear of the lot that were just buckets of rust and decay. This one still had some shine and you could tell what color it was.

The harder they looked at the guy the more certain they were that it was not Pete the hired man. This guy was too tall for Pete. As he hoisted the door onto the back of the wheeler platform, secured his tanks to the side of the passenger seat and started to get on, Olivia let out a shriek.

"Who is he? I've never seen him before and he looks about my brother's age."

Her voice carried right down to the figure on the wheeler. He stopped, looked around and his eyes settled in the direction of the sound. It did not take him long to see the bright blue of Lydia's shirt and Olivia's pink leggings. He stood there, not quite knowing what to do. Jerking himself back to reality, he placed the goggles on the seat of the wheeler and started toward the hill and the two waiting figures. As he got closer he saw that they were two girls, much younger than he was. One was rather tall and gawky and the other had a shock of red hair and was shorter than the other. He came to a stop at the bottom of the hill and looked up at them.

"Well, big mouth," Lydia hissed, "You can do the introductions."

Olivia barely glanced at her partner in trespass and sauntered down the small incline that was much smaller than the one they had just climbed up on the opposite side.

The boy was tall and now, as Olivia looked at him in the late morning light, she saw that he was near Josh's age as she had first thought.

"Hello," she drawled. "We're out for a morning walk. I see you're working here."

He didn't answer. He really didn't know what to say. When customers came to the shop he was quickly relegated to the back room. His father stuck to the policy of no see, no questions.

Lydia quietly approached the boy and stood at Olivia's side. "Hi," she said. "I'm Lydia and this is Olivia."

The boy nodded his head.

"Why aren't you saying something, I mean just anything?" blurted out Olivia. She sounded annoyed.

The boy glanced at the ground and started to speak, but all that came was "ah, ah, ahmm ah, ah."

It was obvious that he was having trouble with the words for as he spoke his head bobbed forward as if to physically throw the words from his lips.

Olivia started to say something but a firm squeeze on her arm from Lydia stopped her.

"That's okay," said Lydia in a soft voice. She didn't want to scare him or give him an excuse to leave. Lydia had heard of people who stuttered. Her mom had told her about a therapy that she used on one of her clients who stuttered when she got excited.

"Take your time and relax," she said. "Take a deep breath and let the words just flow out."

Olivia spun around to face Lydia. "What are you talking about?" she hissed.

Lydia fixed cold eyes on Olivia. "It's obvious to me that this boy is having a problem communicating and I'm using one of my mom's techniques to get him to talk," she said, barely audible but enough for this boy to hear.

"I ca ca ca nnnnntttalk," came the terse reply.

The boy was beginning to like these two. It was obvious they had a special bond and yet each was an individual, and very different individuals at that.

He swallowed hard and then spoke, "Wwhy rrr yuyuyu here? He fixed them with a curious stare. This was a new experience for him. Two strangers, girls, and he was talking to them. He liked this. They weren't making fun of him or cursing or hitting him. He was relaxing a little when suddenly he heard the distant roar of a motor. Glancing nervously around he nodded his head, turned and ran for the wheeler, leaving the two girls looking at him with amazement. He started the motor, spun the wheeler around in the narrow confines of the weedy lane and headed toward the front of the junk yard. He glanced back a few times to still see the pink and blue of the girls' clothing. They were not a figment of his imagination; he had actually talked to them.

Olivia shrugged, "well, if that doesn't beat all."

"I would advise," Lydia said hesitantly, "that we keep this encounter our little secret. There's something about him that makes me sad, and if people get wind that he's here for whatever reason, it won't be good for him."

"I just have a creepy feeling about him," Olivia retorted.

"I have a sad feeling," Lydia mused, "just very sad."

Chapter Nine

Matt drove the squad car on his rounds and stopped at the local newspaper office. As Matt vacated his car, he noticed that it was getting warmer and he was actually sweating. A cool breeze nudged his damp skin and he shivered. Bird songs filled the late morning air. Bird songs always made him feel happy and a bit melancholy at the same time. Why did they remind him of his father and the sorry life he had as a child and of his sister, Sadie? He put the thoughts away and pulled on the handle of a large glass door that led to the counter of the small newspaper.

Owned by its third-generation owner, Richard Perry, the building was bustling with people and activity on this Saturday morning. Perry, as everyone knew him, was an amiable man. He did most of the cold-calling on new prospective advertisers on his own, wrote the editorials, which could get very controversial at times, and kept the mostly local staff very loyal to the paper and their boss.

The paper was printed at another location. The rear of the building that once housed the presses was now relegated to storage and archives. The paper had first been printed here in 1820, so maybe Matt still had a chance of finding something. Matt approached the counter where Margaret, the local insurance agent, was busy giving details about her ad in the upcoming edition to one of the office staff. Besides Perry and three full-time office staff, the paper also employed two full-time reporters and several locals to write editorials, gather news, and write columns of local interest such as history or outdoors. Sally was Perry's part- time saleswoman who was also the local gossip queen and a friend of his wife. She came to the house for Reiki sessions and was thirsty for all things of the occult and beyond.

The paper had lots of hometown news and sports, school news, a swap section, garage and yard sale notices, auction advertising, classified and reader ads and a full human interest section. This section proved to be the boon of the paper, for all the news was good news and much of it quite humorous, and the town's people enjoyed this.

Perry liked news reporters, did a lot to bring quality to the paper and remained completely unbiased about the news, unless you said something negative about his beloved Rotary Club or the Veterans; then he was a force to reckon with.

His star reporter was John Dunn, or Jack as everyone knew him. Jack, the unassuming sort, let Perry talk him into joining anything, including the local Rotary Club. Jack was now the president, much to Jack's chagrin. Every Wednesday you could see them at their meeting place of choice, the café. The meetings became social free-for-alls with anyone's input gladly bantered around. It was said that the Rotarians had as many non-members as members at their meetings.

"Hey, what can I do for you, Matt? This isn't an official call, is it?" said Perry.

"Well," said Matt, "sort of. How far do your archives go back?" Perry looked thoughtful, "Well, in the 1960s, we put a lot of it on microfilm, but mind you it's not indexed to subject, just date, so there's a lot to be desired if you need something specific. We're digitally archiving all we do now, but the rest." he shrugged his shoulders, "There are boxes and boxes of one hundred fifty-plus-year -old newspapers out there. I think there's maybe three weeks missing out of the bunch. This was always a weekly paper, one of the oldest in the country, and I'm proud that my ancestors did it that way. What are you looking for, Matt?"

"Well," Matt sighed heavily and looked at Perry, "there's this legend." Matt stopped in mid-sentence, for he saw Richard Perry's face turn sheet white and the unassuming air between them suddenly turned chilly, almost fearful.

"Oh," said Perry.

"You know about it then?" said Matt quizzically.

"Let's go in the office where we can talk," said Perry.

Richard Perry, shoulders slightly stooped, led the way into a small, but airy office, filled with stacks of papers, camera equipment, coffee cups, a stuffed cat perched high on the top shelf of a bookcase, and more papers.

"Excuse the mess, the habit and clutter of a working fool," he said as he motioned Matt to a seat in an overstuffed chair that Matt wondered if he could ever get out of. It seemed to swallow him whole.

"The paper covers the 1938 event," Perry began, "and it does refer a lot to what happened in the 1800s and 1700s, although there was hardly anyone here before 1700 except a few fur traders, land speculators and natives. Emeryville wasn't officially settled until about 1740. The native accounts, no one ever bothered with getting their stories until about sixty years ago with the renewed interest in Native Americans and their regional histories. That's when the real writings and research began. And that's when our historian began his search into the old papers. He really did dig up some interesting facts from other archives and descendants of the ones whose people were involved in the gruesome carnage of 1938 and earlier."

Matt grew thoughtful. He sighed a deep, long sigh and said, "there's something that bothers me about all this and it's from a strictly police point of view. Could an ancestor be keeping this whole charade alive? I mean someone in the tribe or someone outside the tribe who, for lack of a better scenario just brings someone into the fold who makes sure the dirty work is done every seventy-five years. I mean, it sounds crazy," Matt was stammering now, "but stranger things have happened and I know some people would be thinking that, my boss in particular."

"I've thought of that too but I dismissed it simply because this killing spree has been going on for at least four hundred years, or so I'm told. Now the native population goes back to the early Woodland Period around these parts, and that's way more than four thousand years ago. Hell that's a long time. And to keep a person on the payroll, so to speak, well, that's really farfetched."

"I know, but you know me and my logical, cop brain" said Matt.

"I don't know where to begin, but I heard the story from my grandmother who heard it from her grandmother and let me tell you, my grandmother lived through the 1938 events."

Matt nodded.

"Yes, and she said that her grandmother saw Dave tacked up on that barn wall and that she used to go out every year at the anniversary and put flowers at the side of that dirt road leading past the barn."

"Is the image still there?" Matt asked, the sound of hope in his voice.

"Far as I know it is. Once the family vacated, well, the place fell into ruin. Howard keeps the place mowed and plants corn there but he tells me he doesn't go near the barn if he can help it.

It's about all collapsed now with the exception of that wall that borders the driveway into the pasture and the back wall. Silo's leaning real badly too. Howard says the spot is too creepy and he cuts across the field and goes the long way out when he has to, especially at night."

Matt was thoughtful but hopeful. Here was real evidence. He would check the local, county and state forensic files and police reports as soon as he had time. Sensing it was time to go, he said his farewells and asked Perry if he, by any chance, could get copies of the stories.

"Yup, give me a couple of days and I'll dig them out," he said. "You haven't been the first to ask. Ben's been at it, says it's getting time again. He's like a bulldog when it gets a scent. Don't know when to let go. Just give me a couple days."

Matt grew thoughtful and said, "I can imagine, lonely life he lives, all by himself."

Perry sighed and nodded in agreement. "It's tragic, that's what it is, and him so smart too. He loved that wife of his. It's a real shame how that accident happened and all. Head-on collisions are not fun. Usually no one survives, especially back then. I'll tell ya, if I could get all the information out of that brain of his, I'd have a paper that would run for another hundred years."

Matt smiled, thanked Perry and left the building. He paused at the sidewalk and looked out into the street. It was Saturday and the bank closed at noon, but it was busy.

Matt decided that he would go out to the old farm, the place where Terry's grandfather met his end. He wanted to see it for himself. He would go out as soon as he was off duty.

Chapter Ten

The girls explored around the cars and headed for the back of the property, where the woods started. They found another path, well worn, like the one past Dottie's house and thought that maybe this was the way to the research site and the enormous vine.

Although it was sunny now and a small breeze blew, when they entered the woods, it was dark. The smell of pine and balsa met their nostrils and they breathed deeply. Small animals made scurrying sounds in the underbrush and they heard the distant call of a blue jay.

"I love this place," said Lydia. "It's peaceful here."

The path wound around tree stumps, over downed trees and through a patch of raspberries. Shafts of sunlight filtered through in spots not as dense as others. Red squirrels chattered overhead and small birds flew from branch to branch as if showing them the path. Several small orange surveyor flags marked a spot where a large tendril of vine lay along the ground. Its gnarled and twisted bark was uneven and layered in several shades of dark brown and reminded them of a snake.

"This must be it," said Lydia. "It really does look old, and it feels like a friend, very benign."

"I wonder how many miles it goes back into the swamp. You know the swamp is supposed to be haunted?" Olivia mused.

"Let's go a little further," said Lydia. "It won't hurt and we'll just follow this one vine and when we want to we'll turn around and follow it back out. We shouldn't get lost."

They cautiously stepped over branches and brushed against ferns, all the time using the vine as their guide. Its diameter started to get thicker, the further they walked into the woods. The smell of damp and mold grew stronger. Suddenly, a huge slab of rock barred their way. Carefully they made their way around the rock, and here the vine twisted into several coils, one small coil going up the face of the granite slab on the opposite side. Ahead of them a small clearing filled with moss, ferns and short grasses basked in the shafts of sunlight. On the opposite side of the clearing another slab stood, half leaning. The place seemed magical.

Suddenly, Olivia shivered. "Ooh, I hit a cold spot," she whispered.

Lydia stopped, for suddenly the ground seemed to move around them and something shot up into the air. It was so sudden that both girls gasped, for this force had no shape. It was energy in its most basic form: raw, menacing and dark.

Their feet were rooted to the ground, and they hugged one another, not knowing whether to run or stay. They knew if they ran, they could both get lost.

Olivia let out a scream, but it stuck in her throat.

Lydia shook her. "No," she said.

As they stared into the clearing they saw just a faint mist at first, then that familiar shape of a girl in white. The voice in Lydia's head was faint, but audible. "*Go back quickly but quietly,*" it said. "*It won't hurt you now, it's gone.*"

"What the hell was that and what's happening?" cried Olivia, her face on Lydia's shoulder.

Lydia was visibly shaking, she wanted to cry, to scream, but something deep and primeval wouldn't let her. She started to sweat and then a chill moved over her body, like tiny, icy fingers crawling down her back and neck. Lydia knew that Olivia saw her also and that Olivia felt the same as she did. She grabbed Olivia's arm and pulled her away from the circle, back behind the first slab of rock they had encountered.

Leaning against the cool face of the rock, Lydia regained her strength and composure. At least she stopped shaking, but the uneasy feeling still gnawed at her stomach.

"What, who was that?" Olivia squeaked.

"I'll tell you when we get out of here, now run."

Exhausted, they burst out of the woods and stood, heads bent to knees, gasping.

"Now, that was an adventure!" gasped Olivia." I'm just glad to be alive!" She looked directly at her friend and asked, "Who was that, some guardian angel or something?"

"I don't know who she is, at least not right now. I have a real funny feeling I'm about to find out soon."

She told Olivia about her experience in her parents' room a few days before.

Olivia looked stunned as if she didn't believe her. Finally, Olivia said to her, "I just experienced something, saw something, and I'm really scared but I must admit I'm fascinated too."

"Let's go, it's getting late and we both should be home," said Lydia, wearily.

Olivia started to laugh.

"What's so funny?"

"You, your head is full of twigs and leaves."

"Well, your cheeks are dirty and your face is streaked with mud and tears and your hair looks like it hasn't been combed in a month," Lydia fired back.

They walked through the warren of paths along the rows of cars, came to the end of the property and made their way up the small incline and down the steeper side of the path that skirted the horse pasture. It was growing dark now and they both knew that they should be getting home.

Olivia finally spoke. "Interesting place. It gives me the creeps but you know what?" Lydia gave her a questioning glance. "I want to go back there. It's creepy but fascinating."

"See you sometime tomorrow," said Lydia as they headed for home.

Lydia's mother met her at the door. "Where have you been, dear? I was starting to get worried."

"Oh, Olivia and I just took a walk, mom." She wanted to say more, but she felt that she would find out as much as she could about her ghostly friend and the boy at the junk yard before she ventured into that territory.

Chapter Eleven

The police station was a small, modest brick building housing the dispatcher for the county 911 offices and a police force of the chief, four full-time men, and two part-time officers. These men patrolled an entire county of mountains, small villages, and many acres of state forest and farm lands. Theirs was a large territory, very different from a precinct in a large city. The firehouse was built in the 1850s and sat next door to the police station. Unlike the police, the firemen were all volunteers. There was an ambulance squad that was limited in number, but the dedication of the men and women in the squad stood the test of time.

After finishing his report for the day, Matt signed out and decided that he would get it over with and see his boss, Chris. This would get it all out into the open, or so he hoped. Matt would tell him his thoughts and see if he could shed any light on the subject of the upcoming *anniversary of carnage* as he dubbed it.

Chris was harried, and he looked it. With the upcoming Fourth of July festivities looming in the very near future, this was not a good time until the annual parade and fair was finished, but Matt still wanted to try.

"What is it, Matt?" Chris said, as Matt stood in the doorway waiting for recognition.

"Got a second?"

"Yeah, a second," he said briskly.

Matt closed the door behind him and Chris's brow furrowed. "What is it Matt, problem?"

"No," said Matt quietly. "Not really, but I have to get this off my chest. August is coming up, August 17, 2013 to be exact.

"Yeah, so what?" said Chris, placing his pen down carefully on the desk.

Matt drew in a deep breath and said, "Remember what happened seventy-five years ago on August 17?"

Chris grew quiet and thoughtful. "What old timer doesn't, and of course, the entire backlash that went with it. Oh Christ, could you imagine if something like that..." His voice trailed off. "No. Impossible!"

Matt spoke up. "Every seventy-five years for the last, at least four hundred, so I'm told, there's been this incident here in this town. This is the year, and are we going to turn our back on it? I only just found out about it, and personally, I'm pissed that I wasn't informed."

"Forget it, Matt, this is just a local legend." Chris didn't sound sure of himself as he looked at Matt from over the top of the half-glasses he wore when doing office work.

"I would love to," said Matt, "but if some of our local yahoos got hold of a story like this, who knows what kind of a nut would try to reenact it? Hell, all anyone would need is some half-assed story in a small-town newspaper and it has the potential to go ballistic on the internet."

Chris looked directly at Matt, now giving him his full attention. "Are you the only one who's in on this?" he asked.

"As far as I know I am. You know Ben, he's the one who initially told me. As far as which of the officers has heard about it, hard to tell. If I heard it on the street, they could also. There are only three of us here who have local connections, all the rest are transplants."

33

Chris scratched his head, looked squarely at Matt and said. "Number one, I want this kept under wraps, but I want you to pursue it. I'll also keep my eyes and ears open. My wife and your's travel in the same circle. Some of it I don't approve of, ya know, all the psychic stuff, but Jane said something real weird to me the other night in reference to this and it made my hair stand up. I know this is being talked about. It's only a matter of time before someone gets hold of it that shouldn't get hold of it. Keep your eyes and ears open, Matt, I don't like this one bit," he said slowly.

"I'm going out to the old Ryder place; I want to see that barn wall before it falls down. I think I'll take a few pictures too."

"Wish I could go with you, but it'll be after dark when I get off here. Let me know what you find."

Matt nodded and turned toward the door.

"We're working on it, but we're not working on it. Got it?" were the last words he heard from his boss before he closed the door.

Chapter Twelve

It was late afternoon, sunny with a light breeze. The trees were in leaf, but some of the stragglers, like the ash and butternut trees, were just coming into a glorious yellow green color. The contrast was a pleasant sight. Matt drove north, over the bridge and past the cemetery. Just on the outskirts of town, the scenery opened up into large farm fields. Some of the farmers were plowing and disking. Others had finished and were waiting for the first cutting of hay. The road twisted and turned. Deep ditches filled with sluggish water and grasses formed a barrier into the fields beyond. The old barn loomed in the distance. The house, abandoned, forlorn and long neglected, was the first building Matt saw. Matt slowed down and as he passed the sorry looking structure, he thought about Terry and being born in a place like that. It saddened him. He knew that the house held happier memories, and for just a moment he thought he heard the tinkling sound of children's laughter.

A machinery shed, its roof collapsed onto the hulk of a rusting tractor, sat between the house and the barn. The barn sat off the road, and a well used lane went past the side of it and down into the fields beyond. There was an embankment, overgrown with weeds and burdock, from the lane to the road. This kept some of the barn hidden from view until you were adjacent to it. Matt noticed that Howard, the farmer who now owned the land, had planted corn in the field just beyond the barn. Green, elongated leaves were emerging from the ground forming neat, regimented rows in the brown dirt.

Matt drove the car into the lane, but just far enough for the car to be partially hidden from the road by the high bank of weeds. He sighed, put on his sunglasses and grabbed his camera from the front seat. As he opened the door, birdsongs and that gentle sound of breeze through grass held him mesmerized for a few moments. He had something to do, might as well get it done. Terry was right, the barn was falling down. He looked sadly at the small unmowed area beside the side of the barn where heaps of wooden timbers and metal roofing held the remains of the farm's once stately outbuildings, necessary for the operation of a farm. They sat, like rotting melons in a field, their insides spilling out onto the ground for all to see.

The sun was bright and light reflected off parts of the grey, weatherworn barn. He made his way down the lane and as he passed it, looked up at the old silo standing tall and roofless against the endless onslaught of nature.

Matt reached the back wall of the barn and almost didn't want to look. At first, the light was so bright that it was hard to see any detail, but squinting, he suddenly saw something. It seemed to jump out at him, the almost perfect image of a cross. The burn marks were deep in the wood but years of weathering had faded them. The blood stains were indiscernible, with the exception of a few areas that looked like small discolored puddles to one side of the image. The cross image was tilted, almost as if it was falling over to the right. Matt could now visualize a man tacked to the wall. The barn was large and looking at the cross-like image against the imposing structure, he marveled how small the man must have looked to the person who found him.

He tried to imagine how anyone could get a body up there. Yes, it seemed like an almost impossible feat, and he badly wanted to know how they did it.

Looking at the scene, Matt pondered just how he was going to do this investigation without confronting locals, the local gossip mill and, more importantly, the regional newspapers with their sensationalism, let alone social media. The thought sent shivers down his spine.

~

The moon cast its eerie light, making the shadows deep and long on the dusty ground. Crickets chirped and the restless wind, needing something to play with, created little dust puffs in the night air.

He didn't touch the rusted hulks of metal, he walked through them. It was getting time, he could feel it, that restlessness, the feeling of foreboding when he would be forced to enact the horrible past all over again. He was tired, how much longer could this go on; for all eternity? He felt the urges within him but he was no longer secured with a blanket of flesh, no longer did blood course through his body, but his mind, his mind remembered. It was the ground right here that held his soul, his anger, his rage.

Chapter Thirteen

The day dawned cool and sunny after the evening rain. Matt eased his patrol car onto Maiden Lane, past his mother-in-law's house, and parked in front of Dottie's small house. The white picket fence, unpainted all these years, leaned precariously toward the ground. Matt knocked on the door to the small house. No one answered. Then a shout came from across the paddock. Someone was at the barn door. It was Dottie. "Hold on a minute," she shouted, "I'll be right there."

Her slight figure came across the yard at a run. Gasping, she slid to a stop on the wet walk leading to her doorway. "And to what do I owe the pleasure of this visit?" she grinned. She could see he was troubled.

"I need to talk to you," he said. "How long have you lived here? I mean, you seem to get around, like my mother-in-law, and maybe you heard something about this." He was rambling now.

"Who, what, where, when, why?" she laughed shrilly. "Hold on, boy. Sounds like somebody rode you hard and put you away wet, as we say in these parts."

Taking a deep breath and calming himself, Matt said quietly "There is rumor of an old legend."

"Oh, that," she said, interrupting him. "Come inside and I'll fix tea. The Earl okay?" she asked, referring to the kind of tea she was serving.

"Yeah, that's what Eugenia serves me whenever I'm there, so I'm used to it."

"Nothing like bergamot," she cheerfully countered.

He sat down on one of the kitchen chairs. The cushions were worn and dog-eared but comfortable. The late morning light shone into the room, giving it a somber feeling. She poured the steaming kettle over the tea and as it steeped, began to put out sugar and cream. A plate of cookies miraculously appeared as well as one of many cats.

Settled in a chair, she poured tea and quietly setting the teapot down said, "I heard about it from the librarian at first. You know, when you first come to a place, you want to know everything about it. Well, I got so far into the story and no farther. There seems to be this one thing that binds this community together and it is that or rather those events of the past. It seems there are mysterious happenings here about every seventy-five years or so. It's just like clockwork how it happens. First, someone from the surrounding community, usually a child, or an old woman, disappears. No one hears from them again. Animals and birds are found dead and no one can explain how they died. No bullets or arrows, almost like they were electrocuted. Then a few weeks later strange things are seen in the woods up in back of the junk yard. Now, as I've found out, that woods used to be a sacred grove to the native tribes here long, long ago. Anyway, it ends where several people mysteriously die, some rather gruesomely. The last one, a man, was tacked to his barn wall. There's usually between six and eight people that die. No suspects, no witnesses, no nothing. People around here, the old timers I mean, refer to it as the 'dark time' but no one knows why. At least I don't."

"Ben might be able to shed some light on it," she continued. "I know that he's a plethora of information and he seems to know all about some of it, but as I said before, people are real scared of what happened and are upset that no one was apprehended."

"Ben and I had a talk and that's why I'm here to see you first, before I approach that mother-in-law of mine," said Matt. He was halfway done with the tea and on a third cookie.

"Oh, Matt, she's not that bad, really."

"She reminds me of my mother on a good day. And that isn't good. I really do like her, she's just so hard to get along with, that's all," he sighed.

"Eugenia is really a very nice person, she means well and she's lonely. That's all I can tell you, Matt. Eugenia would know of the matter, because her people were part of the incidents. She is very tight- lipped about it, but if this thing is about to reoccur, you might want to think about how to stop it. I know people are concerned about it now." She hesitated, "and besides, she's my next door neighbor."

"Yeah, maybe that's why I got that call from the state troopers in Milton early this morning on a missing child. It's like they had the disappearance, we have the culprit," said Matt with a slight edge to his voice. He felt sick to his stomach.

"Well, I guess I better go visit Eugenia after I'm through here."

She laughed and said, "You make it sound like you're on official business."

"I have a feeling I am, and I don't like it one damn bit."

"Maybe you should ask your wife first, maybe she would know something more before you approach your mother-in-law."

"Now that's a better idea," said Matt.

Chapter Fourteen

Arriving home, Matt wiped his feet on the doormat and entered the house. Shedding his uniform was one of his first priorities before dinner and he headed upstairs with a shout of "sweetie, I'm home!" He was answered with the clang of a pot, the sweet smell of something baking in the oven and a "hi" from his wife. He reached the landing on the stairs and peeked into Lydia's room. She was sitting on her bed with a look of deep contemplation on her face.

"I don't think you'll solve all the problems of the world in one afternoon," he quipped.

She looked up at him with a questioning look on her face and said, "Why do some people have to bully others?"

He stopped his forward motion down the hall and entered the room to sit quietly on the bed alongside her.

"I guess it's the nature of the beast," he said.

"Beast my ass," she retorted. "Whoops, sorry dad, it's just that Josh and his gang make me so mad. Just because there are people that are different, have different interests and maybe they don't like sports, there are other things in this world besides sports." She almost spit out the words.

"I know you did quite a job on him one day and good for you, but I still don't condone it, the slaying of the Josh dragon, I mean."

"Oh dad," she said. "It's just frustrating."

"Sometimes bullying is a way of getting attention," said Matt, "and many times it's a call for help. He might be saying, look, I can do this because I can, but maybe, just maybe he's hiding a bigger secret he doesn't want anyone to know about. Maybe it's insecurity or an inability to learn."

She smiled a thoughtful smile, nodded her head and briefly placed her head on Matt's arm.

He smiled at his daughter, kissed her on the forehead, got up and left the room. He changed his clothing, went downstairs and found his wife in the kitchen preparing a cup of tea.

"Home early I see," she said in a cheerful, but tired voice.

"Yes ma'am, but this here's more of an official duty call," he drawled in a fake accent.

She laughed and gestured for him to sit down.

"Just out to see Dottie," he said.

She nodded her head and a smile crossed her face. "I really like Dottie and she is one of mom's cohorts."

"Speaking of your mother, I need to talk to you."

"Oh Matt, now what?" said Karen. The tone of her voice was defensive and filled with frustration.

"Nothing bad, well not really, I have to go see her on rather official business."

His wife looked sharply at him and sat down slowly. She rested her elbows on the table and folded her hands, placing her chin on them, looking straight at her husband.

He said, "Ben saw me yesterday, and told me the story of an event that happened here many years ago and somehow he had the idea that this event will be repeated, somehow."

"Oh" was her only reply. She met his eyes. Her hands now rested on the table, but her clenched fists told him everything.

"So you know." His voice was steely.

"There's been talk, you can't help hearing it. The energy fields are changing; I can feel it but not like some can feel it. And yes, they're talking."

"Your mother?" he said.

"Among others," Karen replied.

"Does that include Dottie and Katie and, who the hell else knows who?"

"Matt," she said in a quiet, soothing voice.

He stood, abruptly. "Here is the scenario. Some nut goes out and starts killing people just because of an anniversary, and it's on my watch." His voice was growing louder. "Look, I don't believe in this hocus pocus, my world is black and white. I don't care about energy fields and all the other stuff, I care about murder and who did it."

Karen rose, crossed the room and put her arms around her husband's waist. "I think it's time you became fully aware of what happened and why. It will not be the first time for the incident and it might not be the last but there is more help than you can imagine in seeing that maybe, just maybe this never happens again," she said.

He just grunted. She heard and felt it in his chest. He looked down at her and she smiled.

"Oh lady, let's go to bed," he said as he grabbed her close and hugged her.

She started to giggle and said, "The subject is something that I don't want to carry to the bedroom."

He laughed and kissed her cheek.

"What's your mother doing this afternoon?"

"As far as I know she's home. If you're going over there, I will wait supper as I have a feeling it's going to be a long one."

"Yeah," he laughed, "a long one alright. Call her, tell her I'm coming and tell her she'd better tell me everything," he shouted as he walked out the door.

Lydia quietly stood in the hallway. She had heard some of the conversation and she had to find out more.

Chapter Fifteen

Matt could not help but feel a little queasiness in his stomach. How would she receive him and how would she feel about divulging the information? He'd have to find out. He parked the patrol car in front of the little house which sat in a grove of trees at the edge of town. A gravel sidewalk lined on both sides with marigolds gave it a welcoming feeling. He glanced up and frowned at the noise from behind the large chain link fence that bordered one side of the property. The fence was okay, but the entire length was surfaced with sheets of metal. Some were rusted, some plain grey and others green or red. It looked hideous. But behind the facade was another matter: Tom Pederson's Junk Yard.

Eugenia's property was on the corner of a small street. At the end of the little street was Dottie's house and horse barns. Dottie's property began where Eugenia's property stopped. Dottie's paddocks for her horses lined right up to the fence which went for about three hundred feet before it ended. Where the fence ended one could glimpse the rows of derelict cars lining up to the woods.

Eugenia was waiting for him. She was tall; many called her stately, with the forehead and cheekbones of her daughter. Her hair was once black but now it was more silver and she wore it long and usually braided or pulled up at the nape of her neck. She was the epitome of a native of the Iroquois League, a group of native tribes that populated the Mohawk River Valley in upstate New York. Her people had been here since time began, first as hunters and gatherers and then as agriculturists. Many were displaced during the American Revolution, fleeing to Canada, while others stayed behind and endured.

"I plant climbing vines in the summer, keeps the view nice," said a voice from the doorway. "I try to make it as pretty looking as possible," pointing to the blooming shrubs. "Counters the mess next door." She said it loud as if hoping Tom would hear her.

Matt laughed and hesitantly hugged his mother-in-law. She seemed sad and resigned.

"How do you stand the noise?" he asked.

"Well, some days it's better than usual, but thank God he's closed on Sundays. Thing is, he starts so damned early, so I became an early riser. They used to say up with the birds, I say up with the front end loaders and wrecker trucks."

He smiled.

"I understand you want to talk to me," she said in a resigned voice.

"Yes, I must talk to you."

She led him into a small living room and motioned him to sit down.

She sat across from him, sighed and said, "I can tell you that the legend was mentioned in the 1700's, when the town was settled. Six people died or disappeared all within the time span of several days. Several days is all that the killing spree usually lasts here but there seems to be a host of other incidents, maybe some are unrelated, I don't know. Starts outside of town and moves into it. No one ever elaborated on the method of killing, but the similarities are enough to make you wonder. They, my people, used to call this place a cursed place. Maybe it's because of the legend." She sighed. "My grandfather was Indian and the legend in his tribe says that hundreds and hundreds of years ago, a young shaman, a very powerful young shaman was put to death here for something so hideous that my grandmother usually refused to talk about it. It seems that he had this blood lust, for lack of a better word. He was born to a young couple, actually a daughter of the shaman of the tribe at that time. From the beginning this kid was trouble, something was wrong with him but no one ever elaborated what. They still wanted him as a shaman, at least his grandfather did. Well, after the grandfather taught him everything he knew, he killed and ate him in a blood frenzy at this sacred place in the woods."

She looked at him as if seeing him for the first time and continued. "Just over beyond that last row of cars, there's a path and it leads deep into the woods and to a swamp. Incidentally, there has been activity there lately as our local college and the state university are conducting horticultural assessments. It seems that there's a grape vine living there that is now suspected to be over a thousand years old. It lives in the center of the swamp. The tendrils of this vine coil out over miles in many directions. Some of the tendrils are over a foot in diameter. I'm very interested in horticulture, so of course I'm helping out.

Anyway, getting back to our story," she sighed a long, deep sigh as if contemplating how to say the next words. "The tribe was terrified and there were more killings, well, more people missing. One night, he butchered all the members of his own family including his mother and father. Their deaths were gruesome, and the tribe realized that they had a real problem on their hands. This young man had to be stopped and stop him they did, but it wasn't easy. Being a shaman, he was possessed with all kinds of powers.

"They drugged him and several of the strongest warriors held him while they tied him with vines and then they murdered him. As he was dying, he kept shouting that he would be back. To make sure of him never harming anyone again they cut him up, and to make sure that he was dead, they burned the pieces. Now the next part maybe is a little hard to take, but here it is. As they stirred the ashes of the fire, wanting to make sure he was dead, this bright orange ball of flame came out of the ashes and shot up into the sky. As the ball of flame shot into the air, they heard a laugh, it was loud and unearthly and it was his laugh.

"Initially he was known as the dark force or the evil one. Now, we just refer to him as the dark one. Oh, his eyes were another matter; they were able to hypnotize anyone or anything he looked at."

Matt shivered and looked at his mother-in-law. He found the story a little hard to believe.

"There's been something happening here ever since, every seventy-five years and I don't think it's human in nature. I just have a gut feeling it's far more than that."

She hung her head as Matt asked, "Where was he killed? Maybe that has something to do with it."

"Somewhere in the woods at the rear of the junk yard is where it all happened. That was where the ancient ceremonies were held. There was a stone circle there and mounds or so I've been told. The village itself was where all those cars are parked. I remember the place in the forties and fifties, before Tom and his father got it. There was grass there and someone mowed part of it for a ball field. Along comes Tom, and his father before him, and he puts a junkyard on the site. Can't say I blame him none, his land and all, but to me it's a desecration. Under all those rusting hulks are the remains of a large native village. Ironic, isn't it?" she said sadly.

She stared out the window. The early afternoon sun made deep shadows in the trees. She smiled slightly, sighed and said, "It was about 1930 or so that the last incident happened, and now the time is approaching and all the old ones like me are getting nervous. The new people just scoff at the idea, call it folklore and go on with their lives. Two kids died very hideously and one woman was found in the ditch right in front of the Methodist Church. Her throat was slit and she was burned real badly. I don't remember the rest but I do remember the story about Terry's grandfather being nailed to the barn wall and all those burn marks on the body. It's supernatural, that's what it is."

She hung her head and almost in a whisper she said, "Being involved in the research project in the woods has afforded me the opportunity to hunt for the site of the circle, and someday I will find it."

They sat for a moment, Matt deep in thought and she looking almost visibly relieved. "It's nice to talk to someone who's interested, although in the wrong way," she said quietly.

"No," Matt said, "not in the wrong way. There is no wrong or right in this, it has to be stopped."

She nodded her head and smiled at him.

Chapter Sixteen

Matt entered the house. It had been a long day and he was exhausted. He hadn't done anything particularly physical, but the *mental*, that was sometimes more tiring than anything physical. Hell, even his eyeballs hurt. He had hunted in all the old papers of the village. Yes, it was seventy-five years ago in three months time, on the seventeenth of August to be exact. The murders and whatever happened to those people of long ago…stop, stop his inner voice said. He was getting ahead of himself. Was there really some truth to what Ben had said, and was there a person or persons who were obliged to keep the legend alive, generation after generation?

As he stood in the doorway of the kitchen, he observed the floral pattern of the walls, the whiteness of the cabinets, the chairs and the glass-top table. The whiteness took his breath away sometimes. A green glass bowl of pastel flowers sat in the middle of the table affording the eye a reprieve from the rest of the scene. The curtains, white with a blue and mauve paisley trim, fluttered in the slight breeze.

He heard his wife's soft voice and the voices of Lydia and Olivia engaged in an animated conversation in the dining room. Then he heard it, a voice said quietly, "*Hi Dad, I'll help you.*" He heard it only once and it was as if someone was standing just in back of his shoulder. He froze. There was no mistaking what he heard. Every hair on his head and neck was electrified; he was flushed as if he could feel the prickly heat of the blood in his face. He was momentarily paralyzed, but every sense was on alert, waiting. The steady beat of his heart rang in his ears, and the droning of the conversation in the dining room was a backdrop for his confusion.

He whispered, "yes, little one," and it came out as a hoarse croak in a voice that even he did not recognize. He knew in that instant she, his little daughter Sarah had come to Lydia as well. He did not know how he knew, he just knew. The realization was comforting, and he wanted to laugh. His senses knew what his mind refused to recognize. What were his wife and mother-in-law always saying to him? Oh yeah, "things are not always what they seem."

He took a deep breath, letting out a long and heavy sigh. He felt better, lighter. He was going to have help after all, although from an unlikely source.

Chapter Seventeen

Tom Pederson brushed his shaggy hair away from his forehead. "Hey, boy!" he shouted. "Boy, where are you, you little bastard? I need help here with this here transmission. Let's go, NOW."

There was a scurrying sound and a small-framed young man came up to him silently. "Oh, there you are. Can't talk worth shit so you gotta' sneak up on me, huh?" The boy cast his eyes downward, knowing what was coming.

The slap wasn't a huge blow, not like some of them that left him broken and faint.

He was sixteen years old now, but to look at his gaunt frame was to think of a much younger boy. When was the last time he went to school? Before his mother died. Before his father started into that deep grieving that altered one's mind, before all that. He guessed that in the moment of her death, he had also died in his father's mind. He was only seven then. Now, nine years later here he was, a skinny kid with straw blonde hair and growing ever taller as the months went by. He worked retrieving car parts for his father. The father many said was brilliant. The father who knew an automobile inside and out and where to find a part in that sea of old wrecks in his junk yard. Yes, the father that blamed him for his mother's death.

It was the year before that Gail came along. She seemed like a nice, sweet lady at first. She was rather plump, with blonde, thinning hair, a raspy voice laced with profanity, and huge breasts. His father had delighted in those breasts many times and it didn't bother him where it was. Sometimes, when the boy went to bed, the moans coming from his father's room and the squeak of the mattress springs made him want to vomit.

Soon, Gail became very obnoxious, like she owned the place. She would light up a cigarette, throw food into a pan and curse all the while she was cooking. She went on and on about the "two shits" and how they were sooo demanding. Demanding? He hardly talked because of his stutter, and his father worked most of the time. So Gail found solace in the TV, the vodka bottle, and in chasing him. She would corner him and rub her large, full breasts against his chest while groping for his crotch. He was mortified at first, then he just went along with it for awhile. He was tired of it all, tired of that deep longing that came from a life that even a dog would shy from.

He stayed away from her as much as possible. It didn't always work out. She would occasionally hunt for him, especially when she and his father had a noisy row. Noisy was not the half of it; screaming, threats, crashing pans and glassware and mess everywhere was the result, and his father was getting sick of it.

So one day Gail wasn't there anymore. All vestiges of her just disappeared. "I just gave her a one-way ticket and put her on the train," was all his father said.

He was glad she was gone, now he could at least get back to cooking meals, which he loved, and to reading, his favorite pastime. He was a voracious reader and Gail had the habit of interrupting his reading, so he would go to his car and read with a flashlight. Now he could read without interruption.

Much to his father's unawares, he did have a small circle of friends outside the confines of the compound. Claire the librarian always made sure he had books. There was a small box set in one corner attached to the gate post of the fence. He would find a book or two in there at least once a week. Pete, his father's hired man, would take the books back for him when he left work in the evening.

Sometimes, after dark, especially on evenings when there was no moon, he would sneak out of this place he called home and enter another world. Alex would wander down the main street, looking into shop windows, ducking into alleys when someone passed, careful not to arouse any suspicion.

Some evenings, when his father closed his shop and padlocked the front gate, Alex, the given name on his birth certificate, would go out to his favorite car, a 1968 Plymouth. He didn't know why he liked the car. It was all beat up, one rear door was missing and the front windshield was cracked and shattered around a large hole on the passenger's side. It looked like it was hit from behind. But something about the car and where his father had parked it afforded him a tiny bit of security in his life. The car was parked among hundreds of others but, in a way, by itself. It was a deep gold-brown color and the rather large oak tree it was parked under afforded him shade in the summer and some sort of a wind break in the fall and early spring. A small knoll at the rear of the car kept it from touching the large, metal-covered chain link fence that surrounded most of the compound. Dead leaves and small twigs littered the ground as well as those occasional plastic bags that come floating in on the breeze.

Sometimes, on moonlit nights with the soft glow shedding inky shadows along the junk yard paths, he would see her. At first, Alex thought she was just a figment of his imagination, floating among the cars as if they weren't there. She would stay around a large sedan with a shattered side door and glass everywhere. Black stained the seats and he knew what it was without a second thought. Blood. A tattered piece of pink fabric lay on the back seat. He remembered wanting to take the fabric, caress it against his cheek, but something deep within him told him not to. He respected his inner feelings, sometimes going deep within himself to find comfort in a mother who was no longer there. A mother he could barely remember except for her comforting way and her soft, sweet voice, a sing-song voice that was a small melody in his soul. It was then that he cried, the cry of deep longing and sadness.

Alex knew her only as *the girl*. And then one night she stood there, looking curiously at him as he sat in his space, his comfort zone within his old car. She was very pretty from what he saw of her. In a flash of inspiration he mentally asked her name. It came to him quickly. Sarah. He whispered the name softly, she smiled, and within a blink of his eye she was gone. He would come to the old car with renewed interest and a purpose now. He had to find out more about her.

Alex once asked his father about the cars in his lot. His father stared at him as he stuttered past the sentence that formed the core of his question.

"Every car out there has a story to tell," his father stated matter-of-factly. His father explained that they made a decent living selling parts from the old cars. Many of the parts were no longer available from the auto manufacturers. The parts were not cheap but were fairly priced, and they had enough land to sustain a lot more cars. He also made money from the scrap when the old cars went to the crusher. His father's dream was someday to buy a crushing machine, but for now his parts business was enough for him and his two employees.

When he wasn't drunk, his father was pretty nice, but one drink and then another led him into a world of machismo, intolerance, impatience and violence. A world he wanted desperately to get away from and couldn't.

One day, while talking casually to his father, Alex realized that his father was actually afraid to go out there into that graveyard of twisted metal and broken glass. He would send his son or the hired man, Pete, for a needed part. They were the barrier to whatever was out there that his father was so afraid of.

Alex explored all of the land beyond the main fenced compound, the land outside the regular confines of the fence, the land that stretched all the way across the fields in two directions. Here sat thousands of cars, old trucks and busses, boats, trailers and RVs, all languishing in various states of decay. Some had tires, others the remains of the steel cords that were once tires, while others sat on blocks with wheels and tires removed.

During the daily business routine Pete and Alex drove four-wheelers that could amble up and down the narrow dirt roadways, collecting parts from this car and parts from that car. One of the wheelers had a complete welding shop attached, just in case a part did not want to come off for some reason. Most of the wheelers were equipped with tool boxes with every known wrench and pliers to make the job of parts extraction easier and faster. The parts were delivered to his father's customer service area, where they would be cleaned and inspected. Delivery vans from other car dealers and auto supply houses as well as local repair shops were a daily sight at *the yard's* front door. If anything happened to Pete, his father, or him for that matter, no one would know where anything was. His father's establishment was what one would call "ordered chaos".

Pete would call out to Alex and tell him to go out and fetch a coil or distributor from an old Lincoln Town Car that was the second left turn past the first row of cars, "all the way out to the end where the road splits into three sections."

Everyone in town who had any association with the *yard*, all knew Alex as "the kid". No one asked anything more about him. He was kept away from customers as much as possible and his father held enough weight in the town that no one asked anything further of the "kid's" comings and goings, not even his good friend Matt, one of the local policemen.

Chapter Eighteen

Pete was a short, thin, wiry man. He lived in an old trailer next to the junk yard. His passion was gardening when he was not working. There were always flowers blooming in his yard, and vegetables for the table. He donated much of his summer produce to the local food pantry or gave it to friends. He even had one of the old truck frames hauled up out of the back section of the *yard* so he could fabricate an arbor out of it. Pete carefully placed it 20 feet from his door, so everyone had to walk through if they wanted to find him at home for something. He planted climbing roses on each side, carefully nurtured them, and in the summer the thing was always vivid with blooming roses. His trailer usually took one of the top prizes in the "Best Landscaped Yard in Town" contest run by the local Rotary Club, much to the chagrin of the hardware store owners' over-ambitious wife. It did not please the women of the local garden club either. Pete was always pestering them to let him join. "It's a garden club for Christ's sake, not an old hens circle," he would retort to Mrs. Jackson, who would sniff the air around him in disdain. And the wife of the bakery owner was another one always asking him about this plant and that plant. Finally he invited her over to the house for a talk.

She found the inside of the trailer immaculate but dated. Pete didn't have much more than that old mangy dog of his. She had to admit that he served the best cup of tea and the best scone she ever had in her life. Even though the cup was cracked, she later reported to her friends.

Chapter Nineteen

There was something primeval about the night. The deer grazing at the edge of the woods felt it strongly for they were keenly aware of something lurking just outside their range of hearing and smell, something deadly and malevolent. A doe looked up from her grazing. She was nervous and lifted her leg over the fawn that nursed greedily on her distended udder. She moved further away from the woods into an open field. The fawn, not to be so rudely interrupted, butted her udder hard between her two hind legs and continued nursing. The moon hung low in the sky and dark scudding clouds played hide-and-seek with its light.

She felt it at first, a burning sensation in her throat, then without warning something came into her vision so foul and evil that the small doe was transfixed and had no time to run. Within seconds she was struggling for air as wave upon wave of electrical shocks jolted her body. Her frothy breath came in gasps as her life-blood poured from her nostrils, running down her neck to pool around the leaves of the fresh young grass under her hooves. She heaved a sigh and collapsed on the soft carpet, making one last, futile effort to rise before her heart exploded in her body.

The coppery smell of blood and burning flesh mingled with the pure, sweet scent of spring in the night air.

The little fawn, alone and safe from this predator, nuzzled his mother, but no life was there to comfort him.

Chapter Twenty

Matt had spent his day investigating the usual small town disturbances including Mrs. Allen's umpteenth call about her neighbor burning his garbage in his fireplace, manure spilled on the road in front of the Vesley Farm, problems with teens, a shoplifter and one stray dog.

He was sitting at his desk, finishing the last of his paperwork, when he smelled a familiar odor, but one that was not supposed to be in a police station. He glanced up to see Howard making his way toward him. "Ok, sorry, just got out of the barn," he shouted, for everyone to hear. Matt could hear the snickers of laughter from behind the glass partition that housed the secretarial pool.

"Hey, Howard," Matt stood and extended his hand to the farmer.

"We can talk outside, cleaned calf pens this morning and it was especially ripe," said Howard. "Don't want any of these gals to get asphyxiated."

Matt shook his head and laughed.

As they exited the building, Howard shouted at an exceptionally pretty and petite blonde, who was on the computer, "you can break out the air wicks now," and he let the door close behind them amid gales of laughter.

"What's up, buddy?" said Matt.

"Well, you know where the old place is that I bought several years ago. Ya know, the place where the guy was found hanging on the wall?"

Matt nodded.

"Well, this morning I went out to check on the alfalfa that I got growin' near the woods, in back of where the corn is planted, and darn if there ain't another dead deer back there, third one in so many days. It's weird. No coyote or bear marks on the body and it's black and burned like it was hit with something like an electrical charge. Weird, just thought you'd like to know."

"Thanks Howard," said Matt. "I'll check up on this one."

Howard crossed the street, got in his old Dodge pickup and started the motor. The beast roared to life.

"Howard, I can cite you for that muffler," Matt shouted at him.

Howard gave him the finger and roared off toward his farm.

Matt stood there laughing and at that moment Chris, his boss, exited the building. "How's it going, Matt?"

"Well, just maybe got an interesting lead and I'm off to see it."

"Doesn't that guy ever take a bath?"

Matt started laughing and said, "he just got out of the barn."

"You should hear them in there," said Chris. "I'm on my way to the grocery store for air freshener, gotta keep the girls happy. A lead, huh, let me get the spray and if you want I'd like to go with you."

Matt nodded and they headed for the patrol car.

The barn wasn't far out of town, just three miles. They pulled into the driveway, made their way around the corn field and stopped at the edge of a small alfalfa field that bordered the woods. As Matt turned the corner of the old barn he noticed that Chris craned his neck to see the back wall of the barn.

"Not much visible," said Matt. "It's in the shape of a cross. I'll stop on the way back through, light will be better."

Chris nodded his head.

The smell told them where the deer was. Howard had not bothered to move it yet, so she lay where she died.

"She's pretty bloated but no external signs of any weapon except for the burns on the nose and in the mouth. No animal brought this doe down. She was nursing too," said Matt, and he felt sorry for her.

"What do you make of it?" he asked Chris.

"The same thing you do. I've also been cautiously interviewing people, and Perry has been some help. I understand you and he have an agreement on this subject."

Matt shook his head yes and sighed.

"Well, as the old song goes, 'It's only just begun,'" said Chris.
Neither man smiled.

Matt showed Chris the rear of the barn and they returned to headquarters to finish up needed paper work. As they pulled up in front of police headquarters, they noticed the front door standing ajar, propped open with a large concrete block. As they entered the building, both men realized that air freshener and barn smell don't mix.

Chapter Twenty-One

What were these feelings, these urges that now consumed him? He was turning so mean and resentful, so morbid. The feelings came in waves, washing over him like the ocean's tide; the rhythm of life itself. He had to shake this off, he just had to. It was as if someone else, not him, inhabited his body when he was in these moods.

Seth sat at his desk, restless and very much alone. Most of the teachers and staff had left, but he had grades to complete and it was coming down to the final month of class.

He got up and wandered to the case where the artifacts from area archeology digs were kept. Bone pins and flint knife points, stones used by ancient ones for grinding grains and ending the lives of the animals they would consume. All this, and what use was it? His students became disinterested in this type of thing quickly in today's fast-paced society. Where was the patience and quest for learning that used to be, and where was the respect?

He was contemplating the newest of the artifacts. Odd, it seemed to glow a little! He shrugged, picked up the object. It was smooth, and fit like a glove to his hand. The tiny sacrificial knife was truly a work of art. He flipped it over in his palm. Funny, but it just came to him that when he picked it up, the knife was warm, as if someone or something had recently held it. He couldn't remember who had brought it to him, but he knew what it was almost immediately. It excited him to have such a rare artifact in a school classroom. The state museum people showed a very definite interest when he brought it to them for further identification. He had even showed it to Ben, the local historian.

Ben's reaction to it was a little short of terror. "Where did you get that?" he stammered. This was not at all like Ben, to be so turned off by an historic object. He was more than disappointed by Ben's reaction and mused about that for a few moments before placing it back in the case with the other artifacts.

"Seth?" the questioning voice came from behind. He turned and there stood the high school principle, Amy Goodwin. Tall, slightly stooped and in her mid-sixties for the last how many years, she had a kindly, grandmotherly face and a general's resolve.

She had the habit of looking you straight in the eye with that unnerving stare that unsettled many.

"It's funny that you were looking at the new acquisition," she stated. "Ben says it's a knife used in human sacrifice and that there are just two like it in existence."

He nodded and said, "Yes, I know of its importance, but I still don't know how we acquired it."

"I think it was David, one of the seventh graders in Mrs. Gray's class. He brought it in and one of the children in that class recognized it for what it was."

He jerked up his head. "What, a kid in the seventh grade recognizing this artifact? Impossible."

"Not really," she said, sadly. "These kids are hungering for knowledge and a lot of them have interests outside of the classroom. I do know that Kenny was the one who recognized it. You know Kenny. I am sure you've seen or at least heard of him from some of the other teachers. Kenny even tried to buy it from David with several pieces of candy and gum. He sometimes hangs around old Ben and of course has his own circle of friends which includes Olivia, Josh Walton's sister."

"Oh, the mouth," he said, referring to the tall, gangly girl with the larger than normal ego. A smile crossed his face. "Sorry," he said with a sheepish grin.

"Oh, I just hang around the hall to see what those two are going to do next," she said.

"Two?" he asked.

"Oh, Olivia and her friend Lydia, two real characters, and there's no love lost between the brother and the sister. It's open warfare between Josh and Olivia."

He nodded his head in agreement and said, "Josh can be pretty degrading and he does have a bullying streak." He had seen it first-hand in the classroom.

"Yes," she said sadly, "that's what it's all about. He just won't leave Kenny alone, and those girls will go to the ends of the earth to defend him against Josh and his cohorts."

"I'd sure like to meet this kid," he said, with a note of excitement in his voice.

"Oh, you will, possibly sooner that you think."

He looked at her quizzically.

"He wants to meet you and possibly sit in on your ancient history and folklore classes for these last few weeks of school. He's really into it."

"Oh, now I'm beginning to see the big picture," he exclaimed.

"If you decide to do this," she said, matter-of-factly, "let Kenny into the class, you're going to have your hands full."

He gazed into those blue-grey eyes with the little smile lines surrounding them. The lines deepened momentarily.

"Could be good for you," she said, as she turned and walked away.

Was she smiling, he wondered? He swore she was.

Chapter Twenty-Two

The sidewalk was shaded by the school building, while Seth walked back toward his apartment. Just two more blocks and he would be at the front door. As he neared the house, he could see someone on the sidewalk, hurrying toward him. It was Claire, the librarian. He stopped in front of the brick walk that led to the large old Victorian with the wrap-around porch. The house was shingled a dark brown, worn from years of weathering. It was a comfortable apartment and Claire's mother owned the building. Claire lived with her mother on one side of the structure, he on the other. Shy, quiet and retiring, that was Claire. He liked her in a brotherly sort of way. The sister he never had.

She met up with him, gave him her usual "hi" greeting and looked at him quizzically. "Something bothering you, Seth?" She asked, in that quiet, timbered voice. She had a look of worry and genuine fear on her face.

"Haven't been myself lately, I guess, all the stress in the classroom, regents coming on in another month and a new student coming into my class. It's going to be a mess, these last few months of the term."

"A new student?" inquired Claire, still looking at him with concern, almost fear.

"Do you know Kenny?"

"God, everyone knows Kenny and his aunt and uncle." Claire sighed. "Don't tell me he's moving up to your class?"

"Afraid so, but just for these last few weeks, and just for one class. Trouble is his arch-nemesis is in the class with him."

"I don't want to hear any more. Kenny is a sweetheart, albeit a misdirected one. He's too smart and much too unsure of himself."

"He hangs with Olivia and Lydia, is that right?" he inquired.

"The dynamic duo," said Claire with a laugh.

They were walking toward the house when the front door suddenly opened. Katie, Claire's mother, came out onto the porch and stood there staring at them.

It happened so suddenly, it took his breath away. It was as if something came out of his body, pulling on his insides as if to yank them out in an effort to detach itself from him. He felt light-headed, dizzy, as if some great weight was lifted from him. He stood for a moment, visibly shaken, very tired and quelling the urge to vomit. Then he looked at Katie, who was now standing in the center of the front steps. She looked concerned and very upset. Her eyes shone with a darkness he had never seen before in the several years he had been her tenant.

She came slowly toward him. "Are you okay?" she asked, in a hesitant, high-pitched voice.

"I guess so. I, I don't know what happened, it was like a great weight was lifted from me."

"That's exactly what happened. Come in, I need to ask you some questions and you need to sit down before you fall down," said Katie.

Her tiny, round frame was quick, almost cat-like, and she carried her sixty-seven years like a little whirlwind. He wondered if she could actually shape-shift into other forms, as many of his students whispered that she could. He remembered seeing her in one place, then another, in quick succession and wondered if it was true. Could people really do that?

She led them through the front hall and into the rear of the apartment. They stood in a large, spacious, but very out-dated kitchen. As Katie passed the table, she slid out a chair and gestured for him to sit. Claire sat opposite him at the well worn, wooden table. The kitchen was spotlessly clean, but the one thing he noticed, and it intrigued him, was the row upon row of mason jars lining one wall. They were filled with leaves, buds and twigs of various colors, shapes and sizes. He wondered how many spices one needed when only two people ate here, or was this for something else?

He looked back at the table and the tiny woman. This kitchen was not at all like the kitchen on his side of the house. Having new appliances, fresh wall paper and an island his mother would have killed for were his forte. Here, it was like stepping back in time and as he had been told, Katie liked it that way.

She sat opposite him. "Sugar or cream?" Katie asked.

"No, just plain," he said.

She liberally poured cream and two large scoops of sugar into her cup while Claire poured honey from a spoon into hers.

It came out so suddenly, her words shocked him: "How have you been feeling lately?"

He looked at her with shock at first then lowered his head. Should he tell her?

"Seth," she gripped his hand from across the table. "Tell me everything. I'll know if you're lying or holding back."

He lifted his head and stared into those piercing blue eyes. Her small, round face was without guile and looked at him unsmiling but with kindness.

"Lately, really crappy," he began. "Not sick in the sick sort of sense, but just these violent mood swings. One minute I'm myself and the next, I want to kill someone. It's like someone is living, or more like sharing my body, and it has a completely different personality. I feel really tired after these episodes. I know it is happening, but I can't stop it and furthermore I'm scared. I keep asking myself if I have schizophrenia or manic depression or what? I have never been like this before."

"What you have," she said quietly, "is a bad energy or what some people call a demon or unHoly angel that has, for some reason or another, attached itself to you. It's able to come and to go now, and therefore you have some control over how it will affect you. In other words, it hasn't made you its home yet. It's checking you out. The girls and I have been waiting for this particular entity to show up, because the last time it did, some people in this area suffered and many died. We made the national news in a bad way.

This August will be the seventy-fifth anniversary of our bloodbaths here, and we aim to stop them."

He didn't know if he was hearing this straight. This was something between science fiction and TV horror movies and he wanted to laugh, but he was too tired.

"You mean this is connected with the folklore I hear of the killings in this town and how they started centuries ago?" he asked.

"That's correct," she said, still not smiling. "Now, we must teach you how to protect yourself and you must follow this religiously, because without protection you're endangering yourself and others, including those students of yours."

He gasped and his heart tightened in his chest.

"Are you game or do you want to play hero and think you can do this yourself?" she continued. "Oh, you'll need to pray a lot also, but the most important thing is faith in yourself and your abilities. Do you know Father Munro, our local priest?"

"Of course," he said. "Seems like a nice guy. I attend Mass sometimes, not as much as my mother would want me too, but sometimes."

"Good, Father is a demonologist with the Church. It might be a good thing to talk to him. He'd be able to answer a lot of your concerns, maybe some that I cannot."

He looked straight at her and said, "These girls, as you call them, who are they?"

"Oh, the local good old-fashioned red neck, for lack of a better word, witches. Our ranks include healers, palmists, tarot readers, psychics, your local Reiki master, a Christian minister, and yours truly. We also include Father in the mix." She still wasn't smiling, and she had a look on her face that told him she was very serious.

"Anyway," she continued, "we're helpers, not occult. We believe in the power of healing and in the power of God. Some of us are Christian and others are Wiccan and still others are whatever floats their boat. The bottom line is that we're healers and helpers in things that some people refuse to be aware of. We have God-given talents bestowed on all of us at birth. Many choose not to use these gifts. Some of us have kept or have regained the knowledge of these talents. As I said before, many of us are God fearing, Church-going, ladies auxiliary-type women who just have talents that are not, uh, normal. We are the ones who, in the beginning, have been courageous enough to come out of the closet, so to speak, and say yes, we can do that. Yes we can see ghosts or spirits and we are clairvoyant. Yes we can heal with our hands and we can teach anyone to open up to their God given talents and do the same.

"In the beginning, we endured the labels, gossip, the ridicule and open hostility. Now, after all the dust has settled, we're accepted here. This town is a little bit more forgiving. People here are more open-minded than others. We have had witch covens here since the 1700s and it's funny to say that most of the original settlers of this area were devout Church-goers and members of the local coven at the same time. When one thinks of a coven, they think evil, but there are good and bad witches and we were always for the good."

She looked at him wistfully, smiled slightly and continued, "Did you know that one of our founding members helped her son, a famous local doctor in the early 1800s? She grew herbs and prepared tinctures so that he could practice medicine. Before the advent of modern pharmacology, there were the alchemists and the so-called *good women* who made the tinctures and salves from the herbs they grew and harvested. These women and men helped where they could. They are the unsung heroes of their day.

"We shall begin our lessons in the morning, this Saturday. I expect to see you promptly at 8:30 am. Our friend will not be bothering you any more tonight. I don't expect you to lie awake all night thinking about this either. Get a good night's sleep." He glanced at Claire, who was smiling broadly.

Chapter Twenty-Three

As Seth left the comfort of the warm kitchen, with its wood stove in the corner, he felt confused, but somehow at peace. Heck, he was drained from too-much-information overload. He didn't quite buy into the fact that he could be possessed or was about to be. Demons pick and choose their victims, their hosts, as Katie had called him.

Claire led him out into the late afternoon light. As they stood on the porch a cold wind blew through the branches of the trees that lined the side yard, sending little shivers up his spine. The trees had lost their light green of spring and were already into full leaf. Robins sang their songs and cavorted on the grass in search of worms and larvae for their young. If they were lucky, two broods would be hatched here this year.

He said, "What did she do, put a curse on that, that thing?"

"No," said Claire. "I'm sorry my mom scared you like that, but when you greeted me when I first came up to you, there was something in your aura that was very dark. My mom saw it for what it was."

"My what?" he said. Now he was really exasperated and confused.

"I saw it in your aura, your energy field. All living things have an aura...trees, people, animals, all living things."

"Wait, wait, you can see my aura?"

"Oh yes. Mom never let me lose that little ability. We are all born with the gift. It's just outgrown when we mature. Bless those who never lose it. Now-a-days, many more people are learning how to regain it later in their lives. It's helpful in dealing with people, especially with anger and love."

She smiled up at him. He liked her. Then she quickly grabbed his sleeve and looked directly into his eyes. Her voice was earnest and she spoke quickly as if wanting this one moment over with. "I must make something clear right now; I'll be your friend but never a lover. I'm, I'm a lesbian," she quickly stammered. "I like you very much and I must admit my feelings for you are genuine, except just not in that way. But I would like to be friends with you. There are few people who are aware of my sexual orientation, so to speak, but that's the way it is. I hope you understand. I'm sorry for being so blunt, that is one of my many faults; I can be very blunt."

"Well, two shots in one night are a little hard to take," he said sadly. "I must admit my mind is reeling."

"Just concentrate on the protection. We'll always be around to help. You don't need to be the next evil werewolf in the area. The killing spree will begin soon and we have to be ready. This is something not to be fooled with. As my mother said, go see Father Munro. He'll give you a blessing. Don't be afraid to ask him. He really does understand the situation. And don't forget, 8:30 tomorrow morning."

"This is a lot to take in."

"We wouldn't have done this so abruptly if it weren't for the fact that the attachment to you has already begun. You're going to be going through hell before this is over unless someone else has been chosen, and pity to them. If he had entered you all the way and took complete possession, we wouldn't be talking to you as we are now. Possession is nothing to fool with."

"Oh, like movies involving exorcism?'" he said glibly.

"Worse, "she said. "Those are pure Hollywood fiction. This is not." She wasn't smiling.

"I have a lot of questions, but that's for another day." He sighed wearily.

"I'm afraid so," she said. "It's getting late. And it is the weekend and I have a date this evening."

He smiled, shook his head sadly and said, "What a waste."

She playfully poked him in the rib and he laughed, his brown eyes sparkling.

She turned to go and he grabbed her arm. She spun around to face him. "Thanks, Claire," he said. "I'd like to call you Sis."

She burst out laughing. "It will be nice to have a brother," she said. "Okay Bro," she said laughing. "Mom and I have been alone too long."

He nodded, turned and walked toward the door to his apartment.

~

Damn females, damn imposing females. Those two were too protected, almost as powerful in their energy as he was, but they were of flesh and blood.

He noticed the spirit girl, and suspected that she saw him too, or rather felt him, for his dense energy was unmistakable. When they made contact, he always felt as if she was sending energy to him, but a foreign feeling energy. He only responded to the energy of anger and hatred, this fed him but she was always in a pure light sending him energy that felt different. She was light, he was dark. She seemed to shimmer with a vibration that was very fast. His was a dense energy and his vibration was slow. He was the embodiment of pure hate.

Oh, there were others here in this earth place, other entities. Some came from the source that he was excluded from and others, well, they chose to stay here for whatever reason. He didn't mind them, he rather ignored them. But her, she was a formidable force and he knew that he would someday have to deal with her.

Chapter Twenty-Four

It was a sunny, quiet evening and the conversation at the supper table was the usual. Funny anecdotes about school and friends, what this one and that one were doing in the village and the town. No cell phones were allowed at the dinner table, as Matt said he had to deal with them all day and this was his down time.

Lydia agreed and told her parents that it got annoying when you want to talk about something and your friends all have their noses buried in a piece of plastic. "No one knows how to communicate anymore. I can't tell you how many are flunking English, they talk text talk and wonder why the letter u is not the word y-o-u. They can't even spell."

"You know what happened the other day at lunch?" said Matt, anxiously waiting to finish the food he was chewing. "Well, it was at the Rotary meeting and when Perry came in he told the Rotarians that all cell phones had to be placed in the middle of the table, stacked one on top of another. He told them that the first one to grab for his cell phone during lunch or the meeting after paid the tab for the whole group. The place erupted in applause."

"That's a great idea," said Karen. "I like it."

They feasted on fresh peas from the garden, a salad and roasted chicken with garlic. Lydia had a glass of milk, her father a beer and Karen had iced tea.

After eating, Matt put down his fork and with a resigned look he said, "There's something your mom and I have to tell you."

Lydia bolted up out of her chair with terror in her eyes. "You're not getting divorced, are you?" She shouted.

Both parents were momentarily taken by surprise and then they started to laugh in unison.

"No, nothing like that, in fact this is a sad tale but one that you need to know," said Karen.

"A long time ago a little girl was born," said Matt. "She looked a lot like you. Your mom and I adored her as we adore you. Your mom was driving home one afternoon and there was dense fog at the bridge, on the outskirts of town. Your mom couldn't see anything and neither could the oncoming pickup truck. There was a head-on collision. Your mom spent many months in the hospital and the little girl, who was your sister, died in that accident. Her name was Sarah. It took your mom a long, long time to get over the death of your sister, let alone the injuries she sustained. Then your mom managed to get pregnant again and here you are. We finally realized that you should know." Her father looked expectantly at her and said, "You look like you have a question."

Lydia said, "Well, I kind of knew. Lately this girl keeps showing up in your bedroom and she was with us at the circle in the woods the other day." Karen let out an audible gasp and looked incredulously at her.

Matt looked to his wife, reached for her hand and held it tight. He nodded for Lydia to continue.

"I guess I knew it all along, deep down. No one has ever mentioned a sister to me but I'm really comforted about finding this out," she said.

"Any questions?" said Matt.

"Yes, but it doesn't pertain to Sarah. The other night you mentioned something about a legend and killings. I need to know what's going on. Sarah is here to help us, that I do know, and she keeps telling me we have work to do."

Karen let out a gasp, got up from her seat and abruptly left the room.

Lydia looked imploringly into her father's eyes. "I'm sorry, Dad," she said, and her voice sounded small and far away.

"Not your fault, sweetheart, your mother has to stop blaming herself for that accident, that's all."

Lydia started to cry. Large tears coursed down her face.

"It was no one's fault. Things happen for a reason, we don't know why. But God gives us gifts daily and some are taken away. I don't question anymore," Matt said kindly.

When Karen came back into the room, her eyes were red. She sat down and with a quavering voice said, "I'm sorry. I am getting better."

Karen took a deep breath and said, "The legend, I'm sure you have heard about it from your friends and over heard comments from us. The legend is supposed to reoccur here in our town on August seventeenth of this year. Already things have started to happen, as you realize. The big problem is, what if this is not physical but into the realm of the spiritual or occult or something like it? Then, we'll need all the protection we can get."

Matt rolled his eyes.

Karen increased the timber of her voice and smiled at her husband with a knowing glance. "The police are doing all they can but we, and I mean the group that Mum Mum belongs to, might be the ones to do it. I don't know, but we're doing all that we can, each in their own way."

"So, my girly girl, we love you, and that's all that matters. But we have to keep vigilant and we cannot keep secrets. Anything that happens, no matter how small, should be told to either your father or me. Understand?"

Lydia nodded her head.

"We don't want anything to happen to you."

Chapter Twenty-Five

It was early when Seth knocked on the large, very ornate wooden door. A large carving of a Celtic cross adorned the top panel of the door and a brass door knocker in the shape of a Green Man hung on the panel in the center. He grabbed it, pulled it back and let the clapper clank against the brass button it had covered. The sound was sharp and he winced as it hit his ears.

"Whoa, wait," was the reply on the other side of the door.

Seth felt like running away, and he glanced behind him to see if the path was clear. He turned his head to look back at the door as it slowly opened. There stood a giant of a man. Seth looked up into laughing grey eyes and a thatch of unkempt white hair. It was obvious the priest needed a shave too, but he was still shocked by those kindly eyes. "What the hell is a demonologist anyway?" he thought. Seth stammered a hello and launched into a fast diatribe on why he was there.

"Huld on," boomed a very deep voice that put him immediately at ease. "Firstly you're talkin too fast und secondly I know why you're here, so why not just come in?" came the reply in a heavy Scottish accent.

Seth didn't know whether to run or take that first step into what he perceived as oblivion. It took him three extra coffees this morning to boost his courage, and whatever he consumed last evening; he couldn't remember. He hesitated and then a large arm grabbed him and he was ushered into a small hallway. The priest spun him around and guided him into a sitting room. The room looked comfortable with the early morning light coming in through the blinds and the sheen of pastel curtains fluttering in a slight breeze from the open window.

It was a plain room, with a few scenic photos scattered here and there on the walls, several lamps, a couch and end tables and a few overstuffed chairs. In the center of the room was a large, very low coffee table.

It was obvious that Father was reading in this room, as a book lay open on the seat of the chair closest to the window. A carafe of coffee and a plate of bagels smothered in veggie cream cheese were waiting on a plate on the coffee table. Without much effort, Father guided Seth into the chair nearest the one he had obviously just vacated.

Father sat down opposite him.

They momentarily stared at one another and then they both spoke at once. Both stopping in mid-sentence, they burst out laughing. Father finally interjected, "first meetings are always awkward, Laddie." He spoke with a wonderful Scottish lilt to his voice, like a song.

Put immediately at ease, Seth said, "I suppose the gang has told you I'd be coming to talk to you?"

Father offered Seth half of one bagel and a cup of fresh coffee, but Seth declined.

Father nodded and began. "Yes, Katie told me the situation. The first thing that you must realize is that evil does truly exist. It is tangible und it's real. It's nothing to fool around with, like a Ouija Board or an old piece of furniture you know nothing about.

"An old piece of furniture?" said Seth.

"Huv ya ever noticed how many folk from the other side hang around old antique stores, Laddie? Have ya ever gone into that old barn up there on 28, you know the one that has all the thousands of antiques in und about it, und just walked around und listened? There's a friggin party goin' on in there, twenty-four seven."

Seth's eyes were wide as he looked at the priest. What he was hearing was very upsetting to him.

"But, you're, ah, ah, a priest," stammered Seth.

"Aye, I am, und that gives me great authority to chase away demons in the name of Christ, doesn't it now Laddie?" His eyes were kind and gentle, and his white hair was like a halo surrounding his face. His complexion was rather ruddy and when he smiled, the laugh lines around his eyes and at the corners of his mouth deepened.

"Where do I begin?" said Seth, looking straight into Father's eyes.

"Now, right here, und all you need to do is ask. First of all you must learn to protect yourself, and this is a good exercise for dealing with just about anyone who flips you, you know, makes you mad. It's like countin' ta ten an' seein how the pigs fly."

Seth liked this guy. He spent half a day learning how and when to protect himself and others from the influences of evil from the other side. He learned about energy chakras that are present in all beings, how to deflect bad energy and send good energy through prayer, mantra and meditation. It felt more like a Sunday school lesson from his youth, but it was much more enjoyable. He learned that the opposite of death is birth. He would have said life and he did.

The priest furrowed his brow when he blurted that answer out. "There is no, I repeat no opposite of life," the priest said, "life is never ending, there is no ending, like God und our savior Jesus Christ, they are life itself. All life comes through Them."

Seth nodded his head and said, "It seems like simple understanding from the old Baltimore Catechism, only with a much deeper meaning."

The priest nodded, "yes, much deeper. Und when you fully understand, it goes deeper still. Oh, I forgot one thing, when I said all you have to do is ask for the help, I hope you didn't forget God und Jesus in that equation."

"Ah, oh," said Seth, "I thought of you guys first."

Father shook his head sadly, but he was smiling, "Ach, the foibles of youth," he said.

"Laddie, put God first und the rest will fall into place. Yes, just think of God und the love will flow from him to you und into others und on und on. God's love is never-ending, infinite und real. We have to learn to use that love instead of running from it.

"Well Laddie, I have a one o'clock appointment with the confirmation class und then Mass, so if you will excuse me. Remember, practice, practice, practice, und what do we practice?" He said this with expectation in his voice and raising his finger in the air he tilted his head and raised one eyebrow.

Seth smiled and said, "We practice love, one of the highest vibrational energies."

The priest nodded his head, smiled and showed Seth to the door.

As Seth stepped outside into the bright sunshine and the smell of summer air, the priest said, "Have a good day, son. It's hard to think of this at first, but when you start making what we talked about today a part of your life, magical things start happening." Just before the door closed a booming voice called out, "und don't forget to pray!"

Chapter Twenty-Six

Lydia and Olivia were on a mission. "Okay, okay," said Olivia, "why is it so important to visit the cemetery? I mean, I go there with my mom occasionally, but you seem like you're in another world."

Lydia stopped and turned to Olivia. "Ya wanna know why, because I want to see where my sister's buried, that's why."

Olivia was in shock. In all the years she had known Lydia, there was never any mention of a sister.

"I remember my grandpa's grave," Lydia continued. "I remember when we used to play in here as kids, before we discovered the woods."

They were out on the highway now and their bikes rolled past houses, the filing station and auto repair shop. Suddenly, the bridge loomed ahead.

Crossing the river, they glided through the gates of the cemetery and stopped. Lydia looked back at the bridge. That is where her sister died, she thought. Momentarily mesmerized, she felt sad, but the urgency of her mission beckoned her on.

It was Memorial Day weekend and the cemetery was festooned with flags and flowers everywhere. The American Legion had been there in force and so had countless others to pay their respects to the dead.

It was a large and very old cemetery. The oldest graves were toward the front and the newer ones were in the back part slightly away from the river.

"I think it's somewhere over here," said Lydia.

Olivia looked around in wonder. "I wonder how many kids are in here that are our age," she mused.

Lydia ignored the question. "It would be in the back part. I remember in fourth grade having to look up early settlers and Civil War graves. They were all toward the front."

"Yes, but these are family plots, so some newer deaths could be in those grave plots too," countered Olivia.

"Look for Bell, anything with Bell on it. Oh wait," she slapped her head, "no, it would be my grandma's name, unless we have separate plots. Oh, this is so confusing. My mom's last name was Simpkins, that's it, Simpkins," she shouted. "Look for Simpkins and for Bell."

The day was warm and sunny. Under the tall trees it was cool and refreshing. They exhausted their search in the middle section and looked at several other rows of graves out in the sunlight, away from the trees.

"We'll look at those next," said Lydia, pointing to the graves nearest the edge of the river. Olivia nodded her head and walked toward the back edge of the cemetery. Olivia glanced up and noticed two rows of graves in the very back part of the cemetery. They were near the woods that ended in a myrtle-covered hill with several crypts dug into its bank. Curiously, she approached a particular grave. It was different from the rest. It was obviously the grave of a child. A small lamb graced the top of the stone. A cherub, arms around the neck of a lamb, its fingers interlaced, looked out on a world of silent beauty. "A chubby cherub," Olivia sing-songed in her mind, "chubby cherub, chubby cherub. . ." she began to sing over and over again.

She knelt down and there in front of her was the inscription *Sarah Our Loving Little Angel.*

Olivia stood up and went to the back of the stone. There it was, *Bell*.

"I found her, I think!" she shrieked.

Lydia came on a run. "Wow," said Lydia. "Sarah, yes, her name was Sarah."

Olivia looked at several of the stones next to the tiny grave and found Matthew and Karen Bell.

She also found where Eugenia would someday be buried beside her husband, David Simpkins.

Olivia began reading the names on some of the adjacent gravestones. Pederson.

"Hum," said Olivia, "I didn't know ol' man Pederson was 64." Lydia joined her and remarked that his wife's name was Lorraine. "They had a son. That's funny, there's a birth date and the death date is the same as his wife's but the date on his grave is just scratched in the stone; it's not engraved in, like her death date is. He would be the same age as Josh. That's weird."

"Lorraine is a pretty name, don't you think?" sighed Lydia.

"Okay," said Olivia, sounding like she wasn't quite sure. "I guess it's better than Mihitabel"

Lydia looked sharply at Olivia and said, "Mihitabel?"

"Yes, right over there on that stone. Mihitabel Pederson."

Lydia burst out laughing and then both girls were laughing hysterically.

After a few moments, they sat on the grass and then stretched out on their backs and let the sun warm their faces. They watched the clouds for a few moments before Lydia said,

"Remember in the woods, the other day…the girl?"

Olivia rolled her head toward Lydia and cautiously said, "Yessss. You mean what looked like the figure of a girl that could have been anything, such as ground fog, or mist or...."

Lydia continued in a quiet voice, "She, I think, is my sister."

Olivia suddenly sat up and faced Lydia on the grass. "What?" she cried.

"Yes, I think it's my sister and she's come back to warn us or protect us or something."

Olivia didn't know what to say, and for once kept her mouth shut.

Lydia continued, "The other day my mom and dad were having a discussion about my Gram. Dad mentioned something about a rumor or legend and so the other night I asked my parents about it. Oh, boy, did I ever get an earful. I mean, they were nice about it and all, but I know my dad was concerned, I could just tell."

She sighed, and after a pause continued, "it seems that there was this Indian, many years ago, who was real bad. He did lots of awful things, so his people murdered him. When he died, he vowed revenge on this town, and my mom says it's time again for things to happen."

"Wow," was all Olivia could say.

June

Chapter Twenty-Seven

It was conference day at school, so Josh decided that it would be a good day to see Tom. Attired in jeans, a tee shirt and sneakers, he approached the junk yard and looked at the *part-time-help-needed sign* tacked onto the fence near the entrance. He was tempted to tear it down, but depending on Tom's mood for the day, thought that might be suicidal.

Josh exhaled, took a deep breath and walked into the yard. He crossed the pavement and surveyed the front of the building. It was kept neat and swept. No visible parts lying around like some repair shops he'd been in. As he opened the door to the office, a string of bells hanging on the back of the door sounded his arrival with a clanging that would wake the dead.

The smell of oil, gas and welding flux greeted him in a familiar way and he chuckled. It smelled like the Auto Mechanics room at school, only this looked like the real thing instead of a clean, sterile laboratory for cars.

Tom came out from a large back area and appraised him.

"Hi, I'm Josh. I came to inquire about the part time job," he stammered.

Tom said, "Know who you are. Had any mechanical training?"

"I'm in BOCES. It will be my last year. I'm a good student and very interested in improving my skills."

"Well, I guess you're it. No one else has come along. I'm not the easiest to work for, anyone will tell you that, but I'm fair. Pete, he's my foreman and then we have the boy Alex. Mind your own business around here, don't ask questions unless it's directly related to what I want ya to do, do yer job and you'll work out fine. Can ya drive a wheeler?"

"My friends have some and I get to ride on them sometimes. Never been in trouble with one," Josh added as an afterthought.

"Good. Dress for the outdoors every time. Ya won't know where you'll be, so dress for the weather. I don't want any sissies here, Saturdays to start. We don't run the big machines on Saturday, but we still work till three. If ya don't know where a car is, ask. I don't want anyone running out there willy-nilly, hear?"

Josh nodded.

"Ya get an hour for lunch. There's a picnic table over there under that tree. Crap on it now from winter, just brush it off. We start the day promptly at seven a.m. Any questions?"

"Not yet."

"Don't be afraid to ask. If I'm in a rotten mood, and I bite ya, just let it go. I can be a bear most of the time, but I'm fair. I don't know how Pete stands me. Oh, bring gloves. Cuts are easy here, so bring heavy duty ones. Up with your tetanus shot?"

"I'll have to check with my mom, but I think I am."

"Make sure ya are and one more thing: no sneakers, too dangerous. Hard sole shoes, steel toe preferable. Got it?" Looking at Josh's feet he said, "I'll let it pass now, just don't step on any nails."

"You want me to start now?" said Josh, incredulously.

"You betcha."

Josh nodded. This was going to be a good summer, well, maybe. Either way it would be an interesting one.

He first encountered Alex in the parts yard, an area adjacent to the main building. Scrap parts were heaped all over. Most of these parts were of no use and went into large trucks, which delivered them to the scrap yard. The scrap truck arrived on Thursday and they had to be ready. Alex was changing the oil on a large loader. He glanced at Josh and stared. Josh smiled and nodded. "This kid looks my age," Josh thought. "How come I haven't seen him around?"

Pete came around the corner of the building and motioned for him to follow.

"We're going to get some parts for Monday's delivery. You take one wheeler and I'll take another and we'll go out."

Josh swung his leg over the wheeler that Pete nodded to and started the motor. He waited as Pete started his machine.

"Keys go back on "da board" when you're finished," he shouted at him. "Da boss don't want you to take keys out and leave 'em. He gets real mad, so remember."

They broke out of the trees that surrounded the main building complex and Josh couldn't believe his eyes. There they were, thousands of cars, all languishing in various states of decay. "A virtual sea of cars," he thought.

Pete seemed to know exactly where he was going, and Josh marveled at this.

They stopped in front of a Ford Fiesta and Pete looked at the car. "This one," he said.

"How do you know which cars, there are thousands here?" said Josh.

"I've been here many years," said Pete, "gotten used to it. This section is all Fords. To the right are the Chevys and then the Subarus, Toyotas and the others. The whole lot is divided up into sections. Up nearest the fence are Land Rovers and Jags. We even had several Lamborghinis one time."

Josh nodded, marveled at the somewhat ordered rows and began to understand.

"Your job is to clean the parts me and Alex bring in. I'll be showing you how to do that once we get inside. I'll be showin' you more of the yard in the beginning. You'll go out with me in the morning for an hour or two until you get an idea of where things are. Then you'll go in and clean 'em up."

They extracted several car parts, including a door, and Pete took Josh on a rather long, circuitous route back to the buildings.

"Things run here real quick, especially on Monday and Tuesday when everybody wants things in a hurry. Thursday is scrap day. That's when the big scrap trucks come in. Two days a month the crusher trucks are here and they're real hectic days too. Every day one or more cars show up. We have to assess them and find a place for them. If we know we need a certain part real quick, they are taken out before the car goes into its place in the lot. Those parts are put on the shelves in the main building. Some cars are worth more for parts than others. Big things, like motors and transmissions are taken out in the building across the drive. There's winches and such in there and it makes the job easier. Alex is in charge of that and he helps with putting parts on shelves too."

"Wow," was all Josh could say. He felt overwhelmed. This was some operation.

Pushing a button on one side of a large garage door, Pete waited while the door moved up. Josh's eyes widened at the sight. Row upon row of shelves ran the length of the building with a large area in the center that was clean except for large vats of liquid.

"This is where we clean the parts," said Pete. "Always remember to put the fan on and make sure the ventilation system is working before you close this door. Don't want anything to happen to you in here. Over there are the fire extinguishers and a call button, just in case there's a problem. That call button is hooked up to a siren. Alex hooked that one up. When we first used it, I thought da boss would die. It's loud, really loud, and I thought the fire and police departments would be here. But it was one proud day when the inspectors were coming. Da boss just couldn't wait to show it off, if you know what I mean. One of those damned inspectors started running toward the door when the thing rang. All da boss did was laugh at him."

Josh smiled as he envisioned the scene and noticed Alex looking at him. He was near one of the shelves, picking out parts and putting them in baskets with small tags on each. He had an old, beat-up grocery cart and went down each aisle with efficiency, something like a robot, picking here and picking there. Alex smiled at him and turned to continue his job.

The bell sounded for lunch and Josh went to sit at the picnic table. He brushed off the seat and sat. This job seemed overwhelming but he would stick it out. He wasn't a quitter and he was sure he could do the job, especially if Alex could do it. He wondered how long Alex had worked here.

Suddenly, without warning, Alex was beside him. Alex nodded and Josh stood up. "Hi, I'm Josh."

Alex eyed him carefully and then said, "I Immm Aaa leek." Alex tried to relax but this was a new thing. What did that girl say, relax and just let the words flow? He took a deep breath and asked, "Are you wawawaworkkking here?"

"Yeah, Tom just hired me. I'm trying to get used to the place, but it's sure large and there's lots of things to do."
Alex laughed and nodded his head. He said, "Yayayall gaget used tataoo ...it."

"How long have you worked here?" asked Josh.

"Lalalaoonng tatatime." said Alex.

Josh looked around, as he didn't know what else to say. Alex's stuttering made him somewhat uncomfortable but he really liked this kid. He seemed genuine, not like some of his friends at school. He saw an old basketball hoop attached to one side of the building. "You play ball?" he asked, nodding at the hoop.

Alex's eyes sparkled and he nodded. He ran to an old waste can and, throwing the lid off, produced an old, worn basketball.

Josh laughed, "Go man!" he shouted.

Alex threw the ball to Josh, who dribbled it to the hoop, jumped and with little effort- slid the ball in.

Alex didn't look that impressed as Josh threw him the ball. Alex backed up past the picnic table and kept going.

"Whoa," shouted Josh, "that's half-court. Are you nuts? Half-court? Yeah right. This I have to see."

Josh couldn't help but notice how calm Alex seemed to be. He had a smirk on his face that belied confidence. "Total command," Josh thought, as he looked at this tall, gawky boy who was next to his own age. Without warning, Alex was airborne and so was the ball. Josh looked at the scene as if in slow motion. The ball hung in the air and then, whoosh, it was through the hoop. Josh stood there dumbfounded.

"Holy crap, holy fuckin' crap!" he shouted.

Alex just laughed. He beamed with delight.

"Do that again and I'll really be impressed," Josh said as he threw Alex the ball.

Alex moved over several feet and again without any notice, he shot into the air and the ball fell effortlessly into the hoop.

"This is beyond me," Josh said. "How did you do that? I mean, I haven't seen anything like it."

Just then Tom appeared. "Time for work," he shouted. Josh headed for the parts vats and Alex headed for the back of the building after he deposited his basketball back into the trash can.

Josh worked diligently all afternoon and finally, when three o'clock rolled around, Tom came up to him and told him he would see him next week. Josh told him he really enjoyed it but that it would take him some time to learn all there was to learn.

"Just ask," said Tom, "just ask. You'll catch on."

Josh made a mental note not to get involved, to do his work, keep his eyes and ears open and not to ask questions unless it pertained only to work.

He also made a mental note not to elaborate on all the things that happened at the *Yard* when he came home. He just knew his mom would want to know and that is where the gossip started, especially where she worked.

Chapter Twenty-Eight

Josh walked home in the late afternoon sun. It was starting to cloud up and he would make it home in time for dinner.
As he entered the house, his mother called to him. "Where have you been, and all day?" she whined.

"Well, I did as you said and I went to Tom's and he hired me. So I worked all day," he said proudly.

She gasped, "I just mentioned that he had a sign out front, but I didn't think you would actually go there!"

"Yes, I'm the new hired man and I like it. Saturday's seven a.m. till noon till school is out and then full time. There's a lot to learn, so they're just breaking me in. It's an actual car place, not like school at all, and I really like it. It's the other end of the auto business," he said proudly.

"I would sure say so," said his father from behind him. "How's Old Tom anyway?"

"Pretty decent. I spent most of the day with the hired men. It was really great."

"What did you have for lunch?" his mother asked, rather churlishly.

He rolled his eyes."I'm going to wash up, I bet I really smell."

"Dinner's in ten minutes," his mother said and turned to finish setting the table.

He met Olivia half way down the hallway. "What is that smell?" she shouted.

He slammed the bathroom door, laughing.

They sat at the table discussing the day. As they finished his father said, "So, you really like the job?"

Olivia looked at him, surprised.

"Job," she disdainfully said, "what job?"

"Josh is working for Tom at the yard," said their mother.

Olivia's eyes became saucers. "Really," she gasped. "So you probably met the boy who stutters?" said Olivia, with haughtiness in her voice."

Josh stared at her. "How do you know about him?" he said in a quiet voice.

"Oh, I've met him."

"Really, where?" said Josh, his full attention on her.

"Just around," said Olivia, now appearing nervous.

Josh glanced at his father, who had a look of concern on his face. "Where, Olivia?" her father said, giving his daughter his full attention as he set his coffee cup down.

"We were in the back of the junk yard, a while ago, and he came along on a wheeler. We just introduced ourselves and then he had to go. That's all. We were headed for the woods. Lydia's grandmother is helping with research in the woods and we thought she'd be there."

"What were you doing going through the yard, and besides those woods are dangerous," said her mother.

"Well, that's the shortcut and everyone goes through Dottie's to get into the woods where they're researching."

"Researching, researching what?" said her father sternly.

"There's this vine growing there and they say it's hundreds and hundreds of years old. The college is there to study it. We saw part of it and it is really big," she exclaimed.

Josh just kept staring at her.

She shrugged, "that's all. We just went to see the vine and to see if the researchers were still there or maybe Eugenia. She's helping with some of the work."

"I just don't like the idea of you hanging around with Dottie and Eugenia." said her mom. "They aren't exactly good Christians."

Her daughter looked at her, eyes blazing. "Neither are we," Olivia retorted. "We never go to church either. Not like Lydia and her mom."

"A lot of Sunday mornings I have to work," retorted her mother.

"Alright, enough," her father said sternly.

Looking at Olivia, her father said, "If and when you go over there again, I want you to call us and tell us where you are. Understand? I don't like you in those woods, but I know what I did in there when I was a boy and I'm not going to tell you not to go in them. I do want you to remember that those woods are dangerous and yes, I remember that vine. It's all over the place in there. Now that you mention it, I've never seen where it starts. Some say it's deep in the swamp. Speaking of swamp, you don't go near it, understand? Woods yes, swamp no. Got it? Besides, if Tom caught you going through his junk yard, there would be hell to pay."

"Alex and Pete are the yard men. Tom stays in the office most of the time," said Josh. "I imagine his paperwork is unbelievable. All those wrecked cars coming in and the trucks that have to be loaded, it would be a nightmare. Man, it is some place. Tom said he'll teach me to drive the large loader. When the time comes I'm sure you'll be hearing from him for permission to teach me. That's one thing we don't do in school."

His father nodded.

"Loader?" his mother shrieked.

His father rolled his eyes and let out an exasperated sigh.

"Yes," said Josh. "It'll be good for me and then when I go for my certification, I'll have some experience."

"What?" his mother wailed.

"Our boy is growing up," said his father quietly. "When the time comes, meanwhile, work well and if it doesn't work out, I'll back you."

He looked at his father quizzically.

"You know what I mean, Josh."

Josh shook his head. "It's funny you mention that, I mean about his temper and all. He said the same thing to me this morning. That if he blew off at me to just let it roll off my shoulders. He doesn't mean anything by it. It's his nature, he said."

His father smiled and nodded. "Tom is not by any means a dumb man, it's just that sometimes he gets a little, ah, rough so to speak."

"Okay, okay," laughed Josh, "I know what you mean. I've heard he can be pretty mean, especially when he's drunk."

"I don't like this one bit," wailed his mother.

His father suppressed a laugh, nodded and took a sip of his coffee.

"Oh," said Josh, "I'll need several pairs of work gloves and a pair of steel toe shoes with hard soles."

"What?" his mother said.

"He's really up on safety and he told me not to show up in sneakers. He even asked me about my tetanus shot," he said, eyeing his mother.

"You're up to date, at least I think so. I'll call the clinic on Monday to make sure. Meanwhile, I guess we'll have to go shopping on Monday."

"Thanks Mom," he said.

"Alex, you said. That's his name, Alex?" asked Olivia.

"Yes," said Josh, "his name's Alex. He stutters real bad, but I have a really good feeling about the kid, and boy can he shoot baskets."

Olivia just stared at him.

Chapter Twenty-Nine

It was Tuesday, the sun was still bright on this late afternoon. The day was warm and very humid. There was a threat of rain in the forecast. Tom parked the wheeler in front of the woods and looked at the gaping hole in the bushes to the well worn path. He looked on the horizon and saw the outline of Dottie's barn in the distance. He wondered just what all the commotion was anyway, something about an ancient vine. Things like this didn't interest him, but Alex and Josh had mentioned it, so he should have the right to investigate what all the fuss was about. After all, it was his property. He had closed up at four, followed Alex's lead and headed for the woods.

He headed down the path into the dark interior of the woods. He heard them before he saw them. They were all standing around an elderly man, the same man who had come to him from the university in the first place. He was talking to the small group, one of which was Alex.

His fury knew no bounds, how many times had he told that damned kid to take a low profile, and here he was, right in the middle of the God damned group.

Tom looked closely at the group before they noticed him. Eugenia, those two girls he had seen around, one of them was Matt's daughter and the other one, he didn't know. Alex and the professor made up the rest of the small contingent plus a chubby kid he had seen around a time or two. It was obvious they were getting ready to go as they were packing sample vials into a small black case. Alex was the first to spot him, and he saw the fear in his son's face. The others turned to face him and he nodded.

"Just seein' what you're all up to," he said casually, a little too casually.

"In another day or so we'll be finished here. A very interesting find and a very significant one at that," remarked the professor.

Tom smiled, although a little too much of a friendly smile for Tom, and Eugenia was the first one to catch it.

"Tom, this has been an interesting find. I thank you and I'm sure the college and the professor thank you too," remarked Eugenia, trying to allay the sick sensation in the pit of her stomach. Eugenia sensed something, she didn't know quite what, but maybe it was the way he was looking at the boy they called Alex.

"Anytime I can be of help," Tom remarked nonchalantly. "I'm glad to do it."

They walked out of the woods and onto the muddy, rutted path that ran through the yard and ended up in Dottie's side yard. Alex headed for his house using a different path while the others used the one going to Dottie's.

"How long have ya been coming here?" asked Tom as he caught up with his son.

Alex stopped and turned. "Ah ah ffew tatatimes," he said, "jusssst a ffew tatataimes. IItt is inter..." but the slap knocked him off-balance and his body hit the side of an old derelict car, hard. Tom's voice was now a shout. "Ya stupid kid, how many times have I told ya to keep a low profile?"

Alex regained his balance and then they were there at his side: Olivia, Lydia, Kenny and Eugenia.

When Tom saw them, he bellowed, "Get off my land, this in none of yer business."

"Is so," countered Olivia. "When it concerns one of our friends it concerns us."

Tom lunged at her, but Lydia stuck out her foot. Tom's fall was hard and left him momentarily disoriented. He had landed face-first in the muddy, rutted path. He lifted his head and looked up into the face of a very determined little girl with bright green eyes and carrot red hair. He moaned and looked back at the ground

"You're not dead," Lydia sneered. She wanted to say what an ass he was, but she refrained.

"I thought I was," he mumbled. His head was pounding and he was smeared with grass and mud, for it had rained the night before.

He looked up and saw his son bending over him, ready to help him to his feet. He went to slap his son's hand away as anger now infused his body, but only for a moment. Suddenly, a feeling of calm came over him. He sighed and rolled over on his back, struggling momentarily to sit up. God, his head felt like it had hit a road and bounced twenty times. His eyes even hurt. He looked at Lydia, who still had an authoritative look of disgust on her face. Momentarily, he wanted to slap this kid into the next county if he could. Then something took hold of him, he didn't know where it came from, but he started to laugh and he laughed till tears rolled down his cheeks. His son's look of concern stopped him momentarily. "I look a sight, don't I?" he gasped. Exhausted, he hung his head.

"Now," said Lydia, "my dead sister has a message for you and I think it would be good if you listen."

He was so tired, they could hang him here and now or put him in a barrel of boiling oil and he wouldn't care.

"Okay, okay," he quickly said. "What the hell would a ghost have to say to me?" he thought.

"She has a message from Lorraine," said Lydia.

His head jerked up at the sound of Lorraine's name. Anger infused his body. Lorraine, that sacred name, his secret, his nemesis.

"Before you get all pissy," Lydia chirped, reading the anger in his face, "I suggest you relax and listen to what she has to say."

The sun was setting and as the orb was descending to the other side of the world, it put on a colorful lightshow seemingly just for them. The early evening was turning damp and he shivered. The ripped-off shirt sleeves of his now filthy tee afforded him little comfort. A little breeze touched his cheek and that voice in his head spoke with the gentleness of a whisper.

"*Your wife wants you to let her go,*" were the only words he heard. He wanted her to say more, to clarify what the hell she meant by "let her go." He was now angry, his face turning red with rage. "What the fuck!" he yelled. "Let her go, let her go?" His voice was lost in the still and mournful frames of the watching, waiting vehicles that sat silently by. He raged, he cried, he shouted those words over and over until they rang like thunder in his ears. He collapsed back onto the ground, sobbing. "I can't, I just can't. I loved her so, we were happy. What are you doing to me?" he whispered hoarsely into the now grey-black sky.

He was physically exhausted. He rolled onto his side and hoisted himself onto his hands and knees. He crawled to the side of an old car, its silhouette just discernible in the fading light. He grabbed the door handle and pulled, as hands at his elbows helped him up. He stood there a ragged and broken man. He was in limbo, and his thoughts were jumbled.

Alex had taken a step away from his father, but kept his hand at the ready when he noticed a firm grip on his sleeve. Olivia's hand was still on his sleeve when their eyes met and she shook her head no. His arm fell slowly to his side.

Sarah stood there silently, just the faint outline of her silhouette visible. He looked at her. "What the fffff....," Tom mumbled. "*I will see you when you are ready to see me again*," she said. It was more like a thought that popped into his head, and the thought had a girlish but deep, resonating sound that left his mind befuddled and his heart softened. The sing-song voice of a girl in her puberty, stopped short by time and circumstances.

"What do ya want?" he whispered.

Silence like a vacuum descended. He heard the wind rustling the leaves as night descended, and he could smell the damp hay from mown fields wet by last night's rain. He had spent so long in a cloud of hatred, indecision and anger that he didn't know how to love anymore. Once in awhile a little chink in his armor occurred, and he discovered that at least he was still human instead of this monster he had become. Hiding behind his business and the volunteer organizations he joined and the beer. Yes, lots and lots of beer, that mind-dulling substance, the coward's way out when the truth hurts more than one can bear.

He realized then that it takes courage and guts to face one's own truth. He wasn't sure he wanted to climb out of that comfort zone he had put himself in. The diatribes of hatred, blame and all that went with it. He was comfortable there.

Could he change? It wouldn't be easy, he'd really have to try, try very hard. His mouth was dry. He glanced at his son. The sight revolted him, but why? Why did this boy, who had grown up with all the expectations of youth, why did he hate him so?

Suddenly, he heard a faint whisper. He shook his head and then the faintly audible voice of Lorraine came through as if she were standing right next to him. "*I have never left you, I will always be with you, but it has to be on my own terms, not yours.*" He shook his head: he didn't understand the "my terms, not yours" one bit.

He glanced over Lydia's shoulder and there were Olivia, Kenny and Sarah. Sarah stood a little in front of Kenny and he could see part of Kenny through her image at the same time. He smiled wearily.

"One other thing," said Lydia. "My sister wants you to know that Lorraine is in your son and so are you."

He took a deep breath and saw the image of Sarah fading. It was that quiet time, just after sunset, that darkening period when things are discernible and yet remain in deep shadow. It was just how he felt, in shadow, yet somehow he was beginning to understand. "How come I can almost see your sister and not my Lorraine?" he snarled.

"Because you're not ready to see Lorraine yet," Lydia blurted out. She really, really wanted to know how she knew that.

He looked around and saw Alex, standing quietly near his shoulder, as well as Eugenia, and another woman suddenly appeared. He recognized her as Matt's wife, Karen, yes that was it, Karen. He turned to face the two. "I look a sight, don't I?" he said quietly.

"Nothing that a little water and a lot of love won't heal," said Karen, who had also heard and understood the message.

Karen came close to him. "Let me make something very clear to you," she said quietly but earnestly. "When we grieve someone so much that we have to keep that loved one's soul enslaved, chained to us, we restrict their free will and our own free will as well. One of the greatest gifts a person can give to another person in this life and the next, besides love and respect, is to let go. Letting go is love's greatest sacrifice. It doesn't mean that you love them any less or that they will never be with you again or you disrespect their memory. No. It's the recognition that you've set them free; free to come back to you without the chains and bondage. You'll also find that you have set yourself free, free to love unconditionally and without fear."

Tom blew out a deep sigh. Hesitantly he put his arm around his son's shoulder and they started for the house.

Chapter Thirty

The group followed Tom and Alex through the door and into the kitchen. Eugenia spied a kettle. She immediately began making tea."Where's your tea?" she inquired.

"Never touch the stuff," said Tom, wearily.

"Well you're goin' to now," she said with the voice of a brigadier general.

Karen started to laugh, then looked directly at Tom and said, "Don't even think about disobeying her. She'll bite your head off."

"There's a box up there over the sink," sneered Tom.

"Good," said Eugenia, "now sugar and milk, or are we going Lenten tonight?"

"Mother," said Karen, "really!"

Tom looked from one woman to the other and marveled at the easy dynamics between them.

Alex moved to the refrigerator and produced a small pitcher of half and half. He grabbed the sugar bowl from the counter next to the sink and placed them on the table.

Olivia moved in front of Tom and placed a tray of cookies on the table. She turned and faced him. "I see that you're really human after all. Oh God, it's going to be soooo hard to apologize to that brother of mine!"

Alex burst out laughing.

Tom looked bewildered. "Okay, what's the joke?" He inquired, looking from Olivia to Alex and back again.

"My brother is Josh, and I always believed you were a beastly man, but he says otherwise. So now I have to apologize to him. That is not, I repeat, not good," chirped Olivia.

Tom looked at his son and couldn't believe it. Here was a very amiable and handsome young man, and he was his...son. How could he have been so blind all these years? Tears filled his eyes; he wanted to cry so bad his face hurt. How, just how, was he going to make it up to this kid?

Karen placed her hand on his shoulder. "We're here and we want to help," she said. "We know it will be hard, but you two need quality time alone, by yourselves, away from this place."

Alex spoke up. "You used to take me fishin' before mom died," Alex spoke quietly, slowly, almost wistfully and without a stutter. "Ma ma my mom was mine too, nnnot all yours," Alex blurted out as he turned and faced the counter.

Olivia put an arm on his shoulder.

Eugenia faced Tom from the other side of the table. "You two have a lot of catching up to do and I think that now is a good time to start. One thing," she said, pointing her finger at Tom. Her voice was steel. "Listen, that's all, just listen."

"I've got a lot to work on, ladies," Tom said. Glancing at his son and Kenny, he added, "and gentlemen."

He paused momentarily and continued. "Hate can consume a man and I guess if we don't figure that out here, we have that place over yonder, right?" he said, hopefully. "I want to be alone with my son for a few moments, just a few. Please come back and join us," his voice trailed off.

"It doesn't all have to be said tonight. I think it would be a real good idea if we left the two of you to talk. We'll all come over tomorrow and I'll bring supper," said Karen.

Tom laughed. "This was an awful hard thing to do just to get supper," he remarked thoughtfully as he glanced at Eugenia.

"He's like a little kid," thought Karen as she looked at him.

"Oh, ya old goat," said Eugenia, disgust in her voice.

Tom was laughing as they all left the house.

Alex sat down at the table opposite his father. The silence between them was like a vast universe, deep and intense. Tom looked at his son, as if for the first time since the accident. His son was staring intently at him, a look of expectation in his eyes. Tom was momentarily taken by surprise and by guilt. He remembered back to his own father, who had passed before Alex was born. He remembered the sadness Lorraine felt when she was told that their second child, a girl, would not live and would have to be taken from her womb, and then that horrible accident, when his whole world fell apart.

"I've become a very bitter man," Tom stated. "I feel so guilty that I've wasted your life on my anger," he went on. "I just don't know what I can say, other than that I'm truly sorry. It's going to take time for me, and I'm begging ya to stay with me and maybe we can both learn this together."

Alex smiled thoughtfully, and nodded his head.

"Ya know, I went out there because I, well, I thought you'd be out there and I was just so darn angry about you disobeying me, but, now ya know it just doesn't matter anymore," said Tom as he glanced down at his cup of tea.

"Now," Tom roared, momentarily startling Alex so much so that Alex dumped some of the tea he was about to drink, "I guess I'll have to get in touch with the school!"

~

He looked around at this place that was once verdant forest. Through the centuries it became plowed fields, a ball park and now it was a car grave yard. How appropriate, he mused, oh how appropriate. Rotting, rusting hulks of machines, some newer, some very old, but still the decay amused him. He thought it ironic.

He sometimes watched from the surrounding woods when they brought in a new wreck. Looking at the hulks of twisted metal, hearing the screams of the spirits of the dead as they relived their last moments made him think of his last moments. Some of the spirits stayed for many years, roaming around the weeded paths and rusting hulks, in a limbo of sorts, always questioning, always seeking.

Chapter Thirty-One

It was early morning and Matt sat at his desk thinking, oblivious to everything around him. He was attempting to put the pieces of the puzzle together and started to ask Eugenia and Katie questions that he never thought he would be asking. If a non-physical being could take shape in a physical being, just like in the movies then what? They were telling him a couple of days ago that this was an awakening period. Awakening to what? Another dimension, as Katie called it, or as Eugenia put it, another phase of human consciousness. What about Father Munro? That's it! His feet lifted off the desk like rockets and landed with a thud on the floor. His chair shot backwards and almost ran itself off the floor mat which was placed there to save the floor under its well-worn seat.

Father Munro, yes, clear-thinking Father Munro. He could offer more dimension on this subject, or then again, maybe not. It was something he said one time on the altar when Matt was attending church with Karen and Lydia that piqued his interest; things are real or unreal, it is up to us to figure out which are which, and in all humans the answers are different.

He stood up and noticed Chris coming toward him. Chris didn't look too happy as he brandished a piece of paper in his hand. Matt had a sinking feeling in the pit of his stomach. Chris stood in front of the desk.

"Got some help, although I don't know if I really want it but we could use it, maybe. Oh Christ, I don't know what I'm saying. I made some inquiries and a friend of mine on the police force in the city said he knew a man who was a genius at ferreting out potential crime and the like and that he was a profiler. This guy is retired from the FBI and has agreed to help us. Imagine that, a profiler," said Chris. His voice was sarcastic, as if he was waiting for Matt to say something. "And a retired one at that!"

Matt started to laugh, "I'm sorry, Chief, but that's funny."

"Alright, what do we do with him?" asked Chris.

"Personally, I think he could help us on some of the research for investigating some of the leads we have now. I know we don't have enough men to cover everything. We don't really want this out, but Larry said something to me at the barber shop yesterday."

Chris rolled his eyes. "The barber shop morning coffee entourage, where all the problems of the world are solved," said Chris with disgust.

Matt smiled. He knew every one of those men and opinionated yes, outspoken absolutely, but they were the professionals, business owners, farmers, mechanics and firemen of the town. They were entitled to their opinions. Hell, even the bank manager went in there. You could manage to get roasted and toasted one week and be a regular guy the next. No wonder certain members of the village board didn't go in there.

Matt was smiling when Chris asked him, "What's so funny?"

"I'm just thinking about that barber shop. We should send all our officers there for lessons. Let's face it, if you robbed a bank in the morning they would know who did it, why and the whole scenario an hour later. Those guys are experts at extracting information. They have techniques that rattle my imagination. If they don't ask you straight out they find other insidious ways to wheedle it out of you. They're a fascination to me, a lesson in social infrastructure in a small town. I thought women were bad. Those guys have it all over the gals."

"Okay, take this guy around, see what he can find, we have just a few months to go and that isn't a lot of time," said Chris.

"What's his name?" said Matt.

"Name is Dave, that's all I know for now."

Matt nodded but his face had grown thoughtful. Dave. That was his father's name. His father, how many years had it been? Is he even still alive?

"Something wrong, Matt?" said Chris.

Beamed out of his short moment of thought, Matt shook his head no, but something was still bothering him, and he couldn't figure out why. The queasy feeling in the pit of his stomach wouldn't go away.

"Oh shit," Matt said, hitting his forehead, "gotta issue a citation for Vesley's cows. They caused quite a stir in the fog last night, all standing there in the road. I swear they eat blacktop for dessert or are addicted to it."

"Naw, they're standing there to keep warm. Blacktop retains its heat and cows like that," said Chris. "They also like to lick the salt from the side of the road. When the plows come along in the winter and plow, all the salt ends up at the side of the road."

"Are they even using salt anymore?" said Matt. "I didn't think they did."

"I understand it's a mix of slag dust, salt and coarse sand," said Chris.

"No wonder the bottom of my car looks like hell," Matt muttered.

Chris smiled and said "our boy is due this afternoon. Look out for him would ya?"

Chapter Thirty-Two

Matt grabbed his hat and started for the small parking lot across the street from the station where the county garage stood. He called into dispatch, gave the time and destination, started the car and exited the lot. The air was pleasant but humid. It was slightly overcast as he headed for the Vesley farm. Several miles outside of town he pulled into a large driveway, climbed the hill to the house and parked.

He looked around before exiting the car. The weathered house was well kept but shabby. Flowers were planted here and there. The strong smell of cows and manure greeted his nostrils. The younger Mrs. Vesley came out from the house to greet him. She had on an apron, faded jeans and a tee shirt that was just a wee bit too tight for Matt's taste. Her mother-in-law would be in the barn with the cows, and that is who he came to see.

"Something wrong, Matt?" came a deep voice from behind him.

He turned and looked Sylvia Vesley square in the eye.

"I think you know why I'm here and I don't want to be here doing this, but this complaint came in today and I have to serve you a citation."

"Son of a bitch," replied the older, large-framed, tall woman. "If these damned pissants stay out of my business we could live in peace. Last month it was manure on the road, now what?"

"Cows were in the road last night and almost caused an accident," said Matt, as nonchalantly as he could manage. He did not want to get Sil upset, because Sil's rages knew no bounds.

Her daughter-in-law, Casey, quietly said, "Ma, I'll take care of it."

"Where is Bill this morning?" asked Matt, trying desperately to defuse the situation.

Casey smiled and said, "Out in the back with heifers and..."

Suddenly shouts came from the farm lane that ran between the barn and the house. A large tractor loomed into view and it was going fast. The tractor screeched to a halt and a small, middle-aged man jumped off it.

"Matt, Matt, I'm glad you're here!" he screamed.

Sil's voice, filled with genuine concern, could be heard on top of the shouts of her son, "Settle down, settle down and tell us what's wrong."

Breathing hard and trying to get his thoughts collected, the little man started talking. "I brought the heifers out into the dry cow pasture and I was going to put all of them, including the beefs together for the week. I didn't see the dry cows. There are six of them, so I thought they might be down in the gully by the woods. Not there either. So now I'm thinking that somehow they broke through the fence and may be in the next county. So I start to panic cause that's all I need today is to chase those friggin' cows all over hell. So over the hill I go and there they are, well what's left of them. It was like a slaughter house. Blood everywhere and every one of those cows' looks like it exploded from the inside. I got down real close to number forty-seven," he was now visibly crying, "and she was all burned where her nose and mouth are. I got out of there real quick and here I am."

Matt put his hand on Roger's shoulder as his wife hugged him. When Matt glanced over at Sil, she looked like she was going to explode in rage.

"Calm down," he cautioned.

"Calm down? Calm down? Six cows, thousand dollars each and you want me to calm down? Hell no!" shouted the large woman who looked like she was going to slug someone, anyone.

"Where are they?" asked Matt as he turned to face Roger.

"You want to go out there?" Roger said incredulously.

Matt nodded.

"You actually want to go out there?" said Roger.

"Where?" said Matt, more firmly now. "Let's take the truck."

"Naw, hop up on the tractor, hell of a lot easier," said Roger.

Matt turned to Sil, "Call the station, tell them what happened, and tell them I'm on it. Talk to the chief if possible. Got it Sil?" Matt shouted as he headed for the tractor.

Sil nodded and headed for the house with her daughter-in-law following quickly behind.

"Never saw anything like it," Roger shouted over the roar of the tractor motor.

Matt nodded. He felt for the small tape recorder in his pocket and the radio on his belt. It was better for Sil to call the event in, keep her mind off killing or maiming someone. Sil was generally an amiable woman, until someone lit her fuse, then watch out.

The air was moist with a threat of rain but the smell of fresh-tilled earth and new-mown hay was a delight to the senses as they started down a steep incline near the river. Matt looked up and noticed vultures circling overhead. The huge birds looked so graceful in flight and so ugly up close.

Roger stopped the tractor and shut off the engine. "We'll walk from here," he said. "Not far."

The cows were lying in what seemed to be a circle and Matt was, at first, taken completely by surprise. The carnage was awful. Insides lay about the grass, and huge open wounds in their stomachs exposed dark pink interior. One of the cows was obviously pregnant. The fully developed form of a calf completely encased in its placenta lay on the grass beside her and it had started to wither and blacken in the heat of the day.

Matt took a deep breath and hung his head. He had work to do and he'd best call in the local vet. They would want to know how they all died. It looked like they were hit all at once, but how and with what? These were nine hundred to twelve hundred pound animals and there was no sign of struggle. If these were human beings, oh God he didn't even want to think about it.

He moved among the six animals. He was careful where he was stepping in case they could get a real investigation going. He grabbed the ear of one of the cows; her lolling tongue was stiff when he tilted her head toward him. He noticed the black first, like charcoal around the mouth and deep within the throat, and then he smelled it; burned flesh. Were they struck by lightning? He straightened. "These animals look like they were struck by lightning," he said.

Roger nodded and said, "yeah, but it was a good moon last night, no rain, no thunder or lightning. So now what? "The tone of his voice was sarcastic.

"We'll wait for the rest of the crew to show up."

Matt glanced up, noticed a tall figure walking toward him and immediately recognized Grayson. Grayson walked with the easy grace of a ballerina across a stage. Matt laughed at the local veterinarian as he approached with the little bag he always carried. Grayson stopped short, wincing at the sight. "What the hell," he said in his Georgia drawl.

"That's exactly what I said," countered Matt.

"Looks like a lightning strike, but all six at once and all blown apart like this! Beats anything I've ever seen. Roger," he barked. "is there a fence near these animals?"

Roger looked at him confused and shook his head no.

Matt looked skeptically at Grayson. Grayson put up one finger and said, "Simple, Watson." Matt rolled his eyes; a lecture was coming with all the adjectives of a good Sherlock Holmes skit. "I've seen where lightning hit a fence and the lightning traveled along the fence and into the bodies of cows that were grazing through the fence with the wire resting on their necks. Blew the animals right apart, POW."

"Oh," said Matt, "they acted as the ground. Makes sense, but where is the fence?"

"Brilliant deduction, Holmes," said the veterinarian.

Matt rolled his eyes again.

"Well, time for some answers," said Grayson as he knelt down to put on a pair of rubber boots and snap on rubber exam gloves. "I won't have much sterilization out here but I need certain organ tissue." He grunted as he grabbed one hoof and pulled. "Here, hold this just like this."

Matt grabbed the hoof. He didn't realize that a cow hoof, plus foreleg could be so heavy.

"Roger, get me that tub there," Grayson commanded, "I'll work on this animal, it seems to be the best candidate of all of 'em." Grayson looked up and straight into the face of Roger. "I'm sorry, Roger." he said.

Roger nodded as large tears coursed down his face.

Grayson worked very methodically and occasionally a hum would escape from his lips or an ahhhh accompanied by shakes of the head or scratches behind his left ear.

When the liver was extracted, Grayson just stared at it. "This cow had one hell of a jolt of electricity go through her." With a deft motion he lifted the heavy organ. It made a "thug" noise as it slid to the bottom of the large tub.

Matt sensed others coming down the hill toward them, but he wasn't paying them much attention. His back was to them and he was pushing one hoof into the air so Grayson could get a better look inside the abdominal cavity.

"I wanna get a sample from all four of the stomachs of this animal. I need contents to make tests, so just hang on a little more. I know it's heavy, but try as best you can."

The heat and the smell were starting to get to Matt. He was sweating and filthy. Manure mixed with stomach contents and pieces of organs had a surreal effect on him. He was leaning toward the cow with the hoof held up and away from her open abdomen. Grayson was cutting samples in the space just below his right foot when someone walked into Matt's peripheral vision on the opposite side of the cow. Matt realized someone was there but didn't pay any attention until a familiar voice from a very distant and buried past said, "Hello, Matty."

Matt began to shake as memories of the broken dreams and promises flooded over him like a tidal wave. He looked up into those too familiar blue-grey eyes, the eyes of his father.

Chapter Thirty-Three

Matt was exhausted as he entered the hallway to his house. He smelled, he was dirty and he was tired. His wife met him in the doorway to the kitchen.

She loudly exclaimed, "what is that smell?"

"Cow innards, ma'am," was Matt's reply. "Honey, I'm just too tired to even talk right now and I really need a shower."

"More like two or three," said Karen, looking like she was about to gag.

"Let me shower and then I'll tell you the tale over dinner. Where's Lydia?"

"Oh she's at Mum Mum's; they're doing a girl thing later tonight."

"Good," said Matt, laughing as he dashed up the stairs naked, his clothing heaped in a pile in the small hallway.

Karen opened the washer door and unceremoniously dumped the clothing into the washer. She put in extra detergent, slammed the door closed and started the machine. Then she grabbed the mop and propped open the back door for air circulation.

An hour later, over pork chops, green beans and rice, pie and tea, he related the story of his day. He left out the part about his father. He set down his tea and commented that there were a lot of leftovers.

Karen told him that she had made extra for Tom and Alex and relayed the tale of what had happened the previous evening.

Matt commented that there was a lot going on in their lives.

She asked about Alex, knowing deep down that Alex was Tom's son. "How could Tom get away with not having the boy go to school?" she asked.

"I'm not going to go there. He's been hiding that boy since Lorraine died, and how many years has that been?" said Matt.

"He stutters real badly, but I see he's working on it. That must be why Lydia asked me about stuttering one day, and people being able to overcome it. I told her about the new studies, especially in Sweden, and how successful they are, and I told her about some of the techniques that are being used. I guess she and Olivia have been coaching the boy. Our daughter sure gets around and we don't know it. That's the part that disturbs me."

Matt patted her hand and settled back into his chair.

As he was about to speak, Karen said, "Okay, what really happened today? What have you left out?"

He looked at her and muttered, "Always could read me like a book."

She smiled and nodded.

Matt sighed and said, "Someone showed up today, someone from my past. I knew we would meet again but I certainly didn't think it would be today, or maybe I did. I got a hint this morning when the chief came in to say that a new man was coming here from the FBI. Some sort of profiler. When he said his name, my stomach got real queasy. This man shows up, and sure enough he's my father."

Karen gasped, "Oh Matt!"

"I asked him for some time, and he said we'd have plenty of that. He's staying at the motel just out of town. I told him I'd see him tomorrow," he said wearily.

"Do you want me around?" Karen asked hesitantly.

"Sweetie, I don't know what I want right now."

"Then I suggest you spend some time alone. I'm here if you need me."

"Yeah, I'm gonna take a beer and go sit out on the patio. Fresh air would do me good."

As he walked out of the house, Matt looked up into the early evening sky. The sun had come out from heavy clouds and the yard was at peace. It glowed with a golden shimmer, like a fairy tale. He sat down heavily in his padded deck chair. He was comfortable but not at peace. He remembered his childhood like it was just yesterday. The pain and the hurt and the growing up fast he had to do, all within the madness that was his early life. "Alabama. Never want to go back there again, but . . ." he whispered.

Life with his mother was no picnic. His mother's playing around and foul mouth made it hard to have a normal family life. Matt's father, having no other choice, left and along with his leaving he took Matt's childhood with him.

He remembered one day coming home from school when he met two rather nice-looking young men hurrying along the weedy driveway from his house. He wondered what they would have to do with his mother. It didn't take long for him to find out. There was his mother, in their trash-strewn front yard, topless, in her underwear, laughing raucously at the backs of the two departing men. She had a cigarette dangling from her mouth and she was swinging her bra over her head and shouting something about Jesus bashers and hell and sinning and how dare they tell her how to live.

His mother never drank, wouldn't touch the stuff. Her father had been a very hard-drinking man and frequently beat all six of his kids. She called him a "Bible Thumper". When she left home, she left for good and never looked back.

Then, his mother met Bradley and with Bradley came his son, Garrett, who was fifteen. Matt was twelve at the time and Matt's little sister, Selma was six. It was the year that little Selma disappeared and Matt's life would never be the same. Her body was never found, and when he asked Garrett where she could have gone, Garrett just laughed at him.

Matt was sixteen when his mother told him to get lost. He didn't know how he even got to New York, but after many homeless nights he landed a job as a delivery boy and then worked his way up to finish high school with the help of a local police officer who took a liking to him. He graduated with a GED and applied to the police academy. He got in on his second try. That was over thirty years ago.

He had come a long way from those days, days he did not ever want to repeat. He had reinvented himself, found himself, and now he felt confident to go on. On to whatever life threw at him, including a father that he never really knew.

"Karen always says to let go, guess this is a good time to start," he muttered as he rose from his chair and went inside.

Chapter Thirty-Four

After clearing the dishes, Karen busied herself in the study. Appointments for tomorrow were ready, candles and incense were refreshed, and all was well. Matt came in by her. She turned and smiled. "Better?" she asked

"Yeah somewhat, I guess it's, as you say, time to face my demons and ya know, I don't really think it'll be that bad."

Karen smiled and nodded, "want to go with me?" she asked sheepishly. "I'll need some help and we can walk. Nice night out for it."

"Where we goin'?" asked Matt.

"We're going to Tom and Alex's to deliver dinner, although I have a very intense feeling that we have been beaten to the punch. Mom, Olivia and Lydia are there already but this meal can go in his fridge instead of ours."

"You mean the wily old bachelor has a new following?" asked Matt.

"Well, Dottie's been calling him an ol' bastard for years and my mother follows right along, but ya know, I think they have a new perspective on him now after the other night. We'll see what happens but they both need help, encouragement and good food, although that Alex is a good cook."

They neared Tom's place and Pete was busy with his flowers. Pete lowered his large pruning shears and stared at Karen and her basket and then at Matt.

"What's up, Pete?" asked Matt.

Pete came through his arbor and out onto the sidewalk. "I don't know what to think. What happened to da boss?" he said.

"Let's just say he had a revelation and leave it at that," said Karen.

"A revelation," said Pete in astonishment. "More like hit over the head with a sledge hammer."

"Probably," said Matt with a laugh.

"No, no, you don't understand, things have changed and are changing minute by minute," Pete exclaimed.

"Let's just hope he doesn't revert to his old ways," said Matt.

Karen started laughing, "I don't think that'll happen because he has too many sergeants keeping track of him."

Pete went back to his garden, shaking his head as he retreated, and Karen and Matt walked to the door of Tom's house. They were greeted by Lydia and a chipper "hi."

"Well, we got beat to it," said Karen, laughing.

"My dinner is at six," bellowed Tom, "and you're late."

"Oh ya old fool," countered Eugenia. That was met with a snort from Dottie, who was making iced tea.

"Naw, seriously, I can't thank you all enough, I just can't," said Tom. Alex nodded his head in agreement, taking a large forkful of mac and cheese made with seven types of cheese.

Eugenia turned toward the window and suddenly stiffened. The moon was half–full as it rose slowly over the town. Its silvery threads glimmered on the pavement leading to the warehouse and out buildings of the yard.

Karen noticed her mother's reaction and goose bumps appeared on her arms. She felt a cold sweat on her forehead as she glanced toward the window. They both saw it at the same time, a dark, hunched figure that just floated along the side of the main building. Eugenia bolted for the back door with Karen right behind.

"Mom, no!" she screamed.

Karen heard chairs overturning as she burst through the door and onto a small back porch. Eugenia was way ahead of her now; it was as if she had wings on her feet.

Matt caught up to Karen and pulled at her arm, but she pulled it free. "Get her!" she shouted. "It's too powerful for her."

Matt, momentarily confused, obeyed his wife and charged after Eugenia.

Lydia caught up to her mother and Karen reached out to hug her daughter.

"Mom," said Lydia. "Mom, what is it?"

"It's him is all," Karen said.

Lydia understood.

"What the hell is goin' on?" bellowed Tom as he reached Karen. Karen looked at Tom, bowed her head and said, "Let's go inside and I'll explain."

Matt caught up to Eugenia in the second row of cars. She was muttering to herself about the coward's way out, and Matt almost had to tackle her to get her under control.

"Whatever it is, it's gone, understand," he said firmly, spinning her around to face him.

Resignation on her face, she quietly said, "oh, I'll be a good girl now."

"What in hell were you thinking?" shouted Matt.

"Something just got hold of me and I wanted to kill that thing, that's all."

"Come on, let's go back to the house. You put the scare of Hades in all of us."

"Karen saw him too," she muttered.

Matt rolled his eyes and glanced back one more time. He stopped short and almost fell over one of his feet, for there in the path was the silhouette of a beautiful young girl. She glowed a little in the dying rays of the sun. She was smiling.

Eugenia turned. "Oh Sarah," she said, "did I do okay?"

Matt gasped. "Sarah," he squeaked.

"Who the hell do you think?" said Eugenia.

Sarah smiled and faded from view.

"Listen, I don't know what's going on but I'm sure as hell..." his voice trailed off and he sighed in resignation.

Chapter Thirty-Five

The day dawned sunny, muggy and warm, and the man standing on Eugenia's porch looked a little familiar, his features anyway, like an older version of her son-in-law. This man wore dress pants and a clean polo shirt, "pink of all colors," she scoffed mentally. She looked into his eyes and noticed sadness there, a deep sadness and resignation. He had called her from the police station and she told him to come on up now as she had things to do that afternoon. He assured her that he would only take a little of her time, not long.

He introduced himself as Dave. She escorted him to her kitchen table at the back of the house. He sat and she placed a cup of tea before him. Hell, she didn't even ask him if he wanted a cup of tea. He hadn't had tea in so long he forgot what it tasted like, but this tea was like no other he had had before.

"It's Earl Grey," she said, noticing his interest. "Bergamot is what you taste."

He nodded his head and a warm smile came across his face. He was obviously relaxing.

"As you know, I'm working for the police department here in town. You were one of the people Matt had on his list for me to interview. So, what about this legend? I'm an FBI profiler so…"

But before he could get another word out she said, "You're not looking for a real person. You're looking for a being so evil that he has come back to us time and again."

"Like a possession," Dave countered.

"Yes," said Eugenia, surprised.

He saw the surprised look in her face so he said, "My mother's mother was a seer and a ghost communicator, ghost whisperer so to speak." He shrugged his shoulders. "She initiated us all into that little facet of human, er, universal enlightenment. So I do know something about it. I used to go with her to cleanse people's homes of evil spirits. Learned a lot, but like all things, life gets in the way." He looked at her directly and she felt her skin warming and a flush creeping up her cheeks. He started to laugh, "It's funny, my mom took me to cleanse houses on Saturday and my father took me to Mass on Sunday. No wonder I'm all screwed up."

Eugenia smiled. She was really starting to warm up to this guy, but she still sensed that he had a very, very turbulent past, one that he kept hidden under a good sense of humor and sadness. It was a past that someday he would have to face.

They talked for a while longer and Dave, noticing that time was slipping away, began his exit.

He started to rise from his chair when a "Hi mom," broke both of them out of their thoughts and they turned to see Karen in the doorway to the kitchen. "Oh, I'm sorry, I'll come back later," she said, backing up, a look of chagrin on her face. She looked at her mother with concern.

Eugenia sensed that Karen noticed the first thing she did---the uncanny resemblance of this man to Matt.

"No, no, this is Dave," said Eugenia, "he's helping your husband down at the station. He's an FBI profiler. Right?" she said, looking at Dave.

Dave nodded and stood up, "Glad to meet you," he said, extending his hand.

Karen took a very deep breath and her questioning eyes met his. His mouth formed the word "no" as he lowered his eyes to his hand.

Karen, momentarily taken off guard, grabbed his hand and squeaked, "Glad to meet you. Just came to tell my mom that I'll see her tonight at Tom's, that's all," she stammered.

She started to leave and noticed that Dave had followed her out of the door after saying good-bye to Eugenia. Half-way down the sidewalk, he caught up with her.

He abruptly said, "When I left Matt behind it was the worst day of my life, but I wouldn't have had any sanity if I didn't get out of there."

She turned to face him. "What about Matt, what about him and his sanity?" she said angrily.

"It made him the man he is, and I knew that Matt was a lot stronger than me. He would survive. I made sure of that. I made sure I was in the background when that policeman picked him up, I made sure of a lot of things and now, here we are."

He stuck out his hand. "Hi, I'm Dave." He looked at her from beneath raised brows, a half -smile on his face.

She muttered, "I was really mad and I still don't know the entire story, but I figure time will be on my side. Oh what the hell, hi, I'm Karen, glad to meet you, Dave," she looked at him quizzically. "Dad," she said softly.

"I love the dad thing, but right now I haven't earned that title and especially in your husband's eyes." He smiled sadly.

Eugenia stuck her head out the door and said, "You two have a lot to talk about."

Karen laughed and turned, saying "have a good day," over her shoulder.

Chapter Thirty-Six

The dampness from the previous night's rain made it a little easier walking the path leading from the cars into the woods. The path into the woods looked like the entrance into a cave. How many times had he walked in here? Hundreds, yes hundreds. The darkness enveloped him until his eyes adjusted. He glanced out into the misty grey of dusk. Through the branches he could see the rusting hulks of cars, busses, trucks and the buffer of buildings in the village beyond. It was mid-afternoon when he entered the woods, but as usual he had lost track of time and it was just past sunset when he exited the woods into the overgrown path of the junk yard. He felt some relief as he stepped into the path between the cars.

The moon was rising over West Mountain and the eerie shadows made the whole scene surreal. In the early twilight he could make out the lights of the village and on the right the lights of Tom's dilapidated house and Pete's trailer. What happened next is still a mystery to him. He made his way toward the fence that bordered Dottie's horse pasture. He would go around Dottie's horse barn and then home to his little house next to the library, on the far side of the village. The moon was rising fast and it was good to see that the clouds of the day had dissipated.

Ben buttoned the top button of his sweater and continued walking in the direction of Dottie's. He looked to his right. There was a faint glow in one of the cars, very faint. "Maybe a reflection from the moonlight," he thought. He cautiously made his way toward the light. There stood the faint outline of a small young woman, sad-eyed, her shoulder-length hair framing her oval face. She wore jeans and an open-necked, button-down blouse. She looked familiar, and then a yearning filled him with sadness so profound that he felt his heart breaking. "Ellie," he whispered, "oh Ellie." Tears streamed down his face and a longing filled his aching heart. He almost fell. Then, as quickly as she appeared, she was gone.

He stood there, bathed in moonlight. He felt as lonely as if he were the only man on earth, and the image of his long-dead wife brought that feeling home sharper than he had ever felt it in his life. The faint yips of coyotes were the only other sounds as he made his way toward home on unsteady feet.

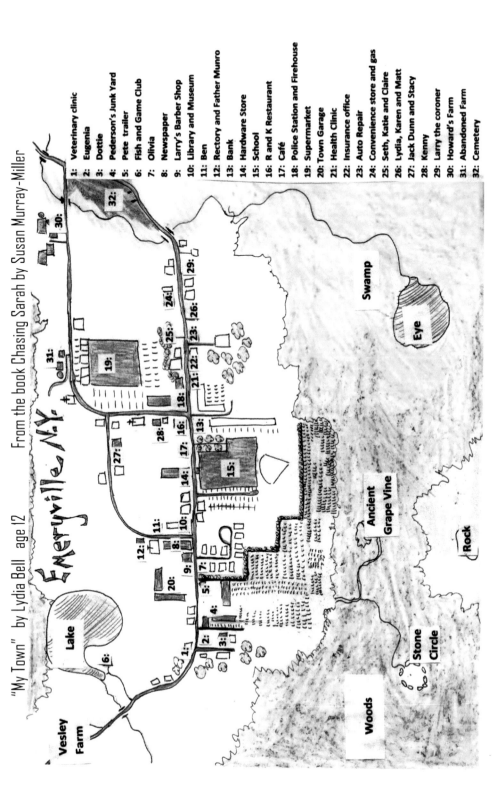

"My Town" by Lydia Bell   age 12   From the book Chasing Sarah by Susan Murray-Miller

Emeryville N.Y.

1: Veterinary clinic
2: Eugenia
3: Dottie
4: Pederson's Junk Yard
5: Pete trailer
6: Fish and Game Club
7: Olivia
8: Newspaper
9: Larry's Barber Shop
10: Library and Museum
11: Ben
12: Rectory and Father Munro
13: Bank
14: Hardware Store
15: School
16: R and K Restaurant
17: Café
18: Police Station and Firehouse
19: Supermarket
20: Town Garage
21: Health Clinic
22: Insurance office
23: Auto Repair
24: Convenience store and gas
25: Seth, Katie and Claire
26: Lydia, Karen and Matt
27: Jack Dunn and Stacy
28: Kenny
29: Larry the coroner
30: Howard's Farm
31: Abandoned Farm
32: Cemetery

Vesley Farm

Lake

Swamp

Eye

Ancient Grape Vine

Rock

Stone Circle

Woods

~

He watched from the shadows. That silly, old man again, the one with the brown eyes, the flat nose and high cheek bones. This man's facial features were like his facial features, and the features of those that put him to death so long ago. Today he chose to be a crow, and he had watched the old man from the vantage point of the tallest limb of a large pine. That was one thing his grandfather taught him, how to be another animal, to shape shift but that eternal fire that consumed him stayed with him from one body to another. Then, before he could blink he was as before, a human shape, walking upright, raw energy and force streaming from his body.

Chapter Thirty-Seven

Jack had heard the rumors and all morning he had waited to approach his boss about a story. Human interest, he would tell him, and good for the paper.

Jack closed the door to the office and Richard Perry looked up from behind glasses that perched half way down his nose.

"Richard, I have to talk to you," said Jack.

"Go ahead," said Perry, an edge of curiosity in his voice.

"There are rumors of a research project going on in the woods in back of the junk yard. Some college is there and they say that there's this vine growing there that's hundreds of years old and they're studying it."

"Is that so?" said Perry. "Hmm, are you game?"

"My thoughts exactly, good human interest story there and I can get some interviews and pictures."

"Go for it," said Parry, "but keep me in the loop."

Jack nodded and bolted for the door.

Jack parked his car in Tom Pederson's parking lot and headed toward the door that said "Office".

He pushed open the door and was startled at the racket made by a bunch of clanging bells attached to the back of the door.

Tom came from a small back room that served as his office. He appraised this man with the eye of indulgence. "What can I do for ya?" he said.

"I'm here from the newspaper. I'm Jack Dunn, by the way."

Tom nodded his head but his face was impassive.

"There's rumor about research being done in the woods out back and I thought that it would be a good human interest story."

Tom screwed up his face and scratched the bridge of his nose. "Yeah, they're doing work out there. Problem is going through the yard with a car. I don't allow it, insurance purposes and all that."

Jack nodded, "I understand, but couldn't I walk?"

"Tell you what, if you go just up the road, Maiden Lane cuts in on your left. Dottie is in the back, last house. She'll show you where to go. I'm sure you can cut across her property and go through that way. Safer. By the way, no hoards of people in there with ya, hear."

"I understand. I know what you mean. Thank you, Tom."

Tom nodded and went back into his office.

Jack started to hum as he approached his car. That was easy, now for the story. He drove onto Maiden Lane and parked at the barn near a small house. He noticed the house was shabby but neat. He knocked and a small woman with white hair answered.

"Tom sent me here," he said.

She looked mildly surprised. "What's that old bastard want now?" she said.

He chuckled. "Not that. He said you might show me the way into the woods where they're doing the research project. Oh, I'm Jack Dunn, by the way." He held out a business card for her to take.

"I know who you are. Go right around the barn and follow the path. I hope you got decent shoes, can be muddy back there."

He nodded. "Thank you so much. Are you Dottie?"

She nodded and closed the door.

The path to the woods was shorter than he thought but it was muddy in some spots. He couldn't help but marvel at all the derelict cars in the lot. Spooky, he thought.

As he entered the woods, camera in hand, he couldn't help but think of fairy tales like Hansel and Gretel and Little Red Riding Hood, going through the deep woods where the big bad wolf resided. He saw a tiny flag stuck in the ground and near it a large tendril of vine. "This must be one of the suckers from the original plant," he thought. "I'll just follow this and when I need to come out of here, I'll just follow it out."

Deeper into the woods he went, following the vine and enjoying his time in nature, which he loved. He liked the deep solitude of the woods, especially when he went cross country skiing. His girl friend, Stacy, didn't like anything to do with the outdoors. She would rather go shopping or to the movies. Neither of those activities interested him, in fact, there were only two things about their relationship that mattered, her cooking and sex. Hardly things to base a long-term relationship on, but there were always others. And let's face it, he had made no commitment, although she certainly thought he had.

He hadn't noticed it at first, but he was in a clearing now. It felt strange, electrifying in an unusual sense. A mist of some sort held low to the ground and there were strange formations of rocks surrounding the outer perimeter of the clearing. He looked for the vine and saw it strangely coiled into a knot and running up the face of one of the stones.

He turned and then saw it. Something, someone was approaching him, only this someone looked grotesque. The first thing that came to mind was an ape of some sort, but this thing was the size of a small man. Whoever it was had dark skin, almost burned, and as it approached Jack, its eyes bore into his hypnotically. Jack couldn't move, and suddenly the thing jumped and instead of knocking him down, seemed to melt into him. His soul screamed out, his eyes burned and his ears rang with a sound so unearthly, he shuddered. Then blackness enveloped him and he fell to the ground.

He woke suddenly. It was getting toward dark. His head was aching as he gathered his camera and note pad that had fallen from his backpack. He felt dizzy. He was so tired he had a hard time putting one foot in front of the other. He progressed out of the circle and toward oblivion.

Chapter Thirty-Eight

After the gossip circulated about the cows, which was not helped by Silvia, who blabbed it all over the town and half the countryside, there was the usual speculation and rumors plus expert advice from the barber shop. Everything from a government conspiracy to aliens became the likely suspects, and the town was on edge. The police station was loaded with calls, some of them legitimate and some wild goose chases. Matt was putting in long hours and he came home exhausted.

Matt was doing paperwork when Mr. Perry from the newspaper came and stood by Matt's desk. He looked concerned.

"Hey," said Matt, as he stood and extended his hand. Perry shook his hand and Matt pointed to a seat.

"What's up, any leads?" said Matt.

"Well, something's been bothering me and I have to get it off my chest. The other day I sent one of my reporters into the woods to do a story on the university and that vine. Thing is, haven't seen him since."

"You mean Jack?"

Perry nodded his head yes. "He never misses a day of work. I keep calling and it just goes to his answering machine. Cell phone doesn't work either."

"Maybe we better get over there. I know he has a girlfriend. I think she works as a receptionist over at Dennis's law firm."

"Paralegal," said Perry.

"Let me call her," said Matt. "Maybe they had a row and he took off or maybe something else."

Matt dialed Attorney Tracy's number and a receptionist answered.

"Officer Bell here, I have a quick question. Jack Dunn's girlfriend, you know her name? "

"Stacy," was the curt reply from the other end.

"Is she there?"

"No, and Mr. Tracy is really boiling mad. She hasn't showed up for several days. We come to trial on the eighth of August and her work isn't done yet. Not good."

Matt was feeling a little queasy as he gently placed the receiver down.

"Where does Jack live?" he said quietly.

"It's 56 Elm."

"Okay. Oh, he's renting from old man McCarthy?"

"Yeah."

"All right, I'm going to go over there. You go back to the paper and if there's anything I'll call you."

"Joe," Matt called to his partner. "Let's go, missing person."

Joe stood up, grabbed his hat and headed for the door. Both men stood for a moment looking to cross the road. When they entered the police cruiser, Joe called Dispatch on their destination and they quietly drove off.

The house was more like a tiny garage, but with the shrubbery and flowers that Mrs. McCarthy planted everywhere, you didn't really notice the smallness of the place.

Matt knocked on the faded door but there was no answer.

"Oh, for Christ's sake what do you want?" came a booming voice from the yard next door.

"Bill," said Matt, putting out his hand to the tall, gruff old gentleman.

Bill, ignoring his hand, said, "Haven't seen them for a few days."

"I need to get in there. I can get a court order or you can let me in. Which will it be?"

Bill looked directly at him with a deepening scowl on his face. His face was craggy enough, and scowling emphasized the prune-like wrinkles that dissected Bill's face even more. "Oh alright, just don't mess with anything, don't want no trouble."

Bill inserted a key into the door deadbolt and tried the handle. "Funny, door wasn't locked," he quietly said.

"Okay, thanks Bill," said Matt. "Go home. If we need you we'll call for you."

Matt opened the door a tiny crack, cautious to keep to the side of the door just in case. He punched the door completely open and the smell assaulted them in waves. It was the smell of heavy lavender perfume, burned meat and decay.

"Holy hell," said Joe.

"My eyes are watering," said Matt. "Call for backup."

Joe sprinted to the car, called in and returned, out of breath. "Chief's coming over and so is that Dave fellow."

Matt stepped cautiously into a small living room. Neat, obviously a woman lived here as well as Jack. Camera equipment was everywhere. He looked into a small dining area where a laptop sat open on the table. The afternoon sun shone in and illuminated the back of a wooden chair that sat in front of the laptop. Its rich grain shined warmly.

It wasn't long before two police cruisers were in front of the house. Chris barked orders and Dave went from room to room, quietly assessing, looking deep in thought.

Joe came from the bedroom. "Nothing, no signs of a struggle."

"Well, let's take a look at the kitchen." They approached the small kitchen and the smell of rot and burned meat was much stronger there.

"This is creepy," said Joe.

Suddenly, Dave called out, "look at this!" He was standing on a small back patio. The patio was covered by an awning spanning the entire width of the small structure. Lawn chairs and a table with glass top stood to one side of the doorway. On the opposite side lay a large black dog in an obvious state of decay. Matt and Dave could see that the nose and part of its face were burned, and the stench of rotting flesh drifted in the afternoon air.

"Get Grayson over here," said Chris.

"Hell," came a gruff voice from the edge of the patio. "That's Dubbs, the mayor's dog. Know it anywhere. What in hell?"

"Take it easy, Bill, it's pretty bad here right now," said Chris. "I suggest you go back to your house and sit tight. We'll have some questions for you in a little while."

Bill looked worried. He turned and headed across the lawn to his house.

Dave and Matt sat down beside one another at the dining table and were quietly looking at the laptop. Careful so as not to erase prints, they both wore gloves and gingerly tapped the keys.

"Well, will you lookey here," said Dave, with awe. Matt only whistled. Across the screen in bold letters were the words "We are human, we are energy, we die, we are still energy, just in another form."

"Where in the hell have I heard that?" said Matt. "Yes, that's it…Eugenia is always saying things like that."

Dave nodded his head. "Sounds like your grandmother. She was always saying things like that."

"I'd like to hear about that sometime," said Matt.

Dave looked down sadly and shook his head.

"What does it mean?" said Chris, coming up behind them.

"It simply means that all living things are comprised of energy. This energy changes form, especially when we die. That doesn't mean we're gone from this world, it means that we exist in another time and another form. Some people become ghosts, some guardian spirits and others, well, if evil exists in their souls to the extent that it warps all thinking, then we're dealing with a very evil entity here," said Dave.

"You mean something paranormal," said Chris quietly, so as not to let the other officers hear.

Dave nodded. "I went to see Dottie, Eugenia and several others yesterday, and I must admit, I got an earful," he said sheepishly.

"You actually believe in this stuff?" said Chris, incredulously.

"Let's just say I was brought up on this stuff, as you call it," said Dave quietly.

Chris shook his head and walked away, shouting orders to have the computer taken into evidence.

Grayson arrived and things started to get hectic. The identification of the dog was a top priority.

Dave tapped Matt on the shoulder and nodded toward the door. "Something was said yesterday and I have to check it out." Matt looked quizzically at his father. "It was something to do with a stone circle and an old vine, many hundreds of years old. Do you know where they are, Matt?"

"The vine I do, but the stone circle..." Matt shook his head. "I'm really stumped by that."

Chapter Thirty-Nine

Lydia rode her bike along the road. It was very hot and she was bored. Thoughts of the woods, where it would be much cooler, beckoned to her. Maybe her grandmother would like to take a walk with her and she could show her the stone circle. It wasn't that late yet, she could at least try.

Lydia arrived at her grandmother's ten minutes later, out of breath. She had pedaled her bike hard all the way. She burst into the kitchen and surprised a busy Eugenia, who was cooking rhubarb on the stove top. "Hey Mum Mum," shouted Lydia, "Wanna go with me?"

"Where to, child?" said Eugenia, rubbing her hands on her apron.

"To the stone circle in the woods, of course," said Lydia.

"Child, what stone circle?" She was obviously alarmed and concerned.

"The one Olivia and I found the other day, the real creepy one where strange things started to happen to us. We got out of there real fast."

Eugenia removed her apron and started for the door. "Let's get Dottie, I'm game," she said over her shoulder.

"Good," chirped Lydia, shrugging her shoulders and following her grandmother out the back door.

Dottie was in her garden pulling weeds and harvesting herbs when they approached and told her where they were going. "Let me get my hat," said Dottie, "and away we go."

They skirted the path along the back of the car lot and entered the large opening in the trees at the edge of the woods. "I hate these paths, they're so gritty, every time I go on one I have to empty my shoes," complained Dottie.

"Oh, quit complaining," said Eugenia. "We're on a mission."

"Okay Lydia, where is the path?" Lydia stepped around the two women and took up the lead. "Let's go slow, there are signs and I don't want to get lost." They came to the first patch of surveyors' stakes in the ground. Dottie started down the path and Lydia stopped her. "Not there," she said. "Over here. Follow this tendril of the vine away from that path."

Dottie looked unsettled. "Did you bring a cell phone with you?" she asked Eugenia. Lydia dug into her pocket and produced a cell phone, and both women look relieved.

The woods were getting dark now, not due to the absence of sunlight but to the heavy canopy of trees.

The tendril snaked along the ground and wound around tree trunks, all the while getting larger and larger in diameter. "We're close," said Lydia, spying the first rock and the dazzling sunlight in the center of the circle.

"Amazing," mussed Dottie. "Just look how this vine wrapped itself around this rock." She was in awe.

"Yes," said Lydia. "Olivia and I stumbled on it by accident and then we had a very scary experience. This man came out of the center of the circle. I don't know if he was a man or a beast but he really scared us. He was coming right toward us, all hunched over and really mean looking and then Sarah appeared and told us to run, and we ran. Thank God we had the vine to follow or we could've ended up in the middle of the swamp."

Eugenia looked concerned as she stepped around the large stone, noticing there were many more like it forming a large circle about eighty feet in diameter. There were no trees growing in the center of the circle, only soft grass.

Dottie noticed the drag marks first and nodded to Eugenia, who made her way gingerly toward the center of the circle. She was not prepared to see the sight that met her eyes. In shock, she couldn't take her eyes off the lifeless body of a charred human being. "No!" she shouted to Dottie and Lydia. "Let's get the police, now."

Fumbling for the cell in her pocket, Lydia tried dialing and shouted, "The cell won't work."

"Then go to the edge of the woods. We'll stay here, if we can," said Eugenia, a quaver in her voice as a mist started to descend into the sunlit meadow.

"That's exactly what happened to us!" wailed Lydia, running for the safety of the car lot.

Then they noticed a girl's shape standing at the edge of the meadow opposite them, looking at them sadly. "*He won't hurt you as long as I am here,*" she said, but the words were not spoken. The two women both heard the message in their minds and realized that she was communicating with them telepathically.

They nodded, neither of them daring to move. Again the voice was in their heads, "*The soul who did this is a lost soul and it is my mission to retrieve him and bring him home.*"

"I'm beginning to understand," said Eugenia, "but why?"

"*No one questions the almighty; we only listen to the wise council that is given to us. Of the millions of beings over here on this side, we don't question, for the almighty one is all-knowing, and full of unconditional love.*"

Chapter Forty

Lydia raced to the edge of the woods and slammed straight into an old rusted hulk. Gasping, she held onto the door handle as if she was going to be torn away from it and eaten. Her hands shaking uncontrollably, she dialed her father's cell number and he answered.

"Lydia, stop screaming, what about a body in the woods at the stone circle? What stone circle, where?"

"Oh dad, it's all charred and gross."

"Okay, stand still, don't move. Are you alright? Who's with you? "

"Dot and Mum Mum," she answered, her voice hesitant and low.

Matt rolled his eyes as Dave came up to his side. "Did I hear stone circle?" he asked, barely above a whisper.

Matt nodded his head and shouted at Chris, "We have a body."

"Where?" said Chris.

"Back of the junk yard, where they're working on the college project, somewhere in there," said Matt.

"Get Tom on the phone, have someone meet us at the yard and we'll all go in together. It's a maze of dead ends in there but the boy and Pete know the terrain."

"On it," said Matt, dialing Tom's number.

A few minutes later Matt shouted at Chris, "Okay, he's opening the back gate now and Alex will go with us with the loader."

"Get the coroner," said Chris, "This might be a nightmare to get a body out of those woods. Let's go."

Lydia saw the flashing lights and wondered if Dottie and her grandmother were okay back at the circle in the woods. She heard the rumble of the big loader and saw the line of cars following it with their lights flashing.

If the situation wasn't so dire, it actually looked funny, like a disoriented parade. It was still several hours before sunset and Lydia was sure she could find the way again.

Matt leapt from the car and hugged his daughter. "What in hell were you doing in here?" he said anxiously.

"I told Mum Mum and Dottie I'd show them the stone circle, that's all."

"Okay," said Chris to Lydia. "You stay here and we'll go in."

"No way," said Lydia, hands on hips. "It's in the opposite direction from the dig site and you'll get lost."

Chris felt the anger flow into his cheeks. Stale-mated by a skinny little red-headed brat.

Before Chris could say anything more Lydia shouted "follow me!" and headed into the woods.

Dave looked amused and nodded toward Lydia's disappearing body. "Like father, like daughter," he quipped, a large smile on his face.

"Let's not go there," said Matt, turning to follow his daughter.

The woods were getting darker now, but Lydia deftly negotiated her way around tree roots and rocks, all the while keeping a close eye on the vine. She could hear the grunts of the men carrying the stretchers from the ambulance squad and the static of the radios of some of the officers. She knew her father was right behind her as she knew his breathing. The labored breathing of Chris was next and then that man. She had glanced at him once and he looked familiar somehow, but the thought didn't stay in her mind long. Maybe it was the way he looked at her, almost with surprise and a lot of curiosity.

"Here we are," an out-of-breath Lydia gasped as she pulled up beside her grandmother and Dottie.

Dottie nodded to Chris and in a quiet voice said, "Over there, in the center of the circle."

Chris started barking orders as the area was secured and policemen searched the ground for clues.

"Christ," said Larry, the coroner, taking a few steps toward the body, "talk about being hit by lightning or burned. Are we secure so I can start working on this body?" he yelled. "I won't know anything until I get it back to the morgue."

"I think we're done here," he said, an hour later. "Getting very dark and we have to find our way out of here."

The morbid procession wound their way along the path, Lydia leading them out into a soft, hazy twilight. Lydia stood by the path and let others go by her, as she waited for her father. She noticed that the strange man was talking to Dottie and Eugenia and they both seemed to know him. She shied away from him and ran solidly into Alex, who smiled down at her and called her the heroine of the day. She smiled sheepishly and nodded to the strange man. "Know him?" she said.
He told her he was some guy from the FBI, which was all he knew.

"I can't get over the fact that they," she nodded toward the two men, "my dad and him, look so much alike, like they're brothers or something."

"I nonoticed that ttoo. Nnnoone of my business. I gottata git this loloder back," he took a deep breath, "or the boss will fire me."

Lydia laughed and smiled, "Yeah, sure, fat chance."

Chris sidled up to Matt and in a quiet voice said, "We won't have anything from the coroner until later. Says he's so fascinated by all this, he's working all night. I just wonder who it is."

"I'm willing to bet it's the girlfriend, but the condition of the body, like it was put on a spit and roasted, it's anybody's guess," said Matt wearily.

"You're supposed to be off tomorrow, but I really need all hands" said Chris.

"That's okay. I'd still be working anyway. I want to find out as much as I can about this stone circle and I'm gonna start with my daughter and her friend," said Matt.

Chris rolled his eyes and said, "Good luck."

"There's something going on here and where the hell is Jack Dunn?"

"I'm putting an APB out on him now. This will be on the news tonight and I think you and your family are going to have to really keep a low profile," said Chris, sadly.

"My standard answer is 'no comment; this is an ongoing investigation'. If they can't understand that then they're free to make up all the stories that they want." said Matt. "I'm not hiding in my home over this."

Chapter Forty-One

Tom saw the group approaching the gates and shouted, "if I see any damned reporters around here, I'm shootin' em, got it?

"I'll back you on it," quipped Chris as he made his way to the patrol car.

Tom wasn't smiling, he was just glaring at Chris as he chewed on a toothpick.

The loader came into sight. Tom ran over to Alex, said something, and Alex nodded and turned the machine off. "See anything unusual out there, son?" he asked.

"Nothing," said Alex. He relaxed and took his time with speaking, and his diction was improving with each day. "Although it was creepy...something about that ha hole in the trees where you go into the woods and then all the darkness."

"Those two old women sure scared the crap out of me the night when they went running out of the house chasing whoever or whatever it was," Tom said. "I'm going down to the hardware store and see if I can put in one of those security systems with a camera."

Alex's eyes lit up. "Really," he said.

"I betcha you'd know just how to install one of them things," said his father, with a half-smile on his face.

Alex's eyes lit up. "Can I go and pick one out?" he said.

"You wanna go and pick one out, hell why not. Just tell James to put it on the bill, but you can go tomorrow. They're closed now."

Chapter Forty-Two

"Well!" said Father Munro as he opened the door. Seth scooted in and went into the sitting room where he and Father had met the first time. "I have to tell you," said Seth, "it's great. I can go into a classroom full of unruly, savage kids and come out unscathed. Yes!" he said, raising a fist into the air.

Father stood there looking at him with an amused look on his face. "Ok, now for the hard stuff," said Father.

"What?" said Seth. "That was hard, thinking about it and then doing it. True, the more I did it the easier it became. But hard stuff, like what?"

"Those were just kids und that was just the everyday stuff," said Father quietly. "Now, what about the people und unholy ones that want to harm you intentionally, make you sick, or are jealous of you? What about that?"

Seth's face fell and Father came over and placed an arm around his shoulder.

"Laddie," he said softly, "you have the ability to think about it, which will make the harder stuff much easier. You've done well und now we have to start the real education for the real evil that's out there. You have to be able to leap into action on the spot, not stand there und think about it und then say, oh yeah, that's what I do next. It's conditioning und always being at the ready, that's what we are going to be doing now. Our natures here on earth are not God-like natures. True, we are made in the image of God but that's where it ends for most of us. Life is like a giant chess game. What moves will you make to create a better place for all living things?"

Seth nodded and said, "Okay, let's begin. But I have to tell you I saw and felt a difference."

"You will und that's the start, now let's finish it. Und remember, this is not a big secret. Share the knowledge with whoever wants help. Don't hoard your skills, use them, that's what God made you for, to use your skills for the benefit of all," said Father.

Two hours later, an exhausted Seth left the rectory and headed home. He was demoralized. Everything he did he felt he flunked. This was more an exercise in martial arts, but Father Munro said he did well for the first time in an advanced situation.

He told the priest he would practice, practice, practice but Father told him it was not necessary, he just had to let it flow; be prepared and let it flow. He understood some of the concept. The priest told him that it had to be part of his nature, an automatic reflex, like a skier moving down a slope; they knew instinctively what to do.

Chapter Forty-Three

Alex was busy installing two cameras, a remote monitoring system, and a control panel, and hooking the system into their computer system. As most of the devices were wireless, it saved on the installation time considerably. When he finished he showed his father how it worked. Pete and Josh looked on in amazement.

The police were on double overtime, news media were probing into the events of the past few days, and the victim in the stone circle turned out to be an elderly woman who lived alone just over the county line. The dog was indeed the mayor's, and a distraught family had to figure out where to bury their family friend.

Chapter Forty-Four

That evening Dave approached his son's house. He had been invited to this meeting by Dottie, more like she blurted it out and Eugenia chimed in that he would be a welcome addition to the group. The monthly meeting of "the Club" started precisely on time at eight p.m. and since it was a club that insisted on rotating venues, it was at Karen's house tonight.

Karen set out a pot of tea, several wine glasses, a beer glass for Ben and assorted finger sandwiches including the club favorite, cucumber. Crackers and cheese, fresh from the dairy rounded out the edibles. It had been hectic with all the phone calls to the house from reporters. Some were asking the dreaded questions, "Is this a tie-in to the murders that happened long ago? Is it someone from the family of murderers that kept the legend alive every seventy-five years?" One reporter even came out with "Well, I guess you can't know everything about your neighbors." One headline had the audacity to name the town *Killer Town,* and the tourist trade was booming. Of course this made the mayor happy and several people were already getting in souvenirs from China, such as key chains and glassware with *Killer Town* engraved on them. Cheap and tacky with a complete disregard for life, mused Karen as she went about preparing for the group.

Eugenia was the first to arrive, followed by Claire, Katie and Fr. Munro. Dottie, James Farrell and Rhonda Elsworth were next, then Larry, the barber, and Dave.

Staring at Dave, Karen stammered, "What are you doing here? "No, no come in," she said, grabbing his sleeve and pulling him into the room. "You might find this interesting."

He nodded, smiled and made his way over to a chair next to the couch near Dottie.

Katie smiled at him, looking very interested and curious. Claire looked directly at her mother, furrowed her brow, pursed her lips and mouthed a silent "no."

"Where's Ben tonight?" said Karen. "He never misses a meeting."

"Haven't seen him all day, now that you've asked," said Larry, "and he always comes in around noon, just after his eleven a.m. brunch at the cafe."

"Well, we'll give him a few more minutes," said Karen, sounding worried.

Chapter Forty-Five

The next morning Matt knocked on the door of the tiny house next to the library and a very shaggy, unkempt Ben answered the door. "Ben," said Matt, "where have you been hiding and why? Folks are worried."

Ben grimaced and motioned Matt to come in. Joe followed.

"Yeah bud," Joe said, "thought we had another unfortunate incident on our hands."

Ben sighed and sat. "I had a very enlightening experience the other night and it has left me rather befuddled," he said sadly.

"Care to talk about it?" said Joe.

"I don't think it's anything you would understand, and I'm sure you'll put it to the quirky imagination of an old man," he said sadly.

Joe nodded.

Matt said, "Someone you really want to talk to?"

"Yyessss" he said hesitantly, "maybe Katie or Dot or Eugenia?"

"Okay, I get it," Matt quietly said. "The dark one hasn't come to you, has he?"

"Oh, no nothing like that. It was actually Ellie." The sound of his dead wife's name made him smile.

"Okay, I'll call on you tomorrow if I don't hear that you've seen one of those women today, understand?" said Matt sternly.

Ben smiled to himself and nodded. "Time to get going, I look a sight and I'm sorry for the scare."

Matt and Joe left the house. On the sidewalk Joe turned to Matt. "What in hell was that all about?" he said.

"Spiritual things, that's all," remarked Matt.

"You're not turning into one of those, are you?" Joe inquired.

"I have to live with it, so some of it does rub off," said Matt.

Joe patted Matt's shoulder. "Time for re-initiation, buddy," he said.

"Nothing like that, but we do have several murders on our hands. The town is buzzing with the reporters and next the FBI will be here in force."

"Yeah, they're due here today or tomorrow," said Joe. "The last time we dealt with them, they took over everything and treated us like a bunch of hicks."

"Chris is really on edge. Dave isn't helping because he's taking the side of the gals," noted Matt. "I have a strange feeling this time will be much different."

"But ya know what?" said Joe. "If anything is going to get done, I betcha they'll be the ones to get it done; those women, I mean."

Matt smiled and nodded his head.

They cruised along the street heading for the station.

Chapter Forty-Six

"Town's really in an uproar about the murder and the missing woman and all," said Josh.

Tom nodded his head and said, "Bad business, real bad business. It seems to be coming from the woods in the back of my property and yesterday Alex found a guy from the New York Times snooping around back there. He told him to git. I would've peppered him real good with my shotgun if I caught him. Kid's out there now putting up 'no trespassing' signs. The only ones allowed back there is the cops, that's it!"

"What about Dottie and Eugenia?" said Josh, smiling slyly.

Tom shook his head, muttered to himself, turned and walked back into his office, slamming the door shut behind him.

Josh burst out laughing and went back to work.

Chapter Forty-Seven

Eugenia, Father Munro and Dottie sat on Eugenia's porch, sipping iced tea and discussing the events of the past few days. "There's got to be a connection between that circle and the evil one, there's just got to be. Maybe it's the vine, after all it was alive when he roamed this earth, maybe that's the connection," stated Eugenia.

"Well, well, look who comes," she said with surprise as the lone figure of Ben came down the sidewalk and sat quietly on the bottom step, not uttering even a greeting.

"Where in tarnation have you been?" said Eugenia.

Ben looked up, eyeing each of them in turn and then said, "Hiding, trying to figure things out. I just don't know anymore. Getting too old I guess."

"We missed you at the meeting and with the missing woman and all, we thought you were numbered in the fold," said Dottie.

Father looked at Ben with concern in his eyes. "See something, Ben?" he asked.

Ben sighed and nodded his head yes. "Saw Ellie in the junk yard the other night. It was almost as if she was coming for me and I finally realized just how lonely I am without her. Sent me into a deep spiral, but the police knocking at my door this morning sure sent me out of it in one heck of a hurry."

"Did she say anything?" said Eugenia, eagerly, now fully attentive.

"No, that's the funny part of it. She just stood there looking sad and then she was gone, just like that."

Eugenia went inside and came out with a fresh glass of iced tea for Ben. "Thanks," he said, "really haven't had a bite in a few days."

"Well that settles it," said Eugenia, "you're staying with us for dinner and no excuses."

Resigned, Ben just looked stoic. He was deep in thought. "There's something I'm overlooking, something important," he whispered.

"That's what I'm saying too," exclaimed Dottie in unison with Eugenia.

"I think it's time to make another trip to the circle, and this time, bring reinforcements," said Dottie.

"All right, we're on for tomorrow," said Eugenia. "I just hope the police don't beat us to the punch."

"What we're doing is very dangerous," said Father, pulling more smoke from his pipe.

Chapter Forty-Eight

He was filthy and he couldn't remember anything except walking out of that place in the woods. Everything was just a big blur after that. He was lying on the floor of what looked like a cave, a very old cave, filled with damp. He could dimly see the sunlight from an opening. Every bone in his body ached. Where the hell was he and why was he covered in what looked like dried blood? He smelled like sweat and smoke, and his elbows were skinned and raw.

He just wanted to lie here and die, but that was not an option and he knew it. "I know, I'll go home and shower, call my boss, see what the gal has for supper and maybe slug back a beer or two."

"Plan one," he said as he hauled his bulk off the floor and went outside. Looking out from the cave entrance, he noticed that he was in an area of the woods where many of the trees touched the rock face of the cliff. The cave was on the opposite side of the swamp. He would go straight through the woods and into the junk yard, he thought, but a few hours later he ended up on a dirt road that intersected with the main town road. He headed in the direction of town. He was not negotiating too well, he had trouble walking and he was more tired than he ever remembered being in his life. Whenever a car went by he managed to stop and not make his disorientation too obvious. He knew he was a mess, but he just wanted to get home. God, he wished he could remember what had happened and how he got where he had just been.

He vaguely recalled Stacy's voice coming from the dining room. She was looking at a strange message on her computer when he came into the room. That was yesterday, or was it? He had lost all sense of time.

He didn't hear the sirens or see the squad cars coming until they were almost on top of him. He looked at them as if they weren't real. His first impression was to flag them down and ask for a ride, but when the officers poured out of the cars with guns drawn, he froze.

"Hands on top of your head!" someone shouted. "Hands on top of your head or we'll shoot." He almost wanted to laugh or crack a joke, but looking down the barrel of a gun was intimidating so he obliged. He felt like fainting, he was so dizzy, and as the officers grabbed him he fell into the arms of Matt, who had all he could do to keep him upright. His mouth was dry and he did try to say, "hi Matt," but nothing came out.

"I'll take this one," said Matt, "and when he's washed and clean he'll be a lot more presentable."

Joe reported into Dispatch and with Jack safely in back of the patrol car and snoring away, they headed for the station.

Jack was led up the steps into a barrage of reporters and cameramen. "He's the murderer," he heard someone say. Confused, Jack shyly said, "murder?"

Matt told him to just keep walking and he was deposited into a tiny interview room. A tall woman, obviously some type of law enforcement officer, stood in one corner, watching him intently. Jack quelled the urge to shout "BOO" at her, he was too engrossed in looking at her well-endowed breasts. She met his gaze with a no-shit look and he thought better of attempting any communication.

Matt soon appeared with another man and the chief, and Jack was asked if he wanted anything. Jack's first words were, "yeah, a rare steak and a beer."

Matt sat across from him and introduced Dave.

"Where were you last night, Jack?" asked Matt.

"Damned if I know. I woke up this afternoon in a cave, a friggin' cave of all places. I mean if anyone wanted to rob me they certainly didn't take my wallet, and my crown jewels are still safe; I can still pee," he said sarcastically. "What the hell is this all about? All I want to do is go home."

"What's the last thing you remember Jack?" said the soft-spoken man beside Matt.

Jack looked from one man to the other and said, "Looking at you two, you'd think you were brothers. Well, Stacy, my girl friend and I went out of the house at the same time. My boss sent me to investigate the vine in the woods, the one the college is studying. I thought it would be a worthwhile human interest story. Well, I get into the woods and I must've made a wrong turn for all of a sudden I'm standing in this beautiful place, like a meadow, right in the middle of the woods. Then, and this is the part I just don't understand, this creature, for lack of a better description," Jack's voice now reached fever pitch, "this thing was there and so help me he leaped at me and that's all I remember."

Dave and Matt looked at one another. Matt started to sweat but Dave looked calm and cool. Matt could imagine those wheels in Dave's brain churning.

"Can I see you for a moment?" said Dave.

Matt and Dave got up and proceeded to the room next door which had a one-way mirror and was used as an observation room complete with cameras and recording devices. Chris looked at both men and blurted out, "you believe him?"

"Under the circumstances," said Dave, "I do. I went to a meeting last evening, not your usual meeting nor your usual subject matter, but I learned a lot and a lot was said that I don't think was supposed to be said in my company. Now I know this superstitious legend is supposed to be a bunch of gobbledy-gook, but you know something, stranger things have happened. Last night two women told me a tale of a local high school teacher who had a similar experience about a month ago, only they got to him in time. I just wonder what they would say about this one."

"What do you mean?" railed Chris with a snort. "Exorcism?"

"Well, more like demonic possession and this guy is just too damn trusting to know the difference and to protect himself," said Dave.

"Jack is generous to a fault," remarked Matt. "He would go anywhere, especially if there's a story involved."

"Look, I've been through the cases from the last one hundred fifty years, and there's something else at play here. Would you just cut me some slack?" said Dave. "I'd like to make a phone call and have someone come over. She's not to step into that room with him, understand, just observe him. Here's the address, go pick her up and tell her I want to see her."

Chapter Forty-Nine

The cruiser stopped in front of the large Victorian house and an officer proceeded up the long, narrow walk to the front porch. Claire met him at the edge of the porch. "Ted, what can I do for you?"

"I need your mom, right now down at the station. Dave sent for her. He said she'd understand."

Katie appeared behind Claire. She untied her apron and handed it to Claire. "It won't take long, sweetie," she said.

"Oh no, you're not going without me," said Claire. "We're both in this together." Claire faced Ted and stated, "All or none."

Ted smiled, nodded and walked to his patrol car with the two ladies following behind.

"Oh, it reeks in here and it isn't cigarettes!" shouted Claire, disgust in her voice.

"Oh, some drunk pissed in the car this morning and I cleaned it up as best I could. It'll be better tomorrow when they go through the car tonight and clean it."

"Think we'll walk," said Claire. "We'll get there just as fast."

"Suit yourself," said Ted, "Meet you at the front door."

"We'll wait for you," said Claire.

Katie and Claire walked into the station with Ted in tow. State troopers and local police were everywhere. It was chaos. Chris greeted them at the door of the small observation room.

"He's in there. You are not to say anything, just observe," he ordered.

Katie nodded and Claire followed her into the small room. Several state troopers, who Chris had called in for assistance, were watching Jack Dunn from inside the observation room. Matt, Dave and a woman state trooper were in the room with Jack. Katie sat for a moment and then sat bolt upright, looking straight at Jack Dunn through the one-way mirror.

"Mom, I see him too," said Claire.

Katie was visibly shaking as she said, in a whisper, "Dear God, help me free this man."

Jack Dunn snapped to a rigid position and looked slowly at the wall which housed the large one-way mirror. "*Well*," he said, "*I see we have company.*" His voice had changed into something very unlike Jack's voice. With a high, breathy, almost surreal pitch to his voice, Jack Dunn became another human being right before their eyes. The woman in the room let out a gasp and stood looking into the most malevolent eyes she had ever seen. Gone were the deep blue eyes of the prisoner, replaced with eyes so yellow they glowed like amber.

In the adjoining room, Katie took sage and a few of her charms, several feathers, a crucifix, and an assortment of stones and amulets from her bag and placed them on the table. She struck a match and made a hoot with her mouth, a sound that was haunting and surreal.

Jack sat bolt upright, his eye color going from blue to amber like the flashing of a traffic signal.

Dave sat motionless, staring at Jack, and said, "Jack, try to gain control, think of something that you like, don't let him come into your mind."

Jack Dunn was crying. He held his hands over his face, large sobs coming from between his fingers. His torso was convulsing in the chair he sat on and his knees hit the underside of the table with rhythmic slaps.

Katie and Claire were still working in the small, adjacent room which was now filling up with smoke from the sage. No one dared to stop them.

Chris was afraid the fire alarms would sound and then all hell would break loose. He raced from the room and ordered everyone out of the building, all fans on and all doors opened.

The officers stood spellbound at the scene playing out in the inner rooms. "I've never seen anything like it," one whispered. "If this is the coming of the new age we're going to have to deal with, I'm retiring now, like pronto," said another.

Suddenly a grey fog appeared in the room in the shape of a medium-sized creature with a hunchback. A snarl emitted from the mouth of the creature and in a flash he was gone. Jack Dunn, who had stood up, collapsed onto the floor of the room, his head hitting the wall. Confusion reigned, and everyone was talking at once. Some saw the creature escape through the back door, others said it was roaming the corridors, and still others didn't know what they saw or where it went.

Katie doused her sage in her sand bowl, sprinkled some onto the floor and asked if she could see Jack and that nice FBI man called Dave. "Lady, I don't know what the hell you just did, but it was some side show," remarked one of the troopers.

"He's just an example of a weak person who has no inkling of how to protect himself from certain things. That man had no idea he was committing whatever crime he committed. The spirit took over and controlled his body through its anger and rage. It's the entity we have to address, not Mr. Dunn."

Katie came into the room slowly and knelt by Jack. "It's okay now, he's gone, but unfortunately not forever. I will tell you one thing: this time we know who he is, why he does what he does, and how he does it, and we're prepared to send him home for good, if it kills us."

Her words sent shivers up Matt's spine and the police woman in the room with them. She stared at Katie in amazement. Katie looked up into her eyes and said, "Your people grew up with this and are much closer to it than some. What do you think?"

"Sweetie," she replied, in a deep southern drawl, "I got into the force to get away from a lot of this stuff, but it seems to follow me."

"It follows those who have the gift, and you, dear one, have it," said Katie, smiling broadly.

The poor woman trooper sighed in resignation, shaking her head, and left the room. Katie could hear her talking to a young trooper by the front desk.

"Mother," said Claire, "no."

"But I think she would add some pizzazz to our group," whined Katie.

Her daughter just glared at her.

Chapter Fifty

Dave was standing, looking out the window of the precinct into the glaring lights of the news vans. Reporters were everywhere he looked. "What a night," he said as Matt approached. "Ever wonder what the future will hold for you when you get my age?" he said wistfully.

"Sometimes I think about the past and how different it is for my daughter," said Matt.

"Whatever happened when I left, I made every possible arrangement to support you. I was under court order, I had no visitation rights, but every month I faithfully sent money. When I found out you left, I went to the local judge and had the court order rescinded. No more child support. I put that money into a fund. There's quite a bit in there and I was wondering if you and your wife would like it to go toward Lydia's education, sort of a college fund?"

He turned to face his son. "Don't think I'm doing this out of guilt. I got over that a long time ago. I'm doing it out of love and respect for you and your wife and you having to endure all the shit I left behind."

Matt put his hand on Dave's shoulder and said, "for what it's worth, I'm glad you're back in my life; our lives."

"Okay, who's telling Lydia and Eugenia our little secret?" said Dave, laughing.

"If we get the opportunity, either of us can drop the bomb shell. No secrets in this town," Matt mused shaking his head.

Chapter Fifty-One

Thursday morning loomed bright and sunny. The girls were enjoying their time casually walking to school. This was the last day and all they had to do was show up for report cards. Just as they reached the end of the drive by the large, brick school building. Kenny and his friend Louis came along.

"Yo," said Louis, "you harassing that brother of yours again?" Somehow, little Louis always wanted to know what Josh and Olivia were up to. Olivia secretly thought that Josh was Louis's idol, and that was too absurd for her to even think about.

"Yes," said Olivia, "I can do anything to him at any time. He's my brother and I hate him, the big oaf. But now that he has a real job, I won't see him all that much. He starts full-time tomorrow, so I can act like an only child, and that will be nice."

"He was nice to me for a change yesterday," interjected Kenny, "but I wonder when the ball will drop from the sky whenever he's like that. Maybe because all his friends had Regents exams and he didn't so he was alone, didn't have to show off."

Chapter Fifty-Two

When Brian Nedo and his men walked into the police station with a barrage of reporters in tow, Chris let out a bellow that sent most of the entourage out the door where they were relegated to wait. The FBI man just stood there, taking it all in stride and smiling. Nedo, as they called him, was the head man at the bureau assigned to this case after Chris had asked for assistance.

Chris and Dave brought him up to speed on the events of the past few weeks, including the past murders and the newspaper accounts. Needless to say, the FBI and the local authorities were stumped.

Matt came up to the group and stood quietly, looking at the large, athletic man.

Nedo laughed and stuck out his hand. "Nedo," he said, "FBI."

"I'm Matt, one of the officers here."

"You're the one who started this whole thing."

Matt put his hands up and said, "Now, wait a minute."

Nedo laughed and said, "Well, what's your take?" looking directly at Dave and then at Matt with a quizzical expression.

"I don't like it, don't like it one bit," mused Dave.

"How so?" said Nedo.

"Too much speculation, too many reporters running around digging up the past and a whole lot of very, shall we say unusual people who believe in this stuff."

"What stuff?" said Nedo cautiously.

"An evil entity coming back for revenge," said Matt.

"Oh," was all Nedo said.

"Matt here is the officer whose daughter, mother-in-law and a friend found the last body," noted Chris.

Nedo nodded. "What in the hell brought them to the spot where they found the body?"

"Apparently, my daughter and her girlfriend were there one day and some interesting things started to happen to them. It's clear in an interview with Jack's boss that Jack also found the spot, only by mistake, and this is where we are."

"How many other people know of this particular place?" queried Nedo.

"Apparently a few, but I can tell you now, I couldn't find it again. I know they could though."

"Ok, first thing tomorrow, you take me there. I want to meet your daughter and your mother-in-law. Maybe they would be game to show me?"

"You're going to need them whether you like it or not," said Matt.

Nedo kept looking from Dave to Matt and back again.

"Anything wrong?" asked Matt with a half-smile.

Dave looked at Nedo and said quietly, "This is my son."

Matt smiled broadly as shock showed on Chris's face. Matt had never seen the chief at a loss for words. All eyes were on Dave and Matt, and Matt suddenly noticed that the entire precinct was quiet.

Nedo, recovering from the bombshell, faintly said, "Ahhh. I see." Chris looked incredulous.

"Matt and I have not seen each other in a very long time," said Dave. "Last night we had a chance to catch up and a lot of things were resolved. This is my son, the only one I have, and I'll endeavor to treat him like I should've so long also, instead of taking the coward's way out."

Matt stood there, a flush slowly creeping up his face. He was proud of his dad, and he realized he had never lost that pride, even in the years he was gone. It was like this invisible cord that connected them through time and space. A cord, he realized, that could never be severed, for it was made with love.

Chapter Fifty-Three

The next morning Nedo, Dave and Matt, with Joe in tow, approached Eugenia's house and knocked on the door. They were met by a shout from Dottie's that told them she was in the horse pasture.

Eugenia was leaning on the fence. Lydia, Olivia, Kenny and Louis were standing at the rails watching Dottie lunging a horse on the other end of a long rope. Dottie let out a whistle and the horse slid to a stop and stood waiting. She approached the horse with soft cooing noises and he put his muzzle into the crook of her arm. She grabbed his halter and approached the fence where the others waited.

"You gotta remember, quiet, no sudden movements," Matt said as he grabbed Nedo's arm and forcefully slowed his approach toward Dottie and her horse. Olivia quickly blocked his way as she looked up and into the eyes of the rather tall and husky man who had an air of someone always in a hurry and was used to barking orders and having people obey.

Eugenia half-turned and gave a sideways glance at Nedo. "Well, well, the big brass is here," she quietly said.

This took Nedo by surprise. This woman had an attitude and he didn't like it one bit. He liked his women small, obedient, and subtle. This one was none of those and he was surprised at his reaction to her.

Dottie saw confrontation coming so she quietly turned and walked the horse out of the small enclosure toward the barn, listening intently all the while.

"You an FBI man?" asked Louis, obvious admiration in his voice. Nedo nodded, all the while not taking his eyes off Eugenia, who had turned and now faced him, her chin slightly tilted upward and her eyes steely.

"Something I can do for you?" she asked. She didn't acknowledge Matt, Dave or Joe but just kept a steady gaze on Nedo.

"Ma'am," he said. "I understand you were one of the ones who found the body in the woods."

"That's correct," she said. "Me, Dottie and Lydia. Lydia is the one who first found the spot along with her friend here, Olivia."

"I read the reports and I've come here to see the spot if it's at all possible. I really need to see it."

"It's a sacred circle," Lydia blurted out. "It's very powerful and sacred. Why do you want to go there?"

"Because that's where the body was found, that's all. There may be some evidence left behind by the killer, you never know, but I need to have a look."

Eugenia looked at Matt.

"Sorry, Eugenia, it's my job," he said.

Eugenia nodded and said, "Alright, let's go."

Nedo looked at her, astonished, and said, "Now?"

Dottie was exiting the barn and she followed the group. Lydia led the way.

Nedo stopped and said, "Ho, wait one moment. " Looking at the kids, he said, "Where do you four think you're going?"

"To the circle," they said, in unison.

"Oh no, no, no," said Nedo.

"Afraid so," said Lydia, disdainfully. "We're the ones who know where it is for certain. End of conversation." They all turned as one and started down the path, into the junk yard, and through the small opening in the trees that afforded coolness from the approaching heat of mid-morning.

"Oh, we all know who the killer is, it's just catching him. He's very powerful, you know," interjected Kenny, who had turned and looked directly at Nedo. Louis nodded.

"Yup, it's the dark one alright," said Louis. "My granny says so."

Dottie and Eugenia cast knowing glances at one another and kept on walking.

"This dark one," said Nedo, "it's the evil guy from the old legend, the legend that has been perpetuated around here for hundreds of years?"

Eugenia nodded, never taking her eyes off Nedo, who had turned and faced her when he asked the question, and now mumbled something under his breath about this whole area being weird and full of crazies.

The small group walked further and further into the impending gloom of the woods. Nedo tripped several times. Dave smiled at him and nodded at his feet. Those loafers were good for office work, not good for the woods. Nedo shot a glance at Dave's feet and noticed he was wearing hiking boots. He rolled his eyes. He also stole a glance at Matt's feet, noticed his high-polished service shoes and sighed. There was some sanity here after all, maybe just a little.

Lydia abruptly halted and turned. "This is the edge of the circle," she said. Nedo slid past her and entered the open light of the meadow. It was a little overcast but the large circle looked like the grass had just been mowed.

"Who takes care of this?" he said.

"What?" said the group in unison.

"Who mows the grass?" he repeated.

Eugenia couldn't believe what she was hearing.

Lydia rolled her eyes. "I guess the spirits do it. I don't know anyone in town who goes here to mow the grass," she said sarcastically.

Nedo turned to look at them. "Am I stupid enough to believe that the grass grows like this? It's like a friggin' golf course."

Matt and Dave both shook their heads. "Yes, Brian," said Dave.

"This circle is very sacred and very old," said Dottie, "and if you're looking to blame some of the locals, we would know about it. So perish the thought."

A branch snapped further into the woods and then another as if something was moving through the underbrush. Matt started in the direction of the sound, unsnapping the safety strap on his holster as he moved forward. Dave instinctively went for his gun also, while Eugenia and Dottie grabbed the four children and huddled them into a small group, each woman taking two of the children.

A form appeared in the undergrowth at the side of the circle. Matt raised his gun and shouted, "who are you? Come out, now." Dave came behind him, gun drawn as more branches snapped and the much-disheveled figure of a woman appeared.

"Oh my God, it's Stacy!" Matt shouted.

"The missing woman?" said Nedo, incredulously.

Stacy's eyes were glazed as if she had been on a drug binge, she was filthy dirty and smelled of urine and body odor. She looked at Matt and Dave as if seeing people for the first time and then she collapsed in a heap before they could get to her.

"Heeeere we go again," whispered Dave, just audible enough for Matt to hear. Matt didn't know whether to laugh or cry so he shouted to Dottie to call 9-1-1.

"No service," said Lydia.

"Then text or do something," shouted her father.

"I'll go and get service," Lydia shouted as she ran out of the circle and down the path toward the junk yard. Keep calm, keep calm, she kept telling herself as Louis, Kenny and Olivia caught up to her. She passed the tree where the stake was that intersected the two paths, one toward the circle and the other toward the research site. She wanted to get out of there as quick as possible and help that poor woman. They reached the narrow opening and burst into the grassy part of the path near several old cars. She gasped as she held onto a door handle and dialed the number.

"9-1-1."

"I need, I need help. I need the police at the back of the junk yard and an ambulance now."

"What is the nature of the emergency?"

"Woman in trouble, badly hurt," she said.

"Do you have an address?" asked the operator.

"Hell no," blurted out Lydia.

Kenny took the phone from her and in a calm voice said, "We're in Emeryville. We're in the rear of Pederson's junk yard and we have a woman here in a lot of trouble. She may be dying."

"I'll tone out your ambulance."

Lydia, shouted, "Tell the squad same place as before and call the police. Chris is the chief. Get him out here too, we'll wait right here and lead them in."

Chapter Fifty-Four

Tom couldn't believe it when Alex came running into the office shouting for him to open the back gate since the ambulance and the police were at the front.

"For Christ's sake, this is a three ring circus," shouted Tom as he ran from his desk and out the front door.

Chris jumped from the squad car. "Sorry Tom, got another one in the back of the yard."

"I'll get the loader but please tell me how a man can conduct business with all this death and weird stuff going on around here? Alex!" he shouted, "Alex!"

But Alex was already heading toward the loader. Instantly, it roared to life as the gate opened and the procession started into the maze of paths that ran through the junk yard.

It was noon and the small group huddled around Stacy as she lay on the grass in the circle. Eugenia and Dottie kept a steady barrage of Reiki going into her body, and Nedo asked what in hell they were doing as the woman seemed to be responding.

"They are giving her Reiki," said Matt quietly, staring straight ahead and not looking at Nedo.

Nedo stared at Matt, unable to speak.

Stacy's eyes flew open and she recognized both women.

"I'm so tired, it's, it's as if all my strength is gagagone," she mumbled.

"Keep still, sweetie," crooned Eugenia, glancing nervously over Dottie's head.

"He's not here, I'd feel him if he were," said Dottie. "Besides, right now, I think I'm mad enough to eat him, the bastard."

"What was that thing?" Stacy mumbled, "Wha, wh," and then she passed out.

Eugenia felt for a pulse and got a strong one. She knowingly nodded her head and Dottie looked relieved.

"I hear a motor," said Nedo, and several minutes later a much-winded Lydia and her friends, accompanied by half the police force and the ambulance squad, arrived. Aaron, the squad captain, approached the two women kneeling on the ground. He knelt as Eugenia and Dottie got up to let him and his team do their thing.

"She's in shock, she looks like she's been running and I don't think she's eaten in several days," Aaron remarked. "Get the stretcher and let's get her out of here. Ed, get the rig ready, we're going to need IV fluids, and call the hospital."

"No," said Olivia, "there's no communication until you are out of the woods."

Aaron nodded as Stacy was strapped in, and the procession of EMTs and medics made their way through the woods, led by Olivia, Lydia, Kenny and Louis.

Chapter Fifty-Five

Dave started walking toward the center of the circle. Looking down, he noticed what resembled charred logs buried in the ground, their ends jutting up to about three inches above the surface. He kicked at one of the pieces of charred wood and the ground moved. He let out a hum under his breath. Matt came and stood beside him.

"Looks like the remains of an old fire pit," he said.

Dave knelt and scratched at the surface, tearing away a few tufts of grass. He grabbed an end of one of the logs and heaved. The dirt, centuries old, moved away from the rotted log and exposed a small depression, similar to a cave created by the maze of rotted logs under the soil. Dave looked like a bulldog, for now he was actively pawing at the dirt under the exposed, rotted logs. Suddenly he stopped, still staring down at whatever it was he had exposed. Carefully he swept away the rest of the soil to reveal a perfectly intact human skull.

Dottie came over and when she saw the find, she gasped. "It could be him, the dark one. If that skull has been burned, it would fit the old legend," she mumbled.

"Get the coroner out here," said Matt wearily. "Get Lydia and her cell phone. Hell, even our radios won't work here."

Half an hour later, the dulcet tones of the county coroner could be heard from the path leading to the circle. Larry Diamond was the chief medical examiner for the county, and although he was much older than most of the men on the police force, he still practiced two days a week at the morgue. He was considered to be a genius at ferreting out diseases and causes of death. He wasn't afraid to call in the big guns if he needed help. His lab at the morgue was small, but the county gave him everything he needed in the way of equipment. His lab, the envy of most of the coroners in surrounding counties, was even better than some of the state labs.

He had one assistant, a young, rather bookish girl who was not very social. Larry often told her to "lighten up."

"God-forsaken place," Larry said in a very audible tone. He stopped short. "Well I'll be damned." He looked around the circle in obvious amazement. A slender young woman with heavy glasses followed him into the circle. She was obviously very nervous and looked like she was going to bolt at any time. "Body bag," said Larry, "and get me that small shovel. Any more bones?"

"Not yet," said Dave.

An hour later more bones had been unearthed.

"This is very interesting. These bones seem to have been cut with a knife, like the victim was dismembered, but I won't know for sure until I get them back to the lab," said Larry.

Dottie and Eugenia sat in the grass near the men and looked around.

"I can just imagine this entire place as a large, native village with all the hustle and bustle of a village's daily life. But this circle would have been away from the village," mused Eugenia.

"Not necessarily," said Dottie. "I would imagine it was near the shaman's home, but I don't know."

Dave sat down next to them on the grass. His pants, shirt, hands and arms were soiled with dirt and he looked tired. "I guess I did my work, now let the experts do theirs, besides, I'm getting too old for this," he said wistfully.

Eugenia stared at Dave and let out a snort. He stared straight back at her and with a cynical smile said "what?"

She let out a deep sigh and said, "Gossip travels around here like wildfire. As you must realize, one cannot fart in this town without someone knowing about it."

"Yeah, and your point?" he said defensively.

"Point, my ass. Why didn't you say something about your relationship with Matt?"

"Oh, that," he said smiling. He was egging her on and she knew it.

Just as Eugenia was about to reply, a voice came from the direction of the fire pit where Larry was busy with his assistant.

"These bones were burned. Many of them are charred," said Larry. He was obviously upset. "Well, my job's done, so let's get out of here. I'm going to send a forensic artist in when I get done finding out if this is one skeleton or many. I would venture a guess it's one person. I'll also be calling in the state anthropologist; friend of mine. Maybe he can look at this skull and tell me a little bit more about it."

Eugenia looked up from where she was sitting and said, "You know as well as I do whose it is and just about how old, ya been here long enough." Then she muttered, just audible enough for Dottie and Dave to hear her, "ya big dumb jackass."

"Eugenia, are we still fighting after all these years?" said Dottie soothingly.

"Yes," Eugenia hissed, "and it will keep on going until," but she was cut short.

Larry put his finger in the air and in a booming, theatrical voice said, "All hell freezes over."

Eugenia threw up her hands, got up, turned her back on the group and marched out of the circle accompanied by snorts of laughter from Dottie, Dave and Larry.

Chris was coming into the circle as they were coming out. He looked exhausted.

"What in hell," he said, eyeing the pile of dirt and rotted logs and the body bag in the center of the circle.

"One more body," announced Larry.

"Oh shit," said Chris.

"This one's very old. I would venture a guess it's not really connected to what's going on."

Eugenia rolled her eyes, looked at Dottie and whispered, "We'll see about that."

Chapter Fifty-Six

Larry got back to the morgue and started cleaning the skull. He noticed a slightly different brow line and different shaped eye sockets from others in the lab, and he couldn't wait until he got his friend Steve in on this. Steve was an anthropologist with the state and quite knowledgeable.

He started to arrange the skeletal remains onto one of the morgue tables and immediately noticed little deformities in the bones. They were old bones, but human bones, and the man in question was short and slightly stooped as if he had a birth defect of some kind. "Goin' to run lots of tests on this one," he muttered. "I don't know about DNA, might not have enough, but other tests could be done," he thought.

It was past seven when he finally called it a day. He called Steve. When he got his answering machine, he told him he wanted him in Emeryville as soon as possible. He knew Steve would call him back, probably at midnight. "Just to piss me off," he thought and smiled.

The phone rang at fifteen minutes past midnight and a groggy Larry answered with "yes, you son of a bitch."

"Now is that a way to greet an old friend?" said a syrupy, sweet voice at the other end. "I know and I bet you're now groping for your glasses because you have to talk to me with them on. Am I right?"

"Bastard," swore Larry, laughing. "You know me better than I know myself!"

Steve just laughed.

"What've you been up to?"

"You know, the usual and married to my work, and never the twain shall meet," came the flippant reply from Steve.

Larry rolled his eyes. "I hear you, but I still miss you."

"Me too," came the sad reply. "Okay, enough of this crap, I'm losing needed beauty rest," he snorted. "What've you got?"

"Well, it's a skull and skeleton. I figured you'd want to see it."

"The last time I was over in your direction, they ran me out of town, you know, the Grant Case?"

"Yeah, yeah, but it all came out fine in the end, if you recall."

"After they tarred and feathered me, you mean," came a terse reply. "I can hear it now as I pop out of my car, with a 'heeeeerrrr we go again, it's your gay anthropologist with another bit of great news!' No way!"

"I really think you're going to like this and it's a whole new set of characters," whined Larry.

"Yeah, is that police chief still there, the blond with the sexy eyes?"

"Yes, a little older and a little balder."

"Paunchier I suppose," mused Steve.

"God, will you just get the hell over here and quit trying to make excuses."

"Okay, okay, I have some vaca time coming. Nothing happens here this time of year but research and all the work in the trenches if the state figures it's going to put up another building on some grave site or something. And then somebody from some historical association gets a bee in their bonnet."

"You sound like you're near retirement. I told you before, you'd really like to live here."

"Only if you retire with me, sweetheart," came the reply, "and then maybe we'll have a deal."

"Deal? Like a business proposition? The last time it was a little different around here. You just don't show up in pink and think you're going to get anywhere with this police department."

"Yes, that was in my boyish and frivolous youth, before life happened to me. Fresh out of the closet, bold, sexy, starving; you know, only the state would hire me. I fit into their minority profile. Black, gay and wearing a pink suit, like the proverbial pink elephant. But look where I am now, tada."

"Knock it off," said Larry.

"Okay, I'll see what my schedule is tomorrow and if I can allot some time, I'll see you real soon, probably sooner than you think. Ciao for now," and the phone went dead.

Larry held the phone to his ear and smiled, floods of memories coming back to fill in gaps of long-ago, bittersweet times.

Chapter Fifty-Seven

Howard entered the large barn that housed the heifers and dry cows. It was dawn and the sky had not quite lost the blackness of night. He loved this time of day and, having left his girlfriend in bed, he was out and about starting the chores that on a large dairy farm began in the early hours of morning.

His booted feet walked noiselessly across the manure-strewn concrete as he approached the feed bunks. Some of the cows were out in the yard in a small group, but where were the rest of them? "Damned cows," he swore under his breath.

He shouted his "Yip Yip" and expected all of them to start their way to the bunkers where the morning silage would be dumped in by the front end loader, but not a cow moved. He was getting annoyed now, as time was everything if he was going to get the milking done before the milk tanker came to pick up the morning's milk. He thought, "Serves me right for going at it a second time," smiling wanly as he thought of the night's events. Yep, this girl could be a keeper if she could keep up with him.

He noticed the headlights near the milking barn and the thud of a truck door closing told him that one of the hired men had arrived. The slam of the milk house door and the flood of lights in the main barn told him that the milking would soon begin as the cows were let in from the free stalls to the milking parlor gates. Sure enough, the steady hum of the compressor began. "Now," he muttered, "getting back to these mother..."

Something wet hit the top of his head. He went to brush it away and noticed that it was sticky and had a funny dark color in the yellow glow of the sodium vapor lights. He felt almost dizzy and the sickening feeling in the pit of his stomach increased as his eyes began their rise upward toward the ceiling rafters of the barn. At first he thought it was a joke. Someone had tied a fake human body to the rafters of the barn. Then he recognized the bloated, darkened face of old Ben.

He looked down, but the dizziness increased and so did the urge to vomit. He looked up and into those darkened orbits where eyes had once been. He looked down. "Oh shit, shit, shit!" he screeched and ran toward the milk house, stopping twice to empty his stomach of the coffee he had drunk an hour before.

"What, hold on, Howard, you're screeching, hold on," said the night dispatcher at the station. "You what?"

"I called 9-1-1, how the hell do I know my damned fire number? I hung up on them bastards. Anyway, I have a dead man hanging from the rafters of my barn. Hell," was all he could manage to say.

"I'll get an ambulance and police right out there. You hang on," said the dispatcher.

"Nothing else to do, just don't block the damned driveway for the milk tanker, will ya?"

The dispatcher rolled his eyes. "Yes Howard."

Another dispatcher called the chief and Chris's wife answered the phone. "It's four in the morning or some ungodly hour," she said sternly. "What is it?"

Chris was already up and grabbed the phone from his wife. "What?" he said anxiously.

"You want to come, another body. This time in Howard's barn, hanging from the rafters."

"Oh shit, no reporters, got it, none and call Nedo and get Dave and Matt out there."

"Oh my God," said Matt as he slammed down the receiver and reached for his pants. "It's Ben, at least they think it's him, dead in Howard's barn!"

"No, oh no," said Karen, thinking about how her mother would take this news. "It's starting early," she said.

Matt fixed her a hard glance and left the room.

"I better get up," Karen mumbled, "can't sleep anyway." This time, as she entered the kitchen, she figured she would fix herself a cup of coffee. Dawn was just breaking and Karen decided to have a one-on-one talk with her number one mentor. She poured two cups of coffee, set out a plate of small scones, a jar of orange marmalade, some cream and sugar and two spoons, two knives and a fork. She sighed as she sat down, rather heavily, tears welling in her eyes. "Keep calm, just keep calm, ask and then just listen." She breathed deeply and said, "Okay God, let's talk because I need answers......"

Chapter Fifty-Eight

Larry entered the heifer barn with a little trepidation. "Be a coroner and see the world," he mumbled under his breath. "Who's cutting him down?" he yelled as he entered the barn.

"It's up to you," said Matt. "Howard's on his way with the loader and the rest of us didn't touch a thing yet. Crime lab is on the way."

"You mean I beat the lab guys for once? I'm gonna write this down in my memoirs," Larry quipped lightly.

The lab men arrived and several officers cordoned off the area and secured the scene. Now it was Larry's turn.

The loader roared into place beside him and Howard, with a half-grin on his face, beckoned him to climb in. "Y' mean I'm going up there in this?"

"Up close and personal," Howard yelled back over the clatter of the loader's motor.

Larry's assistant entered the barn at that moment and he shouted for her to get a body bag and his tools.
As Larry lifted his slightly bulky frame into the loader, he pointed his finger at Howard and shouted, "don't give a shit, smooth ride, understand."

Howard, not used to taking orders, just nodded. He had all he could do to keep himself from vomiting and kept his cool by concentrating on his heifers. He noticed one of the heifers attempting to mount another and mentally took notes. "Looks like two-seventy is in heat, might have to call the breeder tomorrow," he thought.

"Howard!"

His momentary lapse was brought back abruptly with the shout, "A little more to the left and pay attention to me and not that cow, dammit!" shouted Larry.

"If I don't pay attention to that friggin' cow, then I'll puke and you'll have to step in it," shouted Howard right back.

"All right, let's keep it civil here," Chris said in a warning voice.

Larry looked at the corpse. Ben was actually glued to the rafters with his own blood and insides and something else. "Bring me my tools up here," he shouted.

"Demanding bastard," Howard said under his breath.

As Larry poked and prodded with his gloved hands, pieces of the rafter began flaking off. The rafters were charcoal and the entire backside of Ben was burned, as if he was put on fire and burned into the rafters.

"Christ," said Larry. "Ben, you old fool, what were you doing here anyway?" he quietly asked himself.

The sun was rising and the large ventilation fans in the barn came to life with a noisy roar.

"Howard, turn those things off, will ya," shouted Larry, as a blast of cold air hit him in the face. He sighed and glanced into the early morning dawn. "Alright, get that body bag up here, will ya, I just don't want to dump him in the loader, too many contaminants, and besides, you won't want to see this anyway." His voice trailed off in the soft glow of the rising sun as he said, "better to remember him as he was." He barely had time to move when a large coil of rope whizzed through the air and landed neatly over the rafter just feet from the body. "Okay, who's the cowboy?" called Larry.

A small, squeaky voice answered from below and he realized it was his assistant.

"Wow, want a job?" said Howard. "I'm impressed, and you're a woman!"

Larry's assistant gave Howard a sideward, lethal glance and Howard laughed, apparently unmoved by her displeasure.

The body bag began its ascent upward. Larry grabbed the bag and his assistant heard the zipper being pulled. She shouted up, "need help, Larry?"

"No. Just make sure when it comes down that it doesn't hit the floor. I'm taking a sample of the rafter now, and that will be in a separate pack in the bag."

A few minutes later she heard him shout, "Coming down!" over the bellows of cows waiting to be fed. The bag started its descent as the cows' bellows reached a crescendo, and suddenly they all stopped. The bag descended the rest of the way in total silence.

"Jeez, even the cows know," Larry marveled. "Well-trained cows," he quipped to Howard, as the bucket descended and rested just enough above the floor so Larry could jump out. He turned to Howard and said, "My pants were clean, you know."

"Yeah, so were mine a few days ago," was the reply. "Ya know, this is the feed bucket, so the only thing that's been in here is silage. Now the next time I could arrange for you to go up in the manure bucket."

"No next time!" shouted Larry.

"Bitch, bitch, bitch," said Howard, laughing, as he and the tractor headed toward the silo to feed the cows.

"Guess we're done here," said Chris.

Nedo arrived and Chris said, "suppose you want to stay awhile?"

"Me and Dave will be here a while, we want to look around."

"Just tell Howard, I'm sure he won't object."

Matt shouldered up to Chris. "I have a house call to make, you know what I mean," he said.

"Yeah, want anyone else with you?" Chris asked.

"No, this is one I have to do alone," sighed Matt.

"Who's next of kin?" asked Chris.

"A daughter, lives near Albany, all I know. Doesn't have too much to do with the old man, but she has to be notified," said Matt.

Chris nodded, "you sure you're up to this?"

"No, but I have to. No one ever gets used to this." Matt headed toward the squad car, and as he got in he noticed the body bag being loaded into the ambulance. "Goodbye, Ben," he said quietly. "I sure hope you found what you were looking for."

Chapter Fifty-Nine

The squad car parked on the street half way between Dottie's and Eugenia's. He had called Karen and told her where he would be. "Come up in about an hour, I should be finished by then," he told her.

"Oh Matt, why?"

"I'll be damned if I know, but this is better coming from me than from anyone else right now." He was suddenly angry, angry at all the senseless killing.

Eugenia waited on the back porch steps for him to approach. His eyes met hers. She looked concerned.

"This official, Matt?"

He nodded. "Get Dottie over here because I'm only going to say this once. That will be enough," he said quietly.

Eugenia didn't have to go off the steps, for Dottie was running across the small grassy area that separated the two properties. Dottie saw Matt's face and Matt beckoned her onto the porch. The three sat in chairs opposite one another.

"You look tired, Dot," said Matt as he looked into her face.

"Haven't slept all night," she said wearily." Recurring dream. A bad one, but no face on the victim, just that he was flying through the air and he stuck onto something like a part of a building and stayed there. It was like the stories of grandpa being stuck to that barn wall."

"Almost," said Matt, and both women let out gasps. "Ben was found this morning in Howard's barn. Either of you two know why he'd go into Howard's barn in the first place?"

Tears were flowing down Eugenia's face but anger showed on Dottie's. Anger for tears was all she could muster from the shock. "He's in a better place now," was all she could say as she rose and started toward her house across the grass.

Eugenia looked at Matt, but didn't really see him. He knew she was in deep, intimate reflection.

Karen was beside her mother before he knew she was there. She sat on the arm of the large porch chair with her hand on her mother's. Not a word was spoken.

"Ya know, the last time I saw him, I think he knew it wouldn't be long. He went missing for a few days and then ended up here and stayed for dinner. Not like him at all. He was very melancholy, almost fragile. He said something about a little knife used in human sacrifice that he had seen and it was now in the hands of the school, in Seth's room. He said that that knife held the key, but what key?"

"A knife?" said Matt with a frown.

"Yes, a very old artifact that was brought in by one of the school children for show and tell and, as the story goes, another boy recognized it and told the principle or something or other."

Matt started to get a queasy feeling in his stomach. "A knife at the school?"

"Yes, yes," said Eugenia hurriedly. "Ask Seth, Katie's tenant. He knows about the thing."

"Did he say anything else out of the ordinary, and why in the cow barn?"

Eugenia shook her head. "That I don't know." Her voice grew calm. "He did roam around town in the evenings, but why way out at Howard's place? Unless," she shuddered and grimaced, "unless he was transported out there."

~

Just to let them know I'm coming back, he thought. Now that he had their full attention he was going to enjoy this little charade. In the past, he had enjoyed all their attempts to try to stop him, but this time it was different. More people were aware of the inherent nature of good and of evil. But there were still those who didn't believe, maybe those were the ones he could prey upon, the ones that would help him curb his insatiable appetite.

Chapter Sixty

Matt approached his desk at the station. He was surprised to see Richard Perry sitting there with a grim look on his face. Perry stood and said, "Any chance of my star reporter being released? I mean, this is ridiculous."

"Waiting on the judge," said Matt. "Why don't you pursue it with Dennis? He might shed some light on the subject."

Perry nodded. "This is getting crazier and crazier," he said as he headed for the door.

Chris, who was now standing at Matt's shoulder said, "Anything you want to talk to me about?"

"Something has been bothering me. We're looking at the circle but what of the other end? What about where they were doing the research, where that vine begins, or where it gravitates to?"

"You're beginning to sound like Katie and the rest of them. You know, all this psychic stuff." His voice was filled with disgust.

"I have a feeling that what we're dealing with is some form of energy in its most raw form. It's not of this world and it has to be stopped. We're the ones to do it if everyone gets on board. You know the men are talking, you know a lot of them are caught up in this so-called psychic stuff , and the more sensational it gets, the more nuts we'll be getting in here. But somewhere is an answer and it has to do with that circle and the woods behind that junk yard. Something happened in there centuries ago and it's like an imprint on the land and all the emotions that go with it."

Chris was looking at him with an expression of total surprise on his face. "I thought I would never hear you say things like that," he said.

Matt continued, "Go to any Civil War battlefield in the US and sit for awhile. Some people sense that the entire battle is still going on around them. School kids have heard the cry of the Irish Brigade at the Sunken Road, for Christ's sake. And another thing, did you know that there's a knife involved, a small, very ancient knife, and I just got a hunch, but I need to see Larry first. Want to go along?"

"You bet," said Chris.

Chapter Sixty-One

"Larry in?" said Chris as he approached the desk of the hospital receptionist. "I think he is. Let me page him," came the sweet reply from a heavily made-up girl in her mid-twenties. "Yes, ride the elevator to the basement, room twenty, end of the hall."

Matt nodded to her and she smiled in reply, never taking her eyes off the two men as they disappeared down the hall to the waiting bank of elevators.

Larry met them in the hall and escorted them into a small anteroom. He had on a surgical gown and a mask was perched on his balding head. He smelled like charcoal and rotted flesh. "First of all, let me tell you there's a lot with this skeletal body, a lot. Analysis came back from two sources and I have several things of my own. But let's all see what we have and then let's meet and get this all going."

"I might have a bomb-shell for you too, Larry," said Matt quietly.

"Well, not as bad as the one I have now for you. We have company."

Chris got a feeling in the pit of his stomach and looked sideways at Matt.

"Yes," Larry nodded, "I do have help and Chief, I'm sure you remember him."

Chris shook his head from side to side, smiled and said, "Not pink suit."

"The one and only," Larry said, with a laugh.

Chris placed a hand on Larry's arm. "Has he changed?"

"A little older and a lot wiser?" said Larry in a serious tone.

"Okay, I'll be on my best behavior."

"Good," said Larry, "now suit up and follow me."

A man was standing, bent over the bones of an almost complete skeleton lying on a steel table. Body bags lined one wall, and moving carts and the traditional morgue bins lined another wall from floor to shoulder height. The smell of formaldehyde and alcohol permeated the room as well as an underlying smell---that of rotten flash.

"How do you work with the smells?" said Chris.

"Simple," said the figure of the man, and without turning toward them he said, "I put Vicks up my nose or I wear a mask. Some use other petroleum products but I keep away from the perfumes---bad stuff and will make you really nauseous if you have something like a floater where the body is decomposed and the smell of the perfume doesn't get along with the scent of rot."

The man turned slowly, a skull in his hand. There was no mistaking those large brown eyes, the curly hair now turning grey at the temples and that beautiful, full face.

Chris smiled when he saw him, a smile that was warm and without guile.

"Well, well, Chief," the man said.

Chris nodded and looked beyond to the table and its array of bones. Matt and Chris walked to the opposite side of the table and looked down.

The man carefully, almost reverently held the skull for them to see. "What you have here is the skull of a Native American, a full-blooded Indian of the aboriginal tribes that were here from the time before Columbus, or so the text books tell you. But there are a lot of abnormalities with the skull and with the skeleton."

"It's very interesting," Larry interjected. "We have what looks like a strangulation victim, but after or during his ordeal he was cut up, dismembered so to speak, and then his body was burned, or parts of it were."

"But," the man said, "Oh, by the way, I'm Steve and you are?" he said, looking at Matt.

"I'm Matt."

"Your Chief and I go back a ways, so we don't need an introduction," he said sarcastically.

Chris looked him in the eye and stuck out his hand. "I'm Chris."

Steve took his hand, a wan smile forming on his face.

"Well, let's talk about this skull first." He said. "This is the skull of the typical Asian or Native, what you would call a brachycephalic skull. The eye sockets and the shape of the skull are different from that of the Caucasian or Negroid skulls, and each of those skulls would have their differences also. But most intriguing is the back of the skull. It's thinner than it should be and the cervical column is elongated and open."

He placed the skull carefully on the table and picked up the top section of the vertebrae. "This man was a hunchback, oh and incidentally, he also had a club foot. He did not grow as he should have and probably had these conditions from birth. In the days of this man's life, I am sure he went through a living hell of torment."

"He had a congenital condition that we, in this century call spina bifida," said Larry. "There are basically three types of the disease and it's quite common among all human populations, although some races are more prone than others. It's a birth defect."

"I've heard of that," said Chris.

"Now the interesting part is that this man was in his late twenties, early thirties, and someone decided to kill him, for whatever reason. He has several fingers missing on his left hand and the intriguing part is that he was cut up and put in that fire. I don't know of any Native tribe in these parts that would cut up their own. Captives maybe, whites yes, but not their own."

"How old is the body?" said Chris.

"Well, knowing that the skull is Native, Mongoloid, and Asian puts it between 13,000 years to about 200 years ago when the last of the tribe living here was dispersed. The dating just came in but before I go into that I want to tell you what we did. Since the body was burned in a fire we also took samples of the wood from the fire as well as the bones, gives us a more accurate picture. We also took some soil samples which can have an impact on the test. Mineral content of the soil can increase or decrease fossilization, and so can air or the lack of air. These are all variables.

"Tissue and nail samples can now be accurate to within two or three years and some are spot on, but that's another story. All we had to go on was bone and some charred wood and soil samples. With the new techniques used today in removing the impurities in the bone, tests are more accurate. So this fellow here had his unfortunate accident somewhere between 1000 and 1250 this era. So this makes him between eight hundred and one thousand years old."

Larry was unusually quiet and Chris asked him, "Larry, that puts him right smack in the middle of this legend controversy, doesn't it?"

"Afraid so," answered Larry.

"I was really hoping it would be much older, but no cigar," said Chris with resignation.

Steve looked at the men quizzically.

Larry and Chris both saw the look, and Larry said, "Tell you over dinner and drinks. Speaking of. . . how about it, you two?"

Matt and Chris looked at each other. "Oh what the hell," said Chris, "we're off duty in another hour or so, meet you at the R and K."

"Great idea," said Matt.

Steve smiled and nodded. "Sounds like a plan," he said.

Matt called Karen, filled her in on some of the details and told her she had a break tonight as it was just her and Lydia. "Business, and I want to really talk to these two, especially Steve. He may know something and I have to stop by the school before I go anyway."

Chapter Sixty-Two

Seth met Matt at the front of the school. "It's in my classroom in the case," he said. "We had it dated by an expert and it's hundreds of years old, putting it at the late Woodland period."

Matt nodded. "I need to borrow it and I'll tell you why later but this is very important. By the way, when is the next meeting of the psychic group that Katie and my mother-in-law are involved in?"

"I'll find out tonight and let you know."

"If my hunch is right, that knife will be a bombshell," said Matt.

Seth reached for the knife and let out a hum.

"What?" said Matt.

"This knife is usually cold to the touch. I mean the antler handle. The sinew is still intact as well, but the point is as sharp as a razor. But it feels like it was in someone's hands just recently for the handle is warm."

Matt felt his skin crawl and the hair rise on his scalp.

Seth was still frowning at the knife and shaking his head. He carefully wrapped the small knife in a velvet pouch and placed it in Matt's hand.

"Please take good care of this. I could lose my job over this, and remember it's one sharp object."

"Don't worry, I will," said Matt as he exited the building.

Chapter Sixty-Three

Matt arrived a little early at the R and K Restaurant, but that afforded him time to think. Forensics would be done with the investigation at the farm soon, and his father just might meet them here at the restaurant.

He called Dave and left a message as to his whereabouts. A few minutes after he ordered a beer, the door opened and Chris walked in with Larry and Steve right behind him.

"Been here long, Matt?" said Chris.

"No, just came in and ordered for an early start. This may be the last time for any of us to get some rest in a while. Let's take advantage of it."

Steve nodded and sat opposite him. Steve was a tall and lanky man with well cared-for, dark, copper skin and graying hair. Matt was conscious of something about him, but he couldn't put a finger on it. He liked Steve, but maybe just the attitude of the guy bothered him, all business and work or maybe a chip on his shoulder. He sensed some sort of barrier to him, something deep inside the man that only a few knew existed.

Chris sat next to Matt, opposite Larry and they began to talk. Chris said, "You had something to tell me, Matt, and it's been bothering me all day. What is it, and is it relevant to this investigation and the skeleton?"

"Yes and no," said Matt. "Firstly, what do you think about this whole legend thing?"

Larry sighed. "I don't know what to think. The girls are saying it's a force to be reckoned with and a very powerful curse, shall we say."

Matt looked straight at Steve, who nodded slightly, and said, "I've seen all the files from the last case and some of the writings from tribal lore. This is my field so I'm familiar with the legend. Possible, maybe, probable, I just don't know. When you're dealing with a powerful shaman, anything is possible, and even today, tribal elders are very reverential on the subject. It's not voodoo or black magic, it's a force for the good of the tribe, but in this case something went terribly wrong. The man lying in that morgue was a misfit. He could have been bullied into what he did, if it is him, but let's face it, it's only a legend."

Larry began. "When I was a kid we used to play in there, in that part of the woods, only a little farther back. There are old caves there beyond the center of the swamp, beyond the water pool. Yes, there's an eye, we used to call it that, for it's a very deep pool right in the middle of the swamp, and that vine which has always intrigued me grows right up to that pool. From there its tendrils spread for miles and miles. Things happened in there when I was a kid, but you kept quiet about it for fear your old man would whip your ass. We used to call the place the devil's eye. I mean it's a beautiful spot and all, just creepy, like there are things in that small pool you don't want to know about."

The more Chris listened, the more intrigued he got.

"Do you know what type of a blade carved up the body?" asked Matt.

Larry looked at him with concern. "Well, when I sent some of the bones to a friend of mine for analysis, he's a knife expert, he called and told me that he hadn't seen anything like it. The blade had to be from a very insanely sharp instrument like a razor blade, but the blade would have been made from flint and it had several serrated sections and a fork at the tip of the blade, like a double point. He said that this type of knife was used by the ancients here as a form of ceremonial knife for deboning animals or severing tendons, and sometimes warriors carried them concealed on their persons when they went into the woods for vision quests and sweat lodges. He has only seen one sample of an original from that period in his life and I think he said it was in the state museum in Albany in the American Indian Collection housed there. It's made of a flint-like stone of some sort but the color is an unusual pink, lavender. Some knives had a square shaft, and others had bone handles. There are only two or three in existence that he knows of."

The four men sat in deep conversation when their salads arrived accompanied by fresh bread, local goat cheese and brie. Their entrées arrived soon after and Matt looked at the plate with anticipation. Garlic mashed potatoes and hanger steak was just what he needed, filling and seared to a raw perfection. The poached green beans were done just right, a little snap to them, not overcooked.

They were finished eating now and Matt casually reached for the pouch in his pocket. He laid it gingerly on the table and Steve said, "Oh," just audible enough for the other men to hear. Matt smiled at him and winked.

"Could this blade be the blade that did him in?" Matt asked innocently as he extracted the knife from its hiding place.

Chris let out a whistle and Steve just stared at it. Finally regaining his composure, Steve said, "Oh my God, it's a ceremonial dagger or one hell of a reproduction."

"I will attest, and so does the person I borrowed this from, as well as the state, that it's genuine."

Chris looked at Matt and asked, "Where in hell did you get it?"

"I borrowed it for the evening."

"I'll have to photograph it and run tests. In other words, use it on a piece of bone and see if the marks match up. It won't be hard as this is probably one of a kind," said Larry. He looked reverently at the knife that he now held in his hand. "I admire it because of the ingenuity and expertise that went into the making of this weapon," he said. "I'm in awe."

Steve took the knife and said, "I detect a little blood here and lots more into the sinew that binds it. I'd also test for blood protein if I were you. I've heard of this knife. A recent find, am I right?" Steve inquired.

Matt nodded. "Larry, I trust you with this knife, but my ass is on the line if anything happens to it, understand."

Chris looked worried as he glanced at Matt.

After paying the check, they were outside the R and K and Matt found himself talking with Steve.

"You into this stuff?" said Matt.

Steve let out a deep sigh and said, "Well, I'm interested in old legends and before I came here I researched the one you have and that one beats all. But you know all legends have some basis in truth. The skeleton really intrigues me. It's the mortal remains of a man and that man also had a soul, a spirit. I believe that the spirit lives on after one's demise."

"If you think that's unusual, you should see that grove in the woods they call the circle," said Matt.

"I do want to see that. I'm going to Google map it this evening. There's something about the configuration of the land in the back of that junk yard that really intrigues me," said Steve thoughtfully.

Chapter Sixty-Four

Matt stopped the squad car in front of Seth's apartment and got out. He walked casually up the walk and was instantly met by Katie. "Good evening," said Matt casually. "Seth in?"

"Far as I know," said Katie, looking worried.

Matt just laughed. "Don't worry, I'm not taking him in, just a social visit, that's all."

Katie took a deep breath and looked relieved.

The door opened to the apartment and Seth stood in the doorway. "Come in, Matt," he said as he smiled at Katie, who still stood on the porch.

Matt went inside and Seth closed the door. "Larry, the coroner, has the knife at the moment," Matt said. "A few days ago a skull and skeleton were found in the woods. It's the body of an Indian, dead for many years. Larry and I seem to think that that's the knife that did the job on him. He was cut up real bad."

Seth looked worried. He said, "You know I'm going to have to come clean with the superintendent on this. I mean, if it's missing for a week, okay, but longer, not okay."

Matt shook his head. "I had a feeling and I don't want you to have to lie to her, because the Chief is in on this too."

"Great," said Seth, an edge to his voice. "You know I'm going to have to face her, the *Stalwart of Emeryville*."

Matt let out a laugh. "My kid calls her *the old battleaxe* when she gets mad at her."

Seth rolled his eyes and laughed.

"Well, the sooner the better. I'll call you in the next few days and tell you when I'm going to see her."

"Let me know, you might need backup," said Matt, laughing. Matt returned home around eleven and went immediately to bed. The twists and turns in this investigation were beginning to gnaw at him. Karen was already sleeping and he quietly got undressed, slipped into bed and snuggled next to her. She rolled on her side, draped one leg over him and they both fell into deep sleep.

Chapter Sixty-Five

Olivia wiggled her finger in the dirt. "You know," she said absently to no one in particular, "we should find the eye in the middle of the swamp, you know the one that Dottie was talking about the other day, where that old vine comes out."

"I betcha it makes straight for that magic circle," said Kenny, excitement in his voice.

Lydia frowned. "It's in the opposite direction from the circle and that's where that famous Revolutionary War battle was fought.

"Yes, that's right," said Kenny, awe in his voice. "Some people say there are still skeletons lying all over the place in there, and cannon. But getting to it all is a real challenge."

"Not any more, I'm thinking," said Olivia. "How many feet have been tramping all over in there in search of that vine and I really don't think they got to the actual spot. They got to the main vine but there's more to this, I'm thinking."

"Well, what are we waiting for?" said Lydia.

Peddling as fast as they could toward Dottie's, they rounded the corner of her barn and headed for the paths of the junk yard and the woods beyond. At first they didn't know who the person was that sat on one of the rusted hoods of a car nearest the entrance into the woods. Gliding to a stop, they looked at the entrance to the woods and then back at him with questioning eyes.

"Hi," said Steve. "I should have done this yesterday, explore this place, I mean, but I'm such a chicken shit."

Olivia rolled her eyes, not believing what she was hearing.

Lydia looked at him carefully and said, "I've seen you around."

"I'm Steve, the state anthropologist working on this case."

"Wanna come along?" said Kenny.

"I would love to," said Steve. "Where is it you're going?"

"Well, we're going to find the old one, the vine that is, first..." said Kenny.

"And then the devil's eye," said Lydia. "That's the small pond in the middle of the swamp."

"I'm game," said Steve, picking up his backpack.

The hole in the brush at the entrance to the woods was much larger now. They entered the cool of the woods and the myriad of paths that intersected the ancient cedars.

"Be careful of your eyes. Once we get off the main path it'll be easy to poke one out if you're not careful," hissed Lydia.

"What in God's name are you whispering for?" said Olivia disdainfully. "Nobody in here will hear us."

Lydia rolled her eyes and headed for the path that led to the old vine in the woods.

They arrived at the old vine and looked at its dark, shaggy bark and the tangled, gnarled mass of tentacles.

"It's beautiful in a homely sort of way," remarked Lydia.

Steve was in deep contemplation and awe as he reached for his GPS and a compass. "That's absolutely incredible. It's like an old, wise woman," he said. "I've never seen anything like it."

Kenny looked at him and then at his compass and GPS. He was intrigued.

Steve, detecting his interest, said, "Ever hear of sacred geometry?"

"Yes," said Kenny. "Ley lines, the Planetary Energetic Grid Theory, vortices, labyrinths, dowsing. Sure. I find it fascinating."

Steve couldn't believe what he was hearing. He continued, "It's a hobby of mine...pseudosciences, things like that. They tie into my profession as an anthropologist in many ways. Take for instance the paths the original peoples took across the land. These paths connected sacred places of power and were used for thousands of years. They were sacred sites for rituals for the benefit of the tribe and the land. This place is such a place."

Olivia, hands on hips, stared at the vine. "My dad just read that the college is now saying that the vine is somewhere between 3,000 and 3,500 years old."

"That's old," remarked Kenny. "Well before the time of Christ and maybe even the Shang Dynasty."

Steve just looked at Kenny. Here was a walking, talking encyclopedia. He smiled and went back to reading his coordinates.

"Okay, let's circle the vine and see where it comes out of the ground," said Lydia.

Each headed for a side of the vine and with a shout Kenny said, "Here's a large part of it that goes off in another direction from all the rest. It's pretty big."

Olivia nodded her head and said, "let's follow it."

"I don't like this," mused Kenny.

"Yeah, well, we can't get lost, we just turn around and follow it out," said Lydia.

Deeper and deeper into the unknown part of the woods they went. The trees were now all cedar, and the branches nearest the ground were bare and spiked and deadly for the eyes. As they shouldered their way into the trees, brittle branches snapped and created a hollow sound in the noonday air. The ground began to get more sodden and the trees began to thin out a little, and still the vine led them further and further into the gloom.

Kenny suddenly exclaimed, "I see lots of daylight ahead."

Steve nodded, all the while taking notes in a small notebook. He liked these kids, they were genuine and spirited.

The ground was getting very soggy now, but they still pressed on toward the light. Suddenly they broke into a small clearing and there in the middle was a very large pond. Trees had fallen around it so it would be a hard job to get to this pond, but the clearing at least made it possible to see what all the locals called the *eye of the swamp.*

"It looks very black and very deep," mused Steve.

"How many acres is this swamp anyway?" said Lydia.

"I once heard about twenty-five acres," said Kenny.

"I think it's more than that, at least from what I saw on the map last evening," said Steve. "That eye is what many biologists call a bog hole. It's the source of the water that flows under the bridge at the outside of town."

"This is a beautiful spot and I'm really enjoying the feeling of peace here. Did you notice that the vine doesn't grow out of the eye but grows around the eye, like it's protecting that small puddle of water," said Lydia. "And it also grows toward the circle where it snakes over and around the rocks at the edge, but it doesn't enter the circle."

"It's smart," said Olivia with awe in her voice.

Chapter Sixty-Six

Matt, Chris, Dave and Nedo were in the coroner's office the next morning. Larry was giving them a scenario on Ben's body. "Mild shock can cause the heart muscle to lapse into a state of ventricular fibrillation and severe shock, and muscles go rigid causing instant heart and lung failure," he said. "And this is exactly what happened to Ben. Electrical currents can also travel through the nervous system and cause tissue to burn out in patches all along its path. If it's severe enough, neuropathy occurs in sometimes very severe degrees."

Larry continued, "Do you know what Westinghouse said to Edison when they experimented with electrocution at Sing Sing prison? It was an experiment, I might add, and they had a victim---one known murderer, William Kennler. On his day of execution the guards didn't put the straps on his wrists tight enough and they didn't have enough current generated, so the body was still twitching after the initial jolt. They added more current... which caused one of the electrodes to smoke. Westinghouse, who was present for this experiment, turned to Edison and thoughtfully observed that they could have killed him better with an ax.

Ben here, is not the case. It takes two thousand volts and five amps to kill instantly. This current was much more, as the water in his blood was boiled away. Let's look at what I have here. This is his aortic artery, and it looks like a piece of beef jerky. We know how and when he died, and where he died, but we don't know who did it or why."

"Time for more looksies at the scene," said Nedo.

Chapter Sixty-Seven

Chris said he would call Howard and they would all meet at the station. An hour later, Steve showed up in a pair of hiking boots, a faded pair of jeans and an open-necked polo shirt.

"Wow," Chris observed, "I've never seen you..."

"So normal?" interjected Steve, a smile playing on his lips.

Chris laughed and shook his head.

"Hey, Doc, where's the pink tie?" asked one of the desk officers.

"In a safe place," Steve retorted. "We don't want it full of cow poop, now do we?"

Good-hearted laughter erupted from the cubicle.

"I don't use it at the shooting range either," Steve added. "It might get dirty."

Three heads popped around the corners of three different cubicles. "You shoot!" they said in unison.

"Yup," said Steve, "and I bet I could outshoot all of you together if I had a mind to."

"Yeah," came the terse reply from a beefy sergeant, who lowered his phone. "I'll take you up on that."

"Mine's the bet," Steve said. "Give me a time and a place."

"I'll get back to you," the sergeant said gruffly as he thoughtfully eyed the tall, good-looking man.

"Yeah, let's do this," came a chorus of hoots and high-fives from some of the other cubicles.

Chris looked with consternation at Steve.

"I'll beat him so bad he won't know what hit him," Steve said, flippantly.

"He's our senior marksman," said Chris.

"So, I had a chance for the Olympics," said Steve, shrugging his shoulders.

"I want to be present for this one," said Chris.

Matt, who was standing behind the two men, just laughed.

They arrived at Howard's an hour later. Howard came from the milk house and in his usual gruff way said, "cows are eatin' in there, just boot 'em' out of the way." Howard turned and made his way back to the milk house. Over his shoulder he shouted, "Just don't forget to latch the gate."

Matt unhooked the gate and led the small party into the barn. Bovine faces turned, looked at them and then went back to eating, all but one rather large Holstein cow, which looked more curious than the rest. She lowered her head and came to stand quietly at Chris's shoulder. All of a sudden, without warning, her large, pink tongue, rough as sandpaper, whipped out of her mouth and took a great lick of Chris's bald head. Slime and silage juice dribbled down Chris's face. He looked mortified and stood frozen to the spot.

"Hazel!" came a loud voice from somewhere behind a large feed bin. "They're not salt licks!" Hazel turned her head for a moment and looked nonchalantly at the spot where the voice emanated from. Her large head with those deep brown eyes looked at Chris with intense interest. She proceeded to smell Chris, her large nose poking him periodically as gentle puffs of air exhaled from her nostrils. Chris, frozen in fear, started to sweat.

Her large, pendulous udder swinging, Hazel took a step closer to Chris. "Hazel!" came another warning reply, and a small, skinny girl came out from behind the feed bins, smacked her on the backside, and Hazel moved away toward the manger. "She's a pain in the ass," the girl said in a gruff, feminine voice. "She's in heat and if you bend over, you're going to get eleven hundred pounds of cow on top of you."

Steve burst out laughing and said, "The old adage, any port in a storm," and more laughter followed from the group.

Chris's face turned beet-red. He was not amused.

"Nice to be propositioned by a cow," said Joe thoughtfully.

"And one named Hazel at that," retorted Steve.

"Enough!" bellowed Chris as he turned to hide his embarrassment.

The afternoon wore on and, finishing up with the investigation, they left for the station. Steve stayed for a few moments and Matt approached him. "Anything?" he said, looking at the man thoughtfully.

"Just a gut feeling that this belongs to legend, that's all. There's something, we're just missing it."

"You should get involved with Eugenia's group," said Matt. "I think they need all the help they can get at the moment."

Steve looked quizzically at Matt, nodded his head and said, "When do they meet?"

"I'll find out and let you know," said Matt.

"I'll go see her if that's okay."

Matt nodded.

July

Chapter Sixty-Eight

"We have an ongoing dialogue with Father Munro," said Eugenia. Steve was facing her in her small kitchen and was giving her his full attention.

"The Church has priests that act as demonologists. They believe that most, if not all spirits are evil. I do not believe that is the case most of the time. I've encountered mostly good souls in my work. Father agrees, but you won't hear him tell you that in public. This spirit is different. There's so much evil energy here it's like a full AC current running through its body, and it kills."

Steve nodded. "How would one get rid of this spirit?" he said quietly.

Eugenia shook her head. "That's what we're trying to find out, before it gets someone else. The fact that the killings are starting earlier tells me this is going to be a bloodbath."

Steve and Eugenia spent more than two hours discussing the whys and the means of the case, and Steve proposed some of his theories to her. She looked thoughtful. "I guess I just didn't understand how many like-minded people existed in this world," she said with wonderment. "It's so refreshing. Take, for instance, Dave. Now he's one of us and I'm really intrigued about him."

"Dave understands," said Steve, "better than I do sometimes. There's so much we just don't understand anymore. We're supposed to be educated, but the real educated people were the ones who didn't need calculators to map stars or to feel the energies of the land or to heal people," said Steve sadly.

~

He tried to make friends, but others from his tribe repelled him. They said he was ugly, an insult to their tribe, and his mother should have abandoned him when he was born, left him to die. Why the anger and the hate toward those with the slightest reprimand? He was ashamed of his actions when he overheard his parents and the other Shamans talking about him. They knew he was powerful and that his power was not being used for good but for other purposes. He vowed revenge on even his own family, but was that really him or someone or something else?

Chapter Sixty-Nine

Steve laid the piece of skull down. He turned to Larry, who had his back to him. Larry was busy this morning with a hit-and-run victim found at the side of the road in the next town. The body was found by a cyclist in the early morning hours.

"Standard hit by car or large object. Coronary artery disease, obese, diabetic and a host of other things, but blunt force trauma ended it all. That's that report, on to the next," Larry muttered.

Steve smiled and said, "Ever examine this skull? I mean really, really study it?"

Larry winced. "Well no. I mean, not really. Not like you."

"I've noticed more irregularities in this skull. I know, you just brushed them off because of the work load, but now that you're done with what you were doing, come over here and take a look at this. We've been concentrating on the skeleton, but. . ." his voice trailed off.

Larry put down his tools and came over, removing his mask and peering over Steve's shoulder. Steve tipped the skull so that the cranial cavity showed clearly and shined a small light into the interior of the skull.

"Holy shit," exclaimed Larry. "I completely missed that. Wow, classic textbook example of a Bilateral Complete. Look at that hole. I can imagine speech was very limited or at the most very hard to understand, if he spoke at all."

"Can you imagine being hunchback, club foot and severe cleft palate, and what he must have looked like, what he must have endured?" exclaimed Steve. "And the parents, how did they cope? Indian society was very tolerant at that time, still is, but it was his peers that could be very intolerant."

"Wow, talk about a troll," was all Larry could say.

"Yeah," said Steve, "a troll is right. Can you imagine the social stigmas involved with this guy? I can't imagine how he felt, and if that legend is true, and if this is the guy, I can surmise why he acted out like he did. I see another scholarly paper in my future," he said whimsically.

Larry rolled his eyes and headed for the door to write the report that would release his cyclist victim's body to its family.

"Are we going to the July Fourth activities? Should be fun," shouted Steve.

"Yeah, let's go. This place oppresses me sometimes and I need a break," said Larry from the hallway.

"Thought you'd say that," said Steve as he removed his gloves and gave his gown a heave into the soiled hamper.

Chapter Seventy

Seth approached the door labeled Principal. Amy Goodwin's voice resonated with a strong "come in." Seth hesitated and pushed the door open. The handle felt sticky, but he attributed that to his sweating. He walked through the secretaries' room and into the main office where Amy sat at a large, old and worn oak desk. Amy refused to have the desk replaced, saying it was like her, still serviceable but old.

"Seth, you look very nervous," Amy said, "I just hope this call is not about resigning. I would hate to lose you."

Seth shook his head. "No," he sighed, "it's more than that and I hope I didn't just overstep school bounds."

Amy gave him a look of concern and rose from her seat behind the desk.

At that moment, Matt and Joe appeared in the outer doorway with another man who, to Amy, looked intriguing and rather out of place. "Can I help you gentlemen?" she inquired.

"More like we're here to help Seth," said Joe in a booming voice. Matt nodded and the tall black man standing near them with the pink tie smiled, showing perfectly formed white teeth.

"Come in," she said, "might as well make it a party." She was curious and it showed in her face and demeanor.

They pulled up chairs and sat facing her. "Well?" she said with a questioning look on her face.

"Remember that knife we spoke about on the last day of school?" said Seth.

"Yes, the small dagger made of flint. The one Kenny got hold of."

"Yes," said Seth." I let the police borrow it. There was speculation about it being used in a murder, many, many years ago." Seth hung his head and looked at the floor.

Amy looked hard at Seth and then looked down at her desk with surprise as Matt slid a small velvet pouch toward her.

"It's the instrument used in a killing, at least we're ninety-nine percent sure, but it belongs back here in your possession," said Matt.

"Let me get this straight. This knife was involved in a murder? I have a feeling it was the skull and skeleton that I've been personally following in the paper, is that right? The one possibly involved in all this demonic, hocus-pocus stuff?"

Steve nodded his head.

Amy looked directly at Steve and said, "I like the tie. Pink is your color." Steve flushed and smiled broadly.

"Purple and teal are your colors," said Steve, although Amy didn't have a bit of either on today. "And you love turquoise."

"Psychic huh?" said Amy, laughter in her voice.

"Naw," said Steve. "Those are colors that go with your hair and skin tone really well."

Amy looked hard at him. Matt interrupted, "this is Steve from the state anthropology office.

Amy nodded. "Figured as much," she said, never taking her eyes off Steve, who was starting to get uncomfortable under her stare.

Steve spoke. "The skeleton is native and so is the skull. With the deformities he possessed, it's a wonder he survived at all, both physically and mentally."

"People can be cruel, can't they?" said Amy quietly.

Steve bowed his head and Amy nodded her head in understanding.

"Okay," said Amy, letting out a deep sigh, and in an authoritative tone she said, "get that back in the case and if you need it again, please tell me. I don't have a problem but I will not run it by the school board, as a decision from them would probably take us into the next century. Gentlemen," she said, signaling the end of their visit.

Chapter Seventy-One

About noon, Amy left for lunch. As she passed by Seth's classroom, she quietly entered the room and went to the case where artifacts were displayed in a neat arrangement. Shafts of light filtered through the leaves outside the large windows and emitted a soft glow. As Amy looked down at the knife in the case a shaft of sunlight fell momentarily on its blade. She shuddered and turned her back to leave the room.

She didn't see the dark form or sense the energy that was forming behind her as she walked out the door and into the hallway. She was deep in thought as she made her way toward the front entrance of the school, her heels clicking on the polished floor. She knew about the legend, hell who didn't around here? She wasn't here at the time of the last murder spree, but her grandmother was one of the victims and this was one thing she never talked of.

She heard a faint scurrying sound and then the sound of running footsteps, and suddenly Lydia and Olivia burst into the hallway from the direction of the front entrance. Panting hard they slid to a stop in front of Amy.

Gasping, Lydia began with "I need to see my . . ." but her eyes had moved from Amy to something behind her. Her eyes widened and she turned white.

Olivia was like a stone, rooted to the spot. She stood staring at something in the distance. Amy spun around just in time to see a dark shadow in the middle of the hallway. A menacing looking man, short, humpbacked and very ugly, stood there in the shadows of the hallway. His deep eye sockets had a glow that sent shivers down Amy's spine, for the eyes were the eyes of death itself. Instinctively Amy grabbed both girls and kept them from going past her. From behind her she could sense someone in the entrance to the hallway, for the light was getting brighter and brighter as she stood there with the two girls. She kept her eyes on the creature, whom she knew to be a man, but not a man from this world. Before she knew it, the figure of a tall, slim girl stood just in front and slightly to one side of them. The girl emitted an unearthly glow about her in direct opposition to the darkness that came from the man. The man glared at the girl, his eyes emanating a hatred that was palpable in the air. Little shock waves reached the three figures and Amy felt the hair on her arms rise. Lydia said something that sounded like "Sarah," but Amy wasn't sure. And suddenly they were all bathed in a light, a light so comforting, so undeniably loving that Amy lost all her feelings of fear. And as suddenly as the light appeared, it vanished, leaving the three of them in the hallway, alone.

Gone was the man, the girl, the evil feelings and the intense light. There was just the soft singing of birds and the occasional honk of a horn through the open front doors of the school. All strength was gone from Amy, and the girls helped her into her office, occasionally glancing over their shoulders to make sure there was nothing there.

Amy slumped in her chair.

"What was that all about?" she asked breathlessly.

Olivia was the first to speak. "Looks like we came just in time," she said.

Lydia shook her head. "If we hadn't come along, who knows what would have happened. He was really close."

"Who?" Amy said weakly.

"Let's get you some water," said Lydia.

"I'm not going out there alone," said Olivia.

"Oh, for God's sake, you sit, I'll deliver," said Lydia in a huff. She peeked out the door and slowly went outside toward the water fountain. Returning at almost a dead run, she slid the small cup of water toward Amy. The two girls stood with their elbows leaning on the desk as Amy gulped the water down. Amy looked back at both of them through her glasses, which were perched on her nose.

She sighed and said, "what was that? And why?"

"Well, all I can figure is that somehow the evil one visited our school and along came my sister Sarah. And saved you and us," said Lydia. "I think we should go see my dad at the station."

Amy nodded her head and stood. "I'm a little shaky, but I can manage. Wait," she said. "He won't believe us."

"Oh yes he will," said both girls in unison.

Chapter Seventy-Two

They crossed the street, one girl on each side of Amy. They were holding hands. They walked two blocks and entered the station.

Matt looked up from his desk and was surprised to see Lydia, Olivia and Amy Goodwin approaching. Lydia snapped at an officer seated at the front desk as she pushed her way into the inner part of the station and toward her father's desk.

"You won't believe what just happened!" she shouted.

Olivia chimed in with "Oh my God, oh my God!"

Amy looked sheepish and very nervous. Rising, Matt motioned for three chairs to be brought up beside his desk. Amy took a deep breath and sat with a thump. The girls acted like they had ants in their pants and he was ready to burst out laughing when he glanced at Amy and saw her discomfort. He gave her a questioning look.

"Let the girls tell you," she said quietly. "They're dying to tell you what happened after you left."

"Well," said Lydia, "we went looking for you because the officers here told us you were at the school. So we went over to the school, only you weren't there, but the dark man was and he almost got. . ."

"Miss Goodwin," chimed in Olivia breathlessly.

"Huh," said Matt.

Amy said quietly, "I had gone into the classroom to look at the knife. I left and closed the classroom door and started down the hall. Halfway down the hall, the girls met me, only I wasn't alone, so to speak. They saw it, him, whatever, first. I turned and

I just don't know what I saw, but it sure scared the life out of me. At first I thought it was someone playing a trick but the feeling that came over me, I just can't explain."

Matt noticed that Amy was shaking.

"Then . . ." but she was interrupted by Olivia, who blurted out, "Sarah came and rescued us!"

Matt looked directly at his daughter. Lydia nodded. "It was Sarah," she said. "She made the man go away."

"The whole hallway was filled with this brilliant light, like you were in the middle of a stage and all the lights were on you," said Amy quietly.

Matt sighed and suddenly the makings of a headache appeared.

"I hate chasing ghosts, but this is one ghost that is for real. No matter how this sounds, we have to talk to the chief and the FBI, so ladies, are you ready to tell this story?"

"You betcha," said Lydia. Olivia nodded and looked down at her feet.

Amy nodded and said, "I don't know about you but I'm ready to hide and never come out until this is all over. Do you know how ridiculous this sounds, coming from me, an educated, middle-aged woman in academia? Everyone in town is going to think I'm nuts. I have the school board to think about. Oh hell," she said forcefully. "I'm rambling, let's do it."

Matt went to Chris's office and in a few moments signaled for the three of them to enter. Dave and Nedo entered the station and headed for the chief's office. As they entered the office, Lydia groaned. Her father cleared his throat and gave her a warning glance. Dave gave her a questioning look and smiled.

"You all are acquainted with the exception of Amy here. This is Dave, and Nedo, both FBI." Amy nodded and was motioned into a chair by Chris's desk.

"All right, ladies, what happened?"

Amy retold the story, with embellishments from the two girls. When she was done, she sat quietly.

Chris scratched his head. "Coming from you, Amy, I would believe anything, but this is rather far-fetched."

"I know, but all I know is what happened. And that girl, it was like a vision."

Matt cleared his throat. "My wife and several others believe it's my daughter coming back to warn us, save us, oh what the hell, I just don't know. Shit, I just don't know what to believe and this is getting crazier and crazier."

"Yeah, and the time is up soon, people," whined Olivia.

Lydia nodded. "Very soon," she said quietly.

Dave and Nedo stared at the three females. "I have to digest this one," said Nedo. "What in hell do I tell my men? We're looking for a small hunchback evil troll and a girl with a halo around her? Come on."

"I'd like to know how he chooses his victims." said Matt quietly. "Right now it seems random, anything living that gets in his way."

"What do we have, another six weeks?" said Chris.

"Oh hocus, pocus," interjected Nedo. "We don't know when he'll strike again."

"No we don't," said Amy forcefully, "but I do know that I can't even imagine what would've happened to me if these girls or the other girl, or whatever didn't show up. What if he came upon an innocent student, then what?" she shouted angrily.

"Okay, okay," said Nedo. "I just don't come upon this stuff ordinarily. It's usually black and white, involving live people, not dead ones with supernatural powers. I don't know of an exorcist," he said thoughtfully. "Again, I just don't believe in this stuff. Now if my wife was here she would be all over this. Thank God she's not here."

"We do have a demonologist. He's rumored to be good and is affiliated with the local Church," mentioned Dave quietly. "He's a priest with lots of experience."

Nedo nodded. "I want to talk to him."

Dave nodded.

"Father Munro," said Olivia. Her voice was authoritative and she was staring at Dave as if she saw him for the first time. Lydia could just imagine the wheels churning in Olivia's brain. The look, the stare, the pursed lips, and before Lydia could get to Olivia, Olivia blurted out, "you look just like an older version of Mr. Bell."

Matt looked at Dave. Dave burst out laughing and said quietly, "I am an older version of Mr. Bell."

Matt looked at his daughter and immediately saw her confusion. "Lydia, Dave, come with me," he said quietly. Out in the hallway, he put his hand on Lydia's shoulder. "There's something I need to tell you and I, ahh, we have been meaning to tell you, but with all the confusion and everything going on, I just haven't had the opportunity."

"I know you've been busy, Dad," Lydia said, looking questionably at Dave. "Are you my grandfather?"

Dave smiled expectantly and shook his head yes.

"Wow," was all Lydia said, looking at him with wide eyes.

Chapter Seventy-Three

"Where the hell is he?" said Tom in an unpleasant, sarcastic voice.

Alex quietly said, "I'll go t t to the trailer and see where he is. Maaayaabe heeeeeeeees sick." He turned quickly. This was not like Pete, to be absent from his job. Pete hadn't missed a day of work since Alex couldn't remember when.

Alex banged on the door, but no one answered. He pushed the door open. There was something, something sinister that lingered in the space of the old trailer. Alex shivered and pressed further into the space. The trailer had three rooms. He had been in here thousands of times and knew the space like the back of his hand. There was something that he couldn't quite put his finger on. The air felt strange, electric, like the crackle of air just after a thunder storm. He searched the trailer and found nothing, nothing at all. He turned to go and noticed a small piece of rock on the floor near one of the chair legs. He picked it up. It was irregular in shape and pink in color. "Odd seeing this here," he thought. Maybe Pete was gardening last night, found it in the garden and decided to bring it in the trailer. He pocketed the stone and headed quickly out the door.

"Well?" said Tom.

Alex shook his head. "Nothing," he said.

"Where in tarnation could he have gone? He never leaves here."

"I think we should tell someone, "said Alex.

"I hate to waste the time, but if you feel that strongly about it, go let someone know. Police, oh hell, ah no," said Tom. "What about Eugenia, yeah she's good."

Alex trotted up the road and into Eugenia's yard where he found her weeding her geraniums. She looked up and when she saw it was him she stood, a look of concern on her face.

"Pete's missing," was all he said.

Eugenia nodded and headed for Dottie's with Alex in tow. Dottie was in the barn, finishing chores. She looked up, saw the two of them running toward her and met them at the doorway of the barn.

"Pete's missing," said Eugenia.

"I had a bad dream last night. I don't much like this, ya know." She glanced at Alex, who had a look of horror on his face.

Dottie gripped his arm. "These are bad times," she said. Alex nodded and bowed his head.

"We'd better call Matt."

Chapter Seventy-Four

Matt was still contemplating what Nedo was saying when the phone on his desk rang. He excused himself, walked out the door and picked up the receiver. After a moment, "Crap" was all he said into the receiver. Chris started from his desk but Nedo beat him out the door.

"What?" said Chris.

"Pete's missing. No sign of him."

"Pete?" said Nedo.

"Yeah, Tom's hired man. That was Alex. He searched the trailer, came up with nothing." said Matt.

"You ladies stay where we can find you," said Chris sternly.

"I'll stay with them," said Dave, and the four of them watched as Matt, Chris and Nedo hurried out the door.

Chapter Seventy-Five

Alex made his way back to work. "They're on it!" he shouted to his father as he walked to the parts building where Josh was busy filling orders for the following day. Alex picked up a welding torch to finish cutting into the housing to get to the rear transmission of a relatively new truck, when Josh came over and asked him, "What's wrong?"

"Pete's missing," said Alex, "and I, I . . .I'm worried."

"Your father seemed really upset."

"He has a good right to be upset, he's worried too. With all the stu, stu, stuff going on here and in tha, tha, that woods in the back, I just don't know."

Josh shook his head. "I'm really worried about my sister and her friends. They go back there on their picnics and stuff. I don't know what they'll find and I don't like it."

"Alex!" shouted Tom. "Go and get the side panel from that 98' Dodge in the lot, out by the .."

"Yeah, I, I know where it is," Alex shouted back.

His father nodded. "Got a hot one for that door, need it by tomorrow."

Alex smiled, jumped on the wheeler and headed out the gate and into the yard. He gunned the motor and his hair waved across his neck, tickling it. The goggles perched on his head moved slightly with the force of the wind made from the speed of the vehicle. He saw it, faintly at first. He slowed the wheeler and noticed the lump of something on top of one of the cars. It was near the Dodge. It looked like a dead deer. It was bloated and the skin stretched tight over features that had turned black. It suddenly hit him, like a sledgehammer that it was a human being, splayed across the top of the car. Alex's mind didn't want to register at first, then his stomach took over and he vomited. His throat was dry, and he wanted to turn away but he couldn't. Then he noticed the shoes.

"Oh God!" he shrieked, "Oh God, no, no!" He didn't know how he got the wheeler turned around in that narrow space, but before his mind registered anything he was running in the office with Josh close behind him. His father rose from the desk. "Ca, ca, ca call the cops, dead man out bababback," Alex shrieked before he collapsed in Josh's arms.

Matt, Nedo and Chris were already on their way. As they entered the gated yard, Tom emerged, running and shouting, "My son says there's a dead man out back, body on top of one of them cars. Oh Christ, oh shit!" he shrieked.

Matt forcefully slapped Tom's face.

"Sorry, Tom, but you needed that."

Tom, regaining composure, said, "My son, one hell of a shock. He's on the floor in there, just collapsed, don't know what to do."

"Call an ambulance!" shouted Matt.

"We'll need two, I'm afraid," said Chris.

"Where's the body?" said Nedo.

"Out in the yard, over to the left," said Tom.

Alex emerged from the office. He was white and shaking violently. Sweat beaded his brow. Josh supported him by one elbow. "On tthhe leleleeft. Iitts's PaPaete." Matt came quickly over to the boys and put his arms around them.

"Are you sure?" he asked Alex.

"I'dd know ththose shshshoes anywhere," Alex said, quietly looking at Matt with large, soulful eyes.

Chapter Seventy-Six

Dave rose from his chair. "Well, ladies, I think it's time to see Father. I don't know what else to do. There has to be something to allay this evil, a way to appease this creature, apparition, whatever you want to call it."

They started out the door when the siren sounded. All four stopped, as the police scanner announced the call to the junk yard.

"I get a bad, bad feeling with this one," said Lydia.

"So do I." said Dave.

The station was in an uproar. The sergeant was on the radio and announced he wanted one more squad car dispatched to the scene at the junk yard. Two men ran out the door and jumped into a waiting cruiser in front of the station. Everyone else stayed put. There was tension everywhere and it was palpable now.

Amy, Dave and the girls moved through the door without interference and headed for Father Munro's house, next to the church.

Chapter Seventy-Seven

Larry entered the yard slowly so as to not restrict the ambulance that was attempting to go through the gate and into the junk yard. "What's this, the third time in the last few weeks?" he muttered.

"They're waiting for ya, Doc," said a burly policeman.

"Yeah, top of my list to get accomplished today, Walt," he said. The burly policeman smiled sadly and nodded. "I'll walk, not far, and I think I'll need it before I'm finished."

Larry noticed the gritty path was dry and dusty. It was just after noon, he judged, from the position of the sun. Yes, he needed to take his mind off the coming encounter with yet another body. As he got closer he looked at the car and the body, face-up on top of it. Got a good roasting out here in the hot sun, he thought as he smelled the putrefaction already setting in. "Kinda quick," he thought, unless it was in the same shape that Ben's body had been in when it was found in the cow barn, and was fried to the top of the car by a massive electrical force strong enough to adhere flesh to metal.

Larry snapped on gloves and climbed onto the hood of the car. The hood was rusted so he had a decent foot grip. "You gotta get better cars in here, Tom, ya ol' bastard," he muttered. "This is a hell of a way to run a business, with dead people." He looked down on the corpse. It was going to be a mess to get it off the top of the vehicle. The body looked like it was, indeed, welded to the car.

After three hours of steady extraction, Pete was finally moved to a body bag, put into the ambulance and sent on his way to the morgue.

Larry stood quietly for a moment, watching the ambulance pull away. He felt like leaving, like going for a long, long walk away from all this senseless slaughter. His cheeks were wet and he brushed one eye with the back of his hand. He noticed people milling around. Two young men stood apart from the rest. They were on a small side path, quietly looking at the scene. He went over to them.

"This is nothing for you to look at," he said.

The one boy, who was very thin, looked up. Larry could see the intense pain in the boy's eyes as he said, "I found him, he was my friend."

"Mine too," chimed in the second boy who was a little taller and heavier. Larry noticed that this young man had his arm around the shoulders of the thin boy.

"Hell of a business. I hope they get the bastard soon," said Larry.

He turned and as he did the first boy said, "They won't. Same as la la last time, he'll satisfy his blood lust and ga ga go away until the next time."

"He's not of this world," said the taller boy.

"You should talk to my friend, he's an anthropologist and believes in all this hocus pocus," said Larry, scornfully.

"There's your evidence," said the other boy, pointing to the retreating ambulance.

Larry turned and walked away. He looked back once but the two boys were gone.

Chapter Seventy-Eight

Lydia and the group found Father Munro on his porch, deep in thought. A worried look crossed his face as he saw them and he smiled wearily. He rose and stuck out his hand to Amy. "I'm Father Munro," he said.

She took the large hand and held it firmly, not wanting to let go. She looked down sadly at her feet and muttered, "Amy, school principle."

Olivia and Lydia told Father their adventures of the day and he listened intently, glancing at Amy occasionally.

"Ah, you have to understand this situation, ahh, Amy." Father said. "It's not just good und evil at war. It's also our souls at war und at peace. You're in education. How come some kids just want to be trouble und others are fairly decent? Some are, in your opinion, pure evil. Why?"

Amy nodded. "We blame society, their parents or lack of parents, their social status and education or lack of it. Maybe there is something to this, but I would have to see proof."

Father nodded and said, "Just what I would expect an educator to say," and he smiled, and continued.

"When there is evil in a person, or the take-over of a soul by an evil persona, you call it the Devil. We all have free will given by God to use or misuse. Life is our choice, no one else's und especially not the Devil und his un-Holy angels.
"Even more so, when one dies und does not go directly to God, they stay in a limbo, either out of stubbornness, fear, hate, unfinished business, guilt, remorse or any other variety of reasons. Most of these souls are your garden variety type of

ghost, or spirit, as some want to call them. But there are others who are very dangerous, for they are the ones where an un-Holy angel has taken possession of them, und they are still able to wreck havoc on this side of the veil.

A good person, full of love, peace, non-judgment, und honesty, who has gone over to God und because of free will has chosen to return to earth in spirit form, has the ability to help others where it's necessary. It's all about love. Jesus came to this earth to spread the message of love, und that message above all."

"Really," said Dave.

"Yes, really," said Father, "und we have to call that spirit, who is now in our presence und get the evil out of him. When one dies who has the evil in him before death, sometimes it's twice as hard to get it out of him after death. The evil is within many, but most people choose the love und light of the true soul und not bad intentions. The evil sometimes can be so bad that it occupies a body all the way through a person's lifetime on earth und beyond. This soul gets quite comfortable living in that environment of evil und it becomes a habit, a way of life."

"I know of the legend," said Dave. "But Steve, Larry's friend, really made me think. Steve says that the body that was found in the circle was very deformed. If the child grew into a young adult, can you imagine how his peers, his family and relatives treated him?"

Amy winced and said, "It's bad enough at school. Popularity, beauty, sports, it all figures into the equation. I'm just beginning to understand some of it, finally, after all these years."

"Life has many layers, like an onion," said Father. "You have to peel away those layers und when we get all done, we have a very small piece that is the essence of the soul."

"Will this harm you?" asked Dave quietly. "This exorcism I mean?"

"I'm going into this one with a lot of trepidation," Father admitted. "I have exorcised many souls, helping them to go on, but again it's their free will that will eventually take them onward. With this particular soul, evil was present in his body on this earth und now, after he passed, there is still a large amount of evil that exists within his persona. I think if we imagine it like the onion model, I might have a chance. I also think I'll have help from the other side und that could be a blessing."

Father looked at Lydia and said, "Your sister is a blessing und I think she's here for one purpose. If I'm wrong, I may be very sorry.

Well, it's getting dark now, so I'm going to give each of you a prayer und blessing of protection for tonight. Thank God und do not think evil if you can help it. Und Amy, please don't think about what could have happened today, only what did happen if you have to think on it at all," instructed Father.

Chapter Seventy-Nine

Outside the police station a large crowd was gathering in the twilight. News stations, cameramen and reporters were already making reports and presenting fantastic scenarios about the latest killing. "People are frightened," the sergeant heard one reporter say into his microphone.

"Who's going to be next?" wailed a woman in a pair of pink cut-off jeans.

The crowd was getting anxious. When the sergeant appeared on the top step of the station, he asked them to go home and lock their door. The FBI and the local authorities were taking care of the situation.

"Yeah," came a drawl from one of the local men, "sure. Didn't help those two dead men any, did it, or all those cows and whatever else?"

"Listen, we are doing our best. We have the best working on this case. They've been working for several months now and we're getting closer," shouted the sergeant.

"Uh-huh, all getting closer to getting killed," drawled another.

"I'm leaving town tonight, going to my sister's until this blows over."

"Me too," chimed in several other voices from the crowd.

"Please, people, we're trying our best," implored the sergeant.

"Well, let's face it, you can't kill or arrest someone you can't see." They all nodded. Several people were crying.

"It's just an old legend!" shouted the sergeant, obviously irritated.

"Tell that to my grandfather," chimed in Les Mueller. "He was one of the last victims' way back when. This is just the beginning. I say let's get out of here."

The sergeant looked relieved at this statement. "Yes," he muttered to himself, "the less we have in town the less rioting and harassment." He was thinking of his family and suddenly felt sick. He stood for a long while on the top step of the police station, watching the crowd disperse. He would call his wife and ask her to leave with the kids. Yes, he would do that now.

Chapter Eighty

Stacy moved with the crowd. She was scared. Since she had come back, as she liked to tell it, she was absent-minded and her mind wandered into strange, dream-like trances or visions. These were of short duration but left her fatigued and disoriented. The visions occurred several times a day. It was like watching life in little skits in black and white, like old silent movies only much more vivid.

She distinctly remembered that most of these visions were of one individual. He was of small stature with a deformed face and a hunchback. He was taunted and tormented by the others of his tribe and stayed away from them as much as possible, retreating to the cool of the woods at the outskirts of his village where an old, gnarled vine of some sort grew.

As this child grew into adulthood, any human contact elicited foul language and guarded anger from him, so people kept their distance. One day, in one of her visions she came upon him chanting. He was standing near that old vine in the woods, one hand resting on its shaggy bark, the other hand held in the air as if he were pushing someone away. It was then she saw a black form descend into him with lightning speed. He was thrown back against the vine and slid to the ground, dazed. From that time on, a sense of evil surrounded him, and when she looked into his eyes they were the eyes of something so malevolent, it made her shiver.

Chapter Eighty-One

As night fell, several families exited the tiny village and the police station was quiet. Matt came home about eight but, no one was there. He was exhausted. He took a shower and went downstairs to wait for the girls. He had taken two phone calls, one from Olivia's mom asking if he had seen her daughter and another from Jack Dunn, wanting more details on Pete's death and wanting to know if he had seen Stacy. Jack told Matt about Stacy's dreams and medical problems since she had been back.

"It's really weird, some of the things she's telling me," Jack exclaimed. "I told her to go and see the priest, you know, the one at the Church. The doctors are stumped. They told her she was bordering on insanity and that if she kept it up she would have to be hospitalized."

After hanging up, Karen came into the living room. "Hi," she said. "Want some dinner?" "Too tired," he said and smiled sadly. She came and sat beside him, putting her arms around his neck, breathing in his scent, and said, "Tough day, huh?"

He nodded. "Yeah, and we're no closer to solving this case. Actually, he's gaining on us, he's winning. We're clueless."

August

Chapter Eighty-Two

Katie stood on her porch in the early morning sunlight. She was bothered by a sense of foreboding. It started as a small nagging deep in the pit of her stomach. Then she would find her heart racing and she couldn't shake the feeling of imminent danger. She had the same feelings when Ben was killed. She didn't know who would be next, but she knew death was on the way.

Her dreams were vivid last night. She was being chased once more, and once more the dream ended with her hiding near a rock at the circle, the tentacles of the ancient vine protectively encircling her, hiding her from danger. She hadn't visited the vine for quite some time. It stood as a sentinel near the bog in the center of the swamp, its tentacles reaching out a great distance as they crept along the forest floor. "It's about time, ol' girl," she muttered, "it's about time."

Katie meditated for an hour, as she did each morning, and performed a charm that afforded her protection from any evil that might be in the woods. Twenty minutes later, she picked up her medicine bag, which contained sage, incense, assorted semi-precious stones, some rare crystals, a plate and matches, and headed out the door. A crucifix and several amulets hung from a cord around her neck. She had hastily written a note for Claire, telling her where she would be but not to disturb her. She began walking slowly up the road which would bring her to the woods in back of the junk yard.

As Katie walked past Eugenia's she considered asking her to go with her but then thought better of it. As she passed Dottie's, she noticed someone riding a horse slowly around the small paddock on the opposite side of the barn and hoped no one saw her take the path to the woods.

As she neared the entrance to the woods, she heard hoofbeats on the path behind her. Turning, she noticed a horse and rider boring down on her. She squinted as Dottie, her face sweaty, reined the horse to a stop. "Going in," was all Katie said.

"I'll give you to dusk, then I'll be there," Dottie said as she turned her horse and galloped off.

Katie entered the cool dampness of the forest. The path beckoned. At the fork she bore left, and after several hundred feet she looked to her left. There she stood, that ancient vine, towering over the landscape. Katie smiled and whispered, "hello friend, it's been awhile."

Twigs snapped as Katie made her way around the periphery of the vine, careful not to step on its tentacles or trip over branches, until she came to a small place where she could actually get close enough to touch it.

She caressed the shaggy bark and marveled at the gnarled, thick trunk and the tentacles that wrapped round and round before taking off in several directions. "You look like something from outer space," she mused. "Well, what do you have to tell me?"

Katie had surmised that this place where she sat was once within an Indian village and on this spot, at the foot of this vine, many ceremonies were held. This was a sacred place, a place where the veneration of God and nature coalesced into one. She glimpsed a tall, wizened man, an ancient shaman who still visited here in spirit, and now she had the distinct feeling he was here as a guardian for her.

The vine cradled her head, and the moss made a soft cushion for her backside. She was relaxed and let the images and the feelings ebb and flow through her. Some were very disturbing but she was witnessing the story of the lives of a people she admired. They were not much different from people living today.

They had some of the same concerns and many of the same stigmas and sociological taboos. Her most vivid image was that of a young boy. His hair was neatly braided and long. His face was clean and he had vast, deep, intelligent brown eyes and a bright, warm smile. But his face, his face was sometimes so hideous because of the deep cleft in his palate and the discoloration of the skin around one eye, all the way down to his cheekbone. He had a habit of sneering, and that habit rendered him grotesque.

She knew now that the legend was reality in another time, but this reality could transcend even death. This one fact, above all others, scared her.

As Katie sat quietly, the sage and the incense slowly burned to ash. She fingered her amulet and the crucifix she had carried with her. She had gotten many signs and images, but most of all the intense feelings of rage and anger.

The air was getting chilly as she made her way to the entrance of the woods in the deepening twilight. The yip of a coyote met her as she exited onto the gritty path. She glanced toward the front of the junk yard and saw that there was still a light on in the front office. She smiled and thought of Alex and his two new mothers, Eugenia and Dottie. What a combination, she mused as she made her way toward Dottie's and home.

Dottie waited at the end of the path, just short of the barns. She nodded to Katie and asked if she would like tea. Katie was exhausted and shook her head no, for this work was tiring and had a habit of draining energy from a body. Dottie walked silently with her until she was at the end of the street, and as Katie walked slowly toward her home in the deepening twilight, Dottie watched her retreating figure until it was out of sight.

Chapter Eighty-Three

Stacy drew in a deep breath and approached the priest's house. Her sneakers made a soft plopping sound on the walkway as she looked at the tall steeple of the church. She felt sad that she had been away from the formalities of the service for so long, but guilt and remorse did not play into her emotions today. She knew she needed help and this was her last-ditch effort to free herself of whatever this thing was. The early morning sun was oppressive already, but a slight breeze played on her cheeks. She had circled the block twice before she resolved to actually see the priest. It was as if something deep inside was forbidding her to see him.

Father Munro opened the door and came onto the porch as Stacy gained the second step. She looked up, and the look on his face told her something was very wrong, very, very wrong. Her head started to swim and her mouth was dry. She looked pleadingly into his face. She was exhausted. He held a crucifix in one hand, and a cloth stole embellished with green, purple and red stones hung around his neck. He smelled of sage and another fragrance that she had trouble placing, although it was familiar. He clutched in his hand a copy of a well-worn Bible. His eyes were dark and they bore into her as if she was made of glass.

She spoke without meaning to, and didn't recognize her voice or the words. They came with a low, guttural growl. Father quickly laid the crucifix on the Bible he held in his hand and made the sign of the cross in the air with this free hand. He made another sign, quickly, although she didn't recognize it, onto the Bible in his hand. It looked like he was pressing this symbol into the cover of the Bible as he made this motion two more times.

Deep guttural sounds came from Stacy. It was as if her mouth couldn't or wouldn't close on her lips. She was fighting blackness and battling to stay in the moment, but she recognized she was losing.

"Bindings with one's evil, unloose, now," Father said in a menacing and forceful tone.

The deformed face of a boy floated into her mind. The face looked confused, not angry, just confused.

Father repeated the charge and then recited a prayer. The face started to dissolve, replaced by blackness, inky blackness. She was filled momentarily with hatred and rage, and then something really strange happened; there was a bright, blinding light, that made her blink and want to shield her eyes, and then gone were the feelings of hatred and gone was the little boy. She felt euphoric, giddy, and at peace. She gripped the railing, sank to the top step and sat there. Father came, sat and wrapped his large arms around her.

"I, I . . ." she said.

"I know," said Father, "I know. But now you must drink water, nothing else but water."

He stood, patted her on the head and hurried into the house, returning with a tall glass of water. He handed her the glass and she began drinking. As she drank she could feel the water flooding her insides with a soothing coolness, a coolness she hadn't felt before.

They both looked up at the same time. Funny, he thought, he hadn't noticed the police cruiser before. He was so engrossed in Stacy that, until now, no one else mattered. Four men approached, cautiously. "Everything all right, Father?" asked Chris.

Father nodded and said, "Is now."

"What the hell just happened?" said Nedo.

Father looked at the four men and waited for Stacy to finish the water.

"More?" he asked.

She shook her head no and set the glass on the porch. She began telling her story and was very exact and detailed. Father listened as if his life depended on it, and he knew, deep within, that it did.

The others were spellbound by her story. She related how she was feeling and the blackness and the passing out and vivid dreams. Nedo shivered when she was done.

~

He remembered the feel of the flint in his hand. He had watched the other boys while they sat in stony silence, watching their teacher. He ventured to within a few yards of the class and, without warning, several of the boys stood up and began to chase him, throwing rocks at him. He persisted, listening from the quiet of the woods to the dulcet drone of the teacher's voice. He practiced knapping the flint. He would go to the site where the small group had been practicing and pick up larger, discarded pieces, better for him to practice with. His first attempts at knapping flint were not good but with practice he fashioned small utilitarian knives and scrapers. His mother looked at them with wonder and surprise. They were really quite good.

After many tries, his reputation as a maker of fine knives grew. He was sought out and asked to make a knife for this one or that one. He eagerly embraced his new found occupation and found that he was now regarded with awe, but still the stigma of his deformities persisted.

Chapter Eighty-Four

"I don't know where the hell he is or for that matter where my daughter-in-law is either. If I knew, I wouldn't be calling you, now would I?" said the agitated voice on the other end of the phone line.

"Calm down, Miss Silvia," said the dispatcher, "it's still early yet."

"Early my ass" was the terse reply. It was 5 a.m. and the sun was not above the horizon yet.

"Cows are bellering, calves are in a tizzy, and I'm really, really pissed. Where the hell are they?"

The dispatcher wanted to say, "Maybe they ran away, you old bitch," but thought better of it.

"With all the crap going on here I don't know what to believe or do."

"I'll send Matt out, okay," and the phone clicked in his ear. "Matt!" bellowed the dispatcher. "You're needed, missing persons." All eyes looked up at the lone man at the switchboard. He shrugged his shoulders and said, "What?"

"I ain't got a good feelin' about this one" was the terse reply from the sergeant's desk. "It's early yet, Christ it's 5 a.m."

"In light of the current situation, I don't have a good feeling about anything right about now," repeated another officer.

"Where?" said Matt. He had come into the station early this morning as he couldn't sleep.

"Silvia's."

Matt's face turned white. "Silvia's," he choked.

Dave came to his side. "Come on, I'll go too."

"Joe!" called Matt, "time's a wastin'."

Joe slugged down the rest of his coffee and ran out the door with the other two men.

The early morning air was chilly, and a faint glow was forming on the horizon. "When the chief comes in tell him where we are!" shouted Matt.

"He's on his way now, just called him."

They arrived at the farm to the hum of the milking machine compressor and the bellow of cows.

"You want to go it alone and fan out, or do we stick together?" said Matt.

"I think we can fan out a little, but not far enough that we can't hear each other," said Joe.

"Let's start in the barn. Then we'll work to the out-buildings," said Dave.

Cows moved restlessly in their stanchions and Silvia looked anxious, almost scared. Matt looked at her with pity. She looked like a woman adrift at sea with no land in sight.

"I can't imagine what she is thinking," said Joe.

"Yeah," was all Matt could muster.

They looked up to the barn rafters and Dave mentioned the hay loft. Reluctantly they went out of the barn, rounded the corner of the back side of the building and entered the loft from the ramp on the second floor. They took turns looking at the walls of the barn and were relieved at seeing nothing. The sweet odor of hay assailed their nostrils. They searched in the bales, looked up at the rafters, albeit reluctantly, and shrugged their shoulders.

They emerged outside into diffused sunlight. A storm was brewing and with it dense clouds formed over the woods at the back of the barn, where heifers were lounging in a pen.

Matt looked up and groaned. "I see something I just don't like," he said.

Dave looked and saw it too.

Joe looked in the same direction and said, "I don't like the look of that, not with storm clouds brewing. Let's go take a look. I sure hope it's not what I think it is."

The three men moved up the dirt road quickly in the direction of nine to twelve circling vultures.

"They're up real early, must have sighted a good feast," said Joe.

At the top of the hill they looked down on a sight they would never forget.

A large, empty hay wagon with a tractor attached to it was sitting at the edge of one of the fields. The tall frame of the wagon held the bodies of two people, stretched out and tacked to the wooden frame of the wagon.

"Shit, oh shit," said Dave.

"Call in now" was all Matt said.

"I'm on it," said Joe as he started to run down the hill toward the cruiser.

"We got it" was all Joe managed to say into the mike. "We'll need backup and the coroner and an ambulance."

"Over," said the dispatcher. Joe could faintly hear the siren at the firehouse as he leaned against the car. He was sick, and now he understood what his grandfather went through on the police force many years ago when this same scenario happened.

Chapter Eighty-Five

Steve was making coffee when the phone rang. "Larry, Larreeeeee!" he shouted in a teasing voice. "Time to go to workkeeeee."

Larry emerged from his shower and said curtly, "Why in hell are you so chipper in the morning?" Water was puddling at his feet, his head was dripping and the bath towel was sliding down over his waist.

Steve handed him the phone and, as Larry barked into it a sullen "yeah," his face turned pale and he sat down hard. "When? How many?"

Steve looked at Larry and leaned against the counter.

"I'll be right there. Sil's place, right? I know her, she's a good friend."

He handed the phone to Steve. "Well pal, want to go look at some bodies? It's real ritualistic this time."

Steve puffed out his cheeks and blew out the air. "Not really, but I think you're going to need support, and clothes."

Larry was dressed in minutes and on the way to the farm.

"If this is her boy, her only boy, this will kill her," said Larry.

Steve nodded and frowned.

They arrived with the ambulance, three other cruisers, and three black sedans. "Looks like the party's begun," Larry mumbled under his breath.

Larry approached the hill where a group of police and FBI stood. Matt pointed and Larry sighed.

"It's a real mess," said Dave.

Larry noticed some men milling around but no sign of Silvia. "Where's Silvia?" he said.

"Still milking."

"Make sure she doesn't go back there, understand?" he boomed. "Even if you have to tranquilize her. She doesn't have to see this, understand?"

Matt nodded and said, "I'm gonna need back-up guys. We'll intercept her in the barn."

Matt turned to see Silvia approaching the group. "What the hell?" she hollered. Three men immediately surrounded her.

"You don't need to see this," said Matt softly.

"Hell I don't," she barked. She looked confused, almost in pain. It was then that she collapsed onto the grass at the side of the dirt road. "No, no, it can't be," she said quietly, tears forming in her eyes. "All my life I've dreaded something happening, all my life. He's my boy and that wife of his is a daughter to me. What now, what do I do now?"

"They haven't ID'd the bodies yet, Sil," said Dave. "Let's give Larry a chance."

She nodded. "Who the hell else could it be?" she said. "But what were they doing out there in the first place? We all went to bed early. Why would they go looking for trouble?"

"I don't think you have to be anywhere in particular with this monster. He'll find you if you're his next victim," said a young state trooper.

Another ambulance arrived on the scene, and two medics and a driver exited. An old sedan arrived next, followed by news vans and cameramen. "Okay, guys, get them out of here now. No pics," said Chris.

Father exited the sedan with Eugenia and Katie in tow. He sat down next to Silvia as the two women knelt next to her. Silvia looked from one woman to the other. She looked confused as she asked, "Where's Dottie?"

"Feeding your calves," said Eugenia. "The milk tanker is here so she's also cleaning your bulk tank for you." Silvia nodded, dazed.

Larry was finishing up his work. The two bodies were taken down with his supervision, but he did lose several patrolmen to fainting or vomiting. "Think they'd be used to it by now," Larry murmured to himself. The lifeless, charred bodies of Roger Vesley and his wife were packed in body bags and were now waiting for the ambulance crew, who stood at a respectable distance. Suddenly a scream pierced the air from the direction of the woods.

Dave, Nedo and Chris were the first ones to enter the coolness of the canopy and found a reporter from a regional newspaper on his knees with his arms around a tree. He was groaning and his eyes were clamped shut. His camera was on the ground near his side. Drool came from his mouth as he managed to say, "o, over there," and pointed to a small clearing a few yards away.
There, in the middle of the clearing, was the body of a small boy. The skin on his face was burned and his lips were a purplish blue, his eyes were closed. One of the medics appeared at his side and knelt down next to the body. "Get my guys in here. He's still alive, I have a pulse!" he shouted.

Matt ran into the clearing. "It's Louis, my daughter's friend," he gasped.

"He's still alive," said Dave gravely, "burned but still alive."

"Get a Medivac pronto!" shouted the EMT. "I think we can get a helicopter in here, at least on top of the hill, can't we?"

"Storm's coming in fast, real fast," said Matt as he felt the first drops of rain on his cheek.

"Then get the damned stretcher and let's move it!"

Men started running up the hill shouting for medical assistance, and a crew with a stretcher arrived within minutes. IV lines were hooked up and the small body of Louis was lovingly placed on the stretcher for transport to a waiting ambulance. "Get on it, get on it!" shouted another EMT, and men hurried up the hill with their cargo.

Larry waited in the rain, standing on the floor of the hay wagon with the two body bags at his feet as the stretcher disappeared over the hill. The torrent began and Steve arrived.

"Your nose is dripping," he said lightly.

"I love you, man, always a moment of brevity amidst the carnage," said Larry.

Steve smiled brightly as the rain washed over both of them.

"My pink socks are going to get wet, and there'll be hell to pay!" shouted Steve above the din.

Larry burst out laughing, a laugh that could be heard over the rumble of the thunder.

Chapter Eighty-Six

The storm lasted until 10 a.m. and then the sun arrived, along with a brief cooling period.

News media were everywhere. Silvia had lost her temper with one of them, who got a little bit too close to home with her questions. After trying to separate Silvia from nearly strangling the woman, Matt gave up.

Louis was in intensive care with third and fourth degree burns on his face, arms and legs. He drifted in and out of consciousness, mumbling something about a light and a very ugly man.

"I can't understand what he was doing in the woods." said Nedo.

They shook their heads. Louis's parents arrived at the hospital. They didn't even know he had been missing until his mother went to his room to wake him. His brother, who shared the room with him, told her that he never heard or saw Louis leave during the night.

The town was in turmoil. People were leaving to stay elsewhere and the place looked like a ghost town with the exception of the news vans and the reporters, the police and FBI.

Suzie and Terry at the diner and many of the area restaurants were doing well. The owners of the hardware and feed store were complaining that with another week of this business, they would have to shut their doors. The gas station and variety stores were selling souvenirs faster than they could restock, and the gawkers from neighboring towns made traffic a nightmare.

Chapter Eighty-Seven

Father, Amy, Olivia, Lydia and Dave walked along slowly. "Where are we going?" demanded Amy.

"Let's go talk to the group," said Father. "Then we'll start making plans."

They arrived at Katie's house. Seth was outside on the porch finishing up a paint job he had started several weeks before.

"Hello, Mr. Collins," said the girls in unison. He nodded to the small group and was surprised to see Amy as part of the entourage.

"Katie in?" said Father.

"Yea, she's in the garden out back." Seth laid his brush down and followed at a distance.

Katie looked up when they approached. Her straw sun bonnet gave her face a checkerboard look as the light poured in between the weave. "About time," she muttered and put her small scissors down on the bench. They all turned and silently followed Father. They walked up the street quietly but with purpose, and when they reached Maiden Lane they stopped at Eugenia's house. Suddenly, a lone figure came running up the sidewalk from behind, and Lydia knew it was her mother. The small group sat on lawn chairs in Eugenia's back garden.

Dottie sighed and said, "Well, we all know why we're here."

Everyone nodded, even Seth, who had tagged along.

A figure appeared on the lawn and sat on the grass at the periphery of the group. They were startled to see Steve. Lydia and Olivia smiled and waved at him. He nodded and smiled back.

Dave looked at Katie and the other faces in the group, quietly assessing them.

Father spoke quietly. "We need to do this tomorrow," he said, looking around at the group. "On the anniversary. I have everything at the ready but we need to start from here about four, so we can get into the woods before darkness begins. Those of you who want to meet us there, good, but don't go into those woods until we show up, understand?"

A shiver crept down Seth's spine.

"Tomorrow night is the night, August seventeenth." Father reminded them. "It's the seventy-fifth anniversary of the last events, und the window of time is very short. You all know what we're dealing with here und that maybe, just maybe, some of us won't survive this. I don't know how strong my medicine is but we're about to find out."

Eugenia was silent for a moment and then said, "There is someone here who gave me a lot of pause the other day when he visited me. He had a theory and I think we should listen to him."

She nodded to Steve, who shrugged his shoulders and began to speak. "I'm an anthropologist but I also have a hobby. This hobby is the study of energy fields, ley lines and what we call pseudoscience. It involves Sacred Geometry, which is the belief that God created the universe according to a geometric plan or pattern.

"I Google-mapped the spot in the woods and found some interesting patterns. Without getting into a lot of math, let's just say that the spot in back of the junk yard, where I had the privilege of being taken several days ago by two nice young ladies and a young gentleman, has an incredible significance. The circle, the vine and the pond or eye form a triangle. The center of that triangle is where the most energy would be generated and where I think we should be tomorrow. I'll bring my equipment and GPS, and we can find the spot, I'm sure."

Karen looked hard at her daughter, who blushed and turned her head.

"Great idea! That's where we'll head," said Father. "That energy spot must be cleansed, und then I'll need to call him to me und address the evil within him. It's the extraction of that evil, the anger und resentment that we need to address first. I hope the man who is left will listen to us und go into the light. Then maybe those woods und this town will be safe for everyone."

Suddenly, Alex appeared, followed by Tom. Alex held something and as he opened his hand, Olivia noticed it was a chunk of grey rock with a pink tint.

Amy looked at the boy and said, "Hmm, can I see that? Where did you get it?"

"No," said Father, "no. I'll handle it, not you." He was abrupt and it scared Amy.

"Sorry," he said. "Alex, where did you get this?"

"It was in Pete's trailer the day he disappeared," said the boy.

Amy said, "That's the same material that the knife in the case at school is made of. I'd be willing to bet on it."

Seth nodded his head in agreement.

"It's a form of pink flint, very rare and very magical," said Eugenia.

Father nodded and continued, "I had the pleasure of meeting Stacy in person. The demon was within her. I managed to extract him." Father looked around as if listening to something and then looked directly at Katie.

"Katie, what have you seen?" he asked. Katie related her journey to the site of the ancient vine and what she was privy to in her meditation.

"It's all coming together," said Lydia. "Don't you see?"

Father nodded. "We must clear that area of all traces of the young man und the evil forces he has managed to conjure up. We, all of us, have the power und together we can do many wonderful things, including getting this man over where he belongs. He's the one who made the deal with the devil within himself."

~

One day, as he knapped flint for a knife blade in front of his parents' hut, a shadow fell across his lap where the still unfinished blade lay. He looked up into the imposing face of the teacher. He hung his head, but the man sat down facing him. The teacher looked with question at the work in his lap, and the boy held it out for him to see. The teacher took the blade, examined the point and with an approving nod placed it back into his hand. The teacher reached into a large pouch that he had and placed two pieces of flint on the ground next to him. These were like no other pieces of flint the boy had ever seen. They were pink, and the grain lay in undisturbed layers, perfect pieces for knapping. The boy looked at the man with questioning eyes, but the teacher rose, turned and walked away without saying a word.

Chapter Eighty-Eight

The next day the girls were at the Rectory by noon, anxiously waiting for four o'clock and the night to begin.

"First I have to gather my things," said Father.

"Like a Bible and holy water," said Olivia excitedly.

Father rolled his eyes. "That's only part of it," he said wearily. He motioned for them to sit and disappeared into the house. He emerged a few minutes later carrying what looked like a very old doctor's bag. It was well worn, but the sheen of the leather told them it was well taken care of.

"We have flashlights and crystals," both girls said in unison.

"Well, you're prepared then," said Father.

~

Karen had one afternoon client that had just left and, as she made herself a cup of tea, a tiny whisper said, "*it's getting time.*" She poured her tea and sat quietly for a few minutes, just to relax. She knew Matt was still working on the Vesley case. He had called her and told her he'd be very late. But would he come, too? She hoped so. A half-hour later, after saying a few prayers and performing a ceremony of protection, she picked up a few of her amulets and crystals and headed for Dottie's.

~

Larry was busy working on his laptop at the dining room table. The report on the Vesley bodies was open on the screen when Steve came into the room. Larry looked up from the screen into his friend's eyes.

"I have to leave before three. Today's the day," was all Steve said, and he walked out the door.

"Wait!" called Larry. "I'm not going to miss this."

Larry caught up with Steve on the front porch of Larry's large Victorian home. Steve handed him a chunk of what looked like glass.

"What the hell is this?" Larry said.

"A crystal. You're going to need it," said Steve as he walked down the steps, turned and began walking along the sidewalk toward the junk yard at the opposite end of town.

"Are we going to walk?"

Steve nodded and continued walking.

"You know what?" said Larry, sounding over-enthusiastic.

Steve sighed, stopped and impatiently said, "No Larry, what?"

"I prayed this morning."

~

Jack Dunn and his boss Richard Perry were having lunch in the café. They were seated at a small table near the window. As Larry and Steve passed the window, Perry looked at Jack, who nodded. They paid their tab and headed for the door, following Larry and Steve down the street.

~

Kenny caught up with Lydia, Olivia and Father at Eugenia's, just as Katie, Seth and Amy were coming around the corner from an opposite street. Claire intercepted her mother on Maiden Lane. "I closed the library" was all she said as she joined their ranks.

~

Dave looked at Matt from across the desk. They had just gotten back from another visit to the Vesley farm. They were dirty, sweaty and disgusted.

"All this carnage, and for what?" muttered Dave. They looked at one another.

"What time is it?" they said in unison.

"It's three," said Dave quietly. "I know where I'm going."

"Me too," said Matt. As they headed out the door of the station.

~

Chris and Nedo had just entered the parking lot of the precinct when they spotted Dave and Matt walking toward the opposite end of town.

"Where ya suppose they're going?" said Nedo.

"I don't know, but I'm inclined to follow. Something's urging me to follow them," said Chris.

They turned the squad car around and noticed that not too far ahead of Matt and Dave were the two figures of Jack and Richard Perry.

"What in hell is going on?" said Nedo.

"I have a very bad feeling about all this," mumbled Chris.

They parked the squad car and followed the other men at a respectful distance.

Chapter Eighty-Nine

There seemed to be a gathering on the lawn between Eugenia's and Dottie's. Chris frowned. There were a lot of people there.

"We'll start in at four. Steve here has the coordinates for the center of the triangle. He'll lead the way in," said Father.

"I'll need the help of the kids until we get to the path that intersects the circle and the vine," Steve said.

Karen gasped and looked around for her husband. She wasn't disappointed; he was there, standing next to Dave. "What does he think about all this?" she wondered.

They headed for the back of Dottie's barn and the gritty path that led to the woods. It was almost four-fifteen when they stood in front of the opening in the trees. Tom, Josh and Alex were waiting for them.

Steve nodded to Lydia, Kenny and Olivia and was surprised to see Alex and Josh joining them as they began their trek into the darkening gloom.

As they approached the intersection of the paths, Steve said, "Now, this is where it'll get interesting. We'll have to bushwhack some, but we go straight. We don't follow any of the paths from now on."

The children moved ahead and pushed through thick underbrush, hanging vines and fallen limbs from the tree canopy overhead. Lydia's hair snagged more than once on small, thorny bushes in the way, and occasionally she heard a cussword or expletive from someone in the rear of the procession.

"We have about another hundred yards to go until we get to the middle. Kenny, more to the left please, you're getting off course," said Steve.

It was then that Steve noticed that the air temperature was changing. The more they moved forward, the colder it got. Father was at Steve's elbow. He had also noticed the change in the air temperature.

Steve said to Father, "pick a spot straight ahead and stay with it, my GPS is acting strange."

They were no longer in tangled undergrowth but in a grove of huge oak trees, their trunks several feet in diameter. The grove was at least an acre and the further they walked among the trees, the colder it seemed to get until Steve stood still and gawked at his GPS. It was registering one set of coordinates and then another set; each set the opposite of the other.

"My God," he said, "a true energy grid composed of both double black vortexes." He walked forward a little further and noticed that the ground was rocky. Points of rock stuck up at odd angles everywhere. They were in a large clearing in the center of which sat a very large, round boulder, the size of a small house. It sat there reflecting the soft glow from the setting sun.

"Looks like we're here," said Seth. "Father, it's in your hands now."

Yeah, I get the impression we're no longer in Kansas" muttered Larry.

Matt bent, picked up one of the odd-shaped stones and looked carefully at it. "I bet this is the same material that that knife of Seth's is made of," he said.

Seth glanced down at the piece of rock and said, "my God, you're right."

Chapter Ninety

Eugenia, Dottie and Katie placed crystals on the ground around the group and Karen preformed a grid ceremony using sacred Reiki symbols. This act afforded further protection for the group. Father turned and addressed the group. "Whatever happens, try not to go outside this grid. We've made it large enough for all of you to move around freely, but do not step from it."

Father placed a stole across his wide shoulders and took out his prayer book, a small Bible, sage, holy water and a crucifix. Katie lit the sage and Eugenia held the bowl as the sage was ignited. The group formed a semi-circle behind Father and he began his incantation.

The image of a very tall man moved toward them. He moved through instead of around the boulder, seeming to glow slightly as he approached.

Nedo pulled his revolver from his holster but Chris was quick to grip his arm. "No," he hissed.

"*I see you are here for my grandson. He is just as afraid of you as you are of him,*" the tall man communicated sadly.

Several, including Father, heard the voice in their heads. Josh slapped his left ear and frowned.

"*Those who are enlightened will hear me,*" the man's voice said quietly.

Josh's eyes widened. "Oh shit, enlightened, I'm enlightened?" he stammered.

"We're bringing him over in the name of love, not for what he has done but for his soul. Judgment is the realm of only the

Almighty. We must continue cultivating our gardens here, but he must move on. We know his story and it's a tragic one. But he will heal und the anger will leave," said Father in a voice strong with conviction.

"*You are wise,*" said the grandfather sadly. "*Time on this side goes very fast, our energies vibrate higher, and many moons go past quickly for us, but not for you.*"

"We must dissolve this evil within him und take him over to the light," said Father.

The image nodded its head. "*Then begin, for when he is safely over I too can leave this between place.*"

"Oh my God, he's the thing's guardian spirit," blurted Lydia.

"Shhhhhh," Olivia hissed, grabbing her hand.

Dave came over to stand near Karen and placed an arm on her shoulder. "Listening?" he whispered.

She nodded. "It's how we communicate with our daughter, Sarah," she said.

Matt looked at them both and smiled warmly.

Nedo was about to speak, but thought better of it. He stood there in amazement, a dazed look on his face.

Father began his prayers and incantations again, and suddenly the trees and the ground trembled slightly. From the rock came a very dark and menacing being that reminded Lydia of pictures she had seen of werewolves. It had a hunchback and walked with a jerking gait toward them.

"Don't move!" shouted Father.

"Fuck, I'm gettin' outta here!" shouted Tom, but Alex took one of his arms while Eugenia took his other, and they said in unison, "no, you're not." Kenny grabbed a belt loop on the back of Tom's pants and hung on.

"Show me the true self und not the evil within," Father commanded, and said more prayers and incantations. Suddenly, as the daylight began to fade they saw the image of a young man with a disfigured face. He sat on the ground near the large boulder. He worked on a piece of flint, his knife making a rhythmic cadence, and as he looked up his eyes were clear, bright brown and full of understanding and sadness.

The dark image moved closer to the boy, but Father let out a roar so loud that it echoed in the small confines of the circle. The creature stopped and turned to face them, its hands dragging on the ground. Malevolent, yellow eyes fixed themselves on the small crowd, and then the creature crouched.

Jack gasped. His heart was racing as he looked at the creature, the memory of it still fresh in his mind. Jack ducked behind Dave, who was in front of him. Claire reached out a hand to steady Jack as Amy grabbed his other arm.

Larry put a hand on Jack's shoulder and grabbed a handful of shirt. "Just in case you want to run," he mumbled.

Father felt the electricity in the air. Katie, Eugenia and Dottie felt it also. Eugenia grabbed the sage bundle and blew lightly on the tiny ember still cradled within. It released a pungent scent, its smoke drifting lazily within the confines of the circle.

Father raised his hand higher just as the creature leapt into the air and directly at the assembled crowd. The last rays of sunlight glanced off the tip of the crucifix Father held and fell directly onto the airborne figure. A flash of light illuminated the area and undulating flashes of vivid colors rained down. The creature screamed but the screams were lost in the undulation of the light waves. Father kept his hand up and kept saying the prayers and incantations as sparks and light flashed down and around the little group. "Stay where you are!" shouted Father, and the group huddled closer together.

"Christ sakes, it's being eaten alive," said Larry.

The creature and the light were getting dimmer and dimmer when Father suddenly collapsed onto the ground.

Lydia jumped forward, and grabbing his hand, she screamed, "His arm, it's all burned!"

Katie stepped forward from the crowd. She had wrapped a leather strap around her wrist, and on it hung crystals of varying sizes and shapes. Katie took the crucifix from Father's hand and raised it up in her hand. She spoke with authority in her voice. "We thank you for rescuing our brother, for letting him go to the light. All evil within will be neutralized and the earth will not retain this blot upon itself anymore."

An explosion so bright it was almost blinding lit up the area. They watched as the light flashed toward the sky, disappearing into its vastness. Small tufts of grass crackled with electricity as the anxious crowd looked around to assess the damage.

Father lay on his back and Karen knelt over him, administering Reiki on his exhausted body. Claire made him comfortable by placing her sweater under his head.

Karen looked up to see Sarah, bathed in a faint light and standing not too far from them. Several awe struck people looked intently at the figure of the young girl, not knowing what to do.

"He will be okay," Sarah said. *"I have a job to finish now."*

"Here we go again," muttered Tom. Josh burst out laughing only to smother it with his shirt sleeve. Olivia punched him in the arm.

The scene was bathed in a feeling of peacefulness. The young man still worked on the piece of flint as he sat on the ground near the large rock.

They watched as the figure of the young girl approached the young man, bent down and touched him. He looked up at her, smiled and rose, leaving his knife and unfinished piece of flint on the ground. Suddenly a light, like the beam of a flashlight only thousands of times larger and brighter, illuminated the area where they both stood. They moved toward the light;, the grandfather figure following closely behind.

The waves of light became brighter and brighter until many members of the small group had to shield their eyes. Lydia stepped forward as if to follow, but the strong hand of Katie held her back.

"No, it's not your time, my girl," she said sadly.

"Goodbye, Sarah," Lydia called out, followed by a chorus of a dozen voices all saying goodbye.

"*I will always be here. We will always be here,*" was the reply. It was a faint whisper, like that of the wind.

Karen came to stand beside Lydia. She put her arms around her daughter. Dave stood beside Matt and placed a hand on his shoulder.

"Goodbye, Sarah," whispered Matt, and he turned and smiled at Karen. The light began fading and darkness enveloped them as they stood at the edge of a wood, somewhere in a small clearing in a small town in upstate New York.

The moonlight was bright this evening, but the orb hadn't climbed high enough into the sky to clear the face of West Mountain. The yip of coyotes shattered the silence. "God, this is beautiful," mused Kenny, still holding onto Tom's pants. Eugenia and Dottie nodded and each placed her arm around Tom's shoulders.

"Okay, let go, you guys, I won't run anymore," said Tom. Alex and Josh burst out laughing.

"Oh, you old fool," scoffed Eugenia.

Seth, Steve, and Larry helped Father to his feet.

"He's pretty weak," said Larry.

"Yeah, but you're not getting an ambulance in here. Hell, they'll get lost and then we'll have to get a search party out, and shit, we'll have a real mess," said Chris.

Perry took Father's arm and put it around his neck. Seth took his other arm by the elbow and together, they supported Father as he made his way along.

"I still don't believe what I saw," said Nedo.

"Hey Brian, what are you going to tell your men?" said Matt, laughing.

"Damned if I know," said Nedo. "I think I'm going to pack up and leave, now. Don't ever invite me back here again. I won't come."

"Smart man," muttered Chris.

"What?" said Steve, turning to face Nedo. "I'm insulted."

Matt, Dave and Chris were laughing.

Lydia, Olivia, Alex, Josh and Kenny slowly walked behind the group, deep in their own thoughts. Lydia looked at Olivia and saw that Josh had his arm around her shoulder as they moved out of the small clearing and onto the path that would take them through the woods and home.

Ghostlady607@GMail.com

56810720R00166